THE
WITNESS
FOR THE
DEAD

BY KATHERINE ADDISON

KATHERINE ADDISON

THE
WITNESS
FOR THE
DEAD

TOR

A TOM DOHERTY ASSOCIATES BOOK
NEW YORK

THE WITNESS FOR THE DEAD

Copyright © 2021 by Sarah Monette

All rights reserved.

A Tor Book
Published by Tom Doherty Associates
120 Broadway
New York, NY 10271

www.tor-forge.com

Tor® is a registered trademark of Macmillan Publishing Group, LLC.

Library of Congress Cataloging-in-Publication Data

Names: Addison, Katherine, author.
Title: The witness for the dead / Katherine Addison.
Description: First edition. | New York : TOR, a Tom Doherty Associates Book, 2021.
Identifiers: LCCN 2021008738 (print) | LCCN 2021008739 (ebook) |
    ISBN 9780765387424 (hardcover) | ISBN 9780765387448 (ebook)
Classification: LCC PS3601.D4655 W58 2021 (print) | LCC PS3601.D4655 (ebook) |
    DDC 813/.6—dc23
LC record available at https://lccn.loc.gov/2021008738
LC ebook record available at https://lccn.loc.gov/2021008739

Our books may be purchased in bulk for promotional, educational,
or business use. Please contact your local bookseller or the Macmillan Corporate
and Premium Sales Department at 1-800-221-7945, extension 5442, or by email at
MacmillanSpecialMarkets@macmillan.com.

First Edition: June 2021

Printed in the United States of America

0 9 8 7 6 5 4 3 2 1

This book is dedicated to all the librarians I know.

In the jumbled darkness of the catacombs beneath the city of Amalo, there was a shrine to Ulis in his aspect as god of the moon. It was thousands of years old, and the carving of the four phases of the moon on the plinth had become almost undetectable, worn smooth by generations of reverent fingertips. Whatever the plinth had supported was long gone, but the shrine remained.

The shrine was a landmark that every Ulineise prelate in the city knew, and it was frequently used as a meeting place, since it afforded better privacy than the Ulistheileian where formal audiences were held.

Dach'othala Vernezar, the Ulisothala of Amalo, was an elven man of middle age and great ambition. He had his eye on the Archprelacy, and although the current Archprelate was neither ancient nor infirm, it did not do to forget that Vernezar's every move was made with political gain in mind. I had thus received his summons with no little dread, for I was a political sore point, directly appointed by the Archprelate to be a Witness for the Dead for the entire city.

Prince Orchenis had gone to the Archprelate and asked that I be assigned to Amalo for an indefinite period of time, for two reasons. One was that the city had no Witness of my type, who could actually speak to the dead. The other was that the religious hierarchy of the city was, as the prince put it, a nest of vipers, and the Ulineisei were the worst of the lot. The Archprelate had not commanded me to accept assignment in Amalo, but I had agreed with Prince Orchenis that my services were needed. I received a small stipend from the Amalomeire to sit in a cramped box of an office and wait for the people of Amalo to come, which they did in a slow, sad, hopeful stream. I disappointed them, for my ability was not the magic it was always shown to be in operas and novels. But even though I could not discover answers in dust—even though the answers I did discover were frequently inconvenient and sometimes disastrous—they continued to petition me, and I could not leave them unheard.

Today had brought three petitioners whom I could not help (one of whom stood and argued with me for three quarters of an hour); the news that two of the cases for which I had witnessed had been judged unfavorably by Lord Judiciar Orshevar; and a lengthy and fruitless search through Ulvanensee, the municipal cemetery of the Airmen's Quarter, on behalf of a petitioner who believed his sister, and the child with which she had been pregnant, had been murdered by her husband. I had started with the registers, but had ended up walking the rows, reading gravestones, looking for names that the registers did not contain. I was tired and covered in the municipal cemetery's powdery dirt; when Anora Chanavar, the half-goblin prelate of Ulvanensee, brought me Vernezar's message, I did, for a weak moment, consider not going.

Anora came with me, although we argued about that most of the way there. "Thou needst a witness," he said stubbornly. "I know Vernezar better than thou dost."

"There's no need for thee to draw his attention," I said for the third time.

"He cannot harm me," Anora said. "If he takes my benefice away, he only makes a greater headache for himself, because then he has to find some other fool to give it to. Do thou watch. He'll pretend I'm not even there."

Anora was quickly proven correct. Vernezar made eye contact with him for a pained moment, then hurriedly turned away. My heart sank as I took in Vernezar's companion. Othalo Zanarin was the loudest voice in the faction which objected to my presence in Amalo. She was an elven woman of considerable cold beauty, some inches taller than I was, though not nearly as tall as Anora; she was a member of Vernezar's staff, and I knew he was afraid of her. She, too, was a person of connections and ambition, and she had the Amal'othala's ear.

"Good afternoon, dach'othala," I said. I saw Zanarin wince pointedly at my voice, which was harsh and graveled thanks to my surviving the sessiva when it swept through Lohaiso during my prelacy there. It mostly did not bother me, except when someone like Zanarin made sure it did.

"Good afternoon, Celehar," said Vernezar. "I apologize for dragging you down here—not nearly as elegant as what you were used to at the Untheileneise Court, I'm sure—but this really isn't a matter for the Ulistheileian."

"No?" I said, my heart sinking further at his use of "I."

"No need for any formality," Vernezar said with a smile, and I was grateful to Anora for being so stubborn. He was right: I needed a witness. "I just wanted to see if we could reach an accord."

"An accord? About what?"

Zanarin said, "Dach'othala Vernezar has a most generous offer." Zanarin had taken an instant dislike to me, partly because I had been the one—at the behest of the Emperor Edrehasivar VII—to find the Curneisei assassins of the Emperor Varenechibel IV, partly because my appointment came directly from the Archprelate. By one argument, that meant I outranked all the Ulineise prelates in Amalo except Vernezar.

Nobody liked that argument, least of all Vernezar himself.

The other argument was that, as an unbeneficed prelate, I was outranked by everyone except the novices. Zanarin had made that argument first, but others had been quick to back her up. They might have carried the matter, since they were making a much more palatable argument, had it not been for Anora and the other municipal cemetery prelates objecting, for here the relatively trivial question of my rank had crossed a much larger, ongoing contention among the Ulineise prelates of Amalo, that being how a prelate's benefice should be valued. Some prelates argued for wealth; others, prelates like Anora, argued for size. A third faction argued for age. It was a bitterly divisive issue, and I thought the true measure of Vernezar's worth was his inability to resolve it.

"I wanted," said Vernezar, "to propose a compromise. It seems clear that, having been appointed directly by the Archprelate, you are of greater rank than the ordinary prelates, but since you are unbeneficed, you are of lesser rank than the prelates of the Ulistheileian. Does that seem fair?"

It seemed guaranteed to make everyone unhappy, possibly even more unhappy than they were right now. Anora murmured, "The prelates of the Ulistheileian are also unbeneficed," and Vernezar pretended not to hear him.

"You are offering me rank in the Ulistheileian," I said slowly.

"Yes," said Vernezar.

Beside him, Zanarin glowered.

"But in turn," I said, "I would have to concede your authority over me."

There was a pause, as distinct as if it had been measured by a tape.

"Do you *deny* my authority over you?" asked Vernezar.

"I was appointed by the Archprelate," I said. "Not by you."

"Are you claiming you, a mere Witness for the Dead, are equal with Dach'othala Vernezar?" said Zanarin. "Just because your family married into the imperial house doesn't—" Vernezar caught her eye, and she did not finish her sentence.

And there was a third reason Zanarin didn't like me, although what good it did me to be the kinsman of a widowed and childless empress was not at all clear.

"It used to be," Anora said, deliberately not looking at anyone, "that Witnesses for the Dead were honored among the prelates of Ulis."

That sparked a fight out of a tense discussion, as he must have known it would. Vernezar bristled at the suggestion that I was not being adequately honored in his scenario, and Zanarin objected to the idea that I should be honored at all. There was a deeper theological argument behind Zanarin's outrage, and that deeper meaning was the reason I did not say, as I longed to, that I did not care about rank. Zanarin, who was not from Amalo, had brought with her some of the south's skepticism. She doubted that Witnesses for the Dead truly spoke to the dead and thus her belief that we should carry no rank.

Rank was one thing, being called a liar quite another. I could not let Zanarin's ideas gain more ground than they already had. I found myself arguing for status I did not want because the alternative was to agree with Zanarin that I should have no status at all. Across us Vernezar and Anora were arguing, no less heatedly, about the traditions of the Ulistheileian.

We ended finally in much the same place as we had begun, nothing resolved, Vernezar's compromise position neither accepted nor rejected.

I decided to go to the municipal baths. I felt unclean.

X

It was dusk when I got home.

The lamplighters were finishing their rounds, their long poles bobbing on their shoulders. Merchants were locking the grilles of their shops, apprentices and younger sons assiduously sweeping the pavement. In the courtyard of my building, the women were taking down the laundry that had been hanging on the lines to dry all afternoon. They smiled and bobbed their heads at me shyly; I nodded in return. No one wanted to be too friendly with a Witness for the Dead.

I stopped in the concierge's office to check the post. I had a letter, cheap paper and cheap sealing wax, and I recognized the hand.

I climbed the stairs to my apartment, the iron bannister sun-warm beneath my palm. One of the local cats was on the landing, his white paws tucked up neatly beneath him, the cream and red tabby swirls on his sides making him look like a glazed marmalade bun.

He said "mraaao" to me as I unlocked my door, and stood up to stretch. By the time I came back out, he had been joined by two of his sister-wives and a half-grown tom who wasn't old enough yet to be chased away. A third sister-wife lurked halfway up the next flight of stairs, too shy to come all the way down to the landing while I was there. Nine bright blue eyes watched me (the deeply sabled queen had suffered some injury that left her right eye cataracted and blind) as I set down the little saucers, each with a fourth of the can of sardines I had just opened.

I sat in my doorway and watched them eat, amused by how each cat guarded its plate so fiercely from the other three—and the third queen, a dark brown tabby who was probably the biggest of the five of them, watched and waited, one eye seemingly always on me. None of them was entirely tame, but that one had been hurt before.

I had not named them. Names were too much power, given far too easily to animals who wandered the city and returned to my landing only when they felt like it. I did not give them names any more than I let them in.

When the half-blind queen had finished with her sardines, she came over and bumped my shin gently with her head. I rubbed behind her sail-like ears and she began purring, a deep throbbing noise like the engines of an airship. The other cats ignored us and disappeared one by one as they finished their sardines.

Presently, the half-blind queen closed her jaws very gently around my hand to tell me she was done. I watched her go, small and self-possessed, down the stairs, and then went back inside so that the third queen could come down and finish off the remains of the sardines.

I had hung my black coat of office carefully—it was made of silk and probably cost more than all the rest of my wardrobe combined—and now I put on my favorite of my three frock coats, black with a soft gray embroidery down the placket and around the cuffs. I'd had to re-hem it twice and patch the elbows, but the body of the coat was still sturdy and respectable. When I looked in my palm-sized mirror, I saw that my hair was drying in wild curls; I spent five minutes in combing, braiding, and pinning it back into a sober prelate's braid, sliding the pearl-headed hairpins in as I had been taught to as a novice, so that none of the metal showed, only the pearls, almost invisible against the whiteness of my hair, and tying the tail with a fresh black ribbon. The hairpins were probably the most expensive thing I owned—after my coat of office—even though they were really glass, not pearls. My earrings were all brass.

Then I opened the letter I had received in the post.

It did not bother with salutations, merely said, *Meet me in the River-Cat tonight.*

I left my apartment again before it had gotten quite dark enough that I had to light a lamp—the municipal utility metered gas and steam with great severity, and I tried to leave the lamps and radiators off as much as I could. The prelacy of Amalo was obliged to pay me, per the Archprelate's directive, but they did so parsimoniously, grudging every zashan.

The Airmen's Quarter of Amalo was rich in teahouses. There were five within easy walking distance of my apartment: the Red Dog's Dream, the Circle of Pearls, the Hanevo Tree, Mendelar's, and the River-Cat. Six if you counted the manufactory-owned Tea Leaf, which I did not. My favorite was the Hanevo Tree; the River-Cat was less a place for quiet contemplation and more a meeting place for families and courting couples.

The River-Cat was one long room divided up into deep booths; I walked past two nervous young couples, a rowdy family of six (seven? the tow-headed children were hard to count), a venerable man and his even more venerable wife, sitting together on the same side of the booth and passing one cup slowly back and forth—a very old courting ritual that my Velveradeise grandmother had told me about when I was a child. Two women, sisters by the look of it, were both reading the same copy of the *Herald of Amalo,* spread flat on the table between them, one sister reading right side up and one sister reading upside down.

The back-most booths were the least popular; I liked them because I could lean against the warm-veneered wood and know that no one was coming up behind me. It was easy to make enemies as a Witness *vel ama,* and I did not have a conciliatory tongue.

A very young tea-server brought pot and cups and the tiny sand-clock that marked how long the tea had been steeping. I drank for preference the dark, bitter orchor, but it was stiff enough that if I drank it after sunset, I would still be awake at dawn. This evening I had chosen the more delicate isevren, and I indulged myself with a generous spoonful of honey.

I put the honey spoon in the second cup (which the staff of the River-Cat could not be trained out of bringing—unlike at the Hanevo Tree, where you had to specify if you wanted more than one) and briefly tormented myself by imagining a companion who would smile across at me and happily lick the spoon clean. Neither of my lovers had had such a sweet tooth—that was the only thing that made my imaginings even remotely safe. A purely made-up lover was foolish; conjuring the dead was something else entirely.

I reminded myself that Zhemena was not dead, merely far away and uninterested. Oddly, it did not make me feel better.

Drink thy tea, Celehar, I said impatiently to myself, *and cease repining.*

I was halfway through my little pot of isevren, trying to focus on the question of Mer Urmenezh's dead and missing sister and not on a sweet-toothed imaginary lover, when a shadow fell over the end of the table, and I turned to look.

Subpraeceptor Azhanharad of the Amalo chapter of the Vigilant Brotherhood was a tall, broad man, half goblin, dark and scowling, his voice thick with the upcountry consonants of the Mervarnen Mountains. He did not like me.

The feeling was mutual. I thought Azhanharad brutal in his methods, preferring force to subtlety—and at that I had a higher opinion of him than of many of his brethren. The Vigilant Brotherhood served a necessary purpose, both in cities like Amalo and in the long stretches of empty fields and copses where they patrolled, but their recruitment efforts did not attract men of either great intelligence or sensitivity. One was only lucky if one's local chapter had succeeded in attracting men of integrity.

Azhanharad was always uncomfortable when he had to talk to

me—still close enough to his Mervarneise roots to be superstitious about my calling rather than incredulous. Little as I liked him, I had to respect the courage that brought him back to me every time he thought I might be able to help. He said, "Good evening, Othala Celehar."

In the emperor's court, the honorific "othala" was considered hopelessly provincial and out of date. Here—in the provinces—it was common politeness.

"Good evening, Subpraeceptor," I said, and gestured him to the other bench. "We received your note."

He sat, eyeing the second cup warily, his ears flicking. "Are you expecting a companion, othala?"

"No. Would you like some tea? It's isevren—though we regret that you will have to accept the honey."

"No, thank you." He folded his hands together on the table—big hands, with big scarred knuckles. "A patrol pulled a body out of the canal this morning. None of us recognized her."

Which meant very little, but did provide negative evidence. She wasn't an inhabitant of the Airmen's Quarter—or, at least, she wasn't a troublemaker. The Vigilant Brotherhood was very familiar with rowdy drunks and chronic brawlers, with the prostitutes who could not afford the dues to work in a Guild brothel and with the Guild enforcers who chased them off the streets. The prostitutes ended up dead sometimes.

Azhanharad sighed and said bluntly, "Will you come?"

And I said, feeling suddenly less despondent, "Yes, of course."

⚭

The Chapterhouse of the Amaleise Brethren was a very old building, probably as old as the mystery of Anmura the Protector, from which the Brotherhood sprang—and which, in all probability, they still practiced. The Church did not recognize the four Anmureise mysteries; I was careful not to ask. The Chapterhouse was built out of massive blocks of stone, carved at eye-level with the names of the dead Praeceptors who lay in the Chapter-house crypt. In the six or seven hundred years since that practice had started—at a time centuries after the Chapterhouse was built—they had filled twenty-nine blocks.

Azhanharad led me to the alleyside door rather than the grand front entrance on General Parzhadar Square. I followed him down the twist in the areaway stairs, waited at the bottom while he threw his weight against the ancient lock on the basement door.

The basement of the Chapterhouse had never been fitted out for gaslight; the brethren kept a rack of lanterns hanging by the door. Azhanharad took one down and lit it, his thick fingers careful and precise as he touched his lighter to the waiting wick. The lantern did not provide very *much* light, being what they called in Amalo an owl-light, as it was roughly the size of the tiny screeching owls that nested in the city's eaves. But it was better than candlelight, and far better than no light at all.

We descended another flight of stairs, and then another, down to the floor of the Brotherhood's vast crypt. The Chapterhouse crypt was the only place in the Airmen's Quarter where a body could be stored for long. This woman had to be identified before anything could be done with her—without identification, no one was willing to prepare the body for a funeral. Unlike the southern and western communities where I had begun my prelacy, Amalo had three main sets of funerary practices and a dozen others with smaller followings. It might well be more; no one could keep track of the splintering sects and hero-cults and the secretive kindreds that came down out of the mountains. Each tradition required the body to be prepared in a different way, and the wrong preparation would, at *best,* offend both kin and congregation. I knew of cases where the luckless officiant had had to petition for a change of benefice.

The other reason the Brotherhood might keep a body in their cold room was if it took an unusual amount of time to identify the cause of death—a question which often made the difference be-tween unfortunate happenstance and murder. For this body, if she had been pulled out of the canal, it was less about cause of death than about where she died, and therefore about who she was.

They had laid her out carefully on a clean white sheet. Black was better for sanctity, but black dye that would hold through repeated, frequent washings was expensive, and no one would waste it on mortuary sheets. White was almost as good, signifying that this woman, like all the dead, was under the protection of the emperor.

She was a young elven woman, no more than thirty judging by her hands and face. She showed no signs of childbearing, and her hands were uncallused. Her white hair hung in a tangle over the side of the table and nearly to the floor. She was no kind of cleric, not a liveried servant, not a manufactory worker. She might be the wife of a nobleman or the daughter of a well-off burgher. She *might* be a prostitute, but if so, she had to come from one of the elegant houses in the Veren'malo, to show no signs of poverty or disease in her face.

Her dress, a ruined mass of dark green velvet, had probably been expensive. The cuffs were stained with dye from the embroidery of flowers that decorated them, but they were silk: second grade probably, although it was hard to tell after the canal had been at them. I investigated and discovered a pocket hidden in the folds of the skirt and inside it, a wad of paper.

"What's that?" said Azhanharad.

"We do not know," I said, unfolding it cautiously. There was no need for caution; the ink had run into a purplish gray blot, with no words still legible. "Nothing useful."

I touched the body on the forehead—cold, helpless flesh, a house condemned but not yet torn down. Not quite yet. The inhabitant had not entirely fled.

"Can you?" Azhanharad said.

"Yes," I said. The prayer of compassion for the dead was worn and familiar. The woman no longer knew her name, nor who had wanted her dead, nor why. But she did remember her death. She had been alive when the water slammed the breath from her body. She remembered the fall from the dock, though she had been more pushed than fallen and more thrown than pushed. She remembered the cold dark water, the way her panicked gasps for air had echoed off the bricks.

She hadn't known how to swim. Despite the lake and the canal and the river, most Amaleisei didn't.

I felt the memory of her clothes dragging her down, heavy velvet getting heavier very quickly. She tried to scream for help, but got a mouthful of foul-tasting water, and before she even had time to realize she was going to die, there was a sudden crushing agony deep into her head and then nothing.

She had not drowned after all.

I lifted my hand and stepped back, out of range of the sympathy I had created between the corpse and myself. It would take a moment for it to fade enough that I could touch her again without being dragged back into the memory of her death.

"Anything?" Azhanharad said, without much hope.

"No name," I said, since that was what he most wanted. "But this was definitely murder, not suicide. And *not* an accident."

"The poor woman," Azhanharad said, with a ritual gesture of blessing.

"She was alive when she went into the water," I said. "But she didn't drown. Here." I felt my way gently around to the back of her skull, where there was a deep divot, and tilted her head so that Azhanharad could see.

He almost managed to hide his wince, but his ears flattened and gave him away.

"It was a better death than drowning," I said.

He said dryly, "We will remember not to tell her family that. If she has one. Since we do not know, and time is precious, we make petition to you on her behalf. Can you witness for her?"

"Yes." I considered the alien memories in my head. "We think that we can find where she was pushed into the canal."

Azhanharad nodded. "We will keep her as long as we can."

Even in the cold of the Brotherhood's vault, they could not keep her forever.

※

As I knew they would be, my dreams that night were full of drowning. Sometimes it was I who drowned; dreadful as that was, I preferred it to the other dreams, in which I stood helplessly on the brick bank of the canal and watched Evru struggling in the cold dark water, knowing he would drown and knowing I could not help him. I woke before dawn and was grateful for it.

I got up in the darkness, dressed by touch. I did not light a candle until I was in the tiny michenmeire I had created out of my apartment's only closet. There I lit the seven candles one by one, saying the silent devotions I had been taught as a child.

In the cult in which my Velveradeise grandparents worshiped and into which I was initiated when I turned thirteen, just before I began my novitiate as a prelate of Ulis, we knew that Ulis was not the true name of the god of death, of dreams, of mirrors and the moon. His true name was never spoken aloud, save only for the initiation of each child into the mysteries. We worshiped unspeaking, and for myself, I continued the rituals of silence, kneeling in the light of the seven candles before an altar made out of an old dressing table and a black coat too threadbare to be worn. The only precious thing I owned lay on the old black coat on top of the dressing table, the long silky coil of Evru's hair, as white as moonstone, which I had shamefully stolen when they cropped his hair for his execution. I had no right to it, but I could not have given it up if the emperor himself had demanded it.

I had called him Evrin, after the mastiff-sized white deer that foraged in the wheat fields of the south. He had never seen one; I described them to him, their long delicate legs, their wide, lambent eyes. They were not hunted, unlike their bigger cousins, and they were sacred to a goblin sect with a strong following in the border cantons. They were shy, crepuscular creatures, but if one had the patience to remain still, they would eventually come close enough to show the white-on-white dapples of their coats, dipping their heads to graze, then looking up again. If startled, they bolted with astounding swiftness, faster than any horse. Evru, shy and long-legged, was in truth very much like an evrin. If only he had bolted when he had the chance.

I scrubbed my palms up my face and moved through the Devotion of Folded Hands, blowing out the candles and accepting—or trying to accept—that the past was the past and could not be changed.

I walked to the Red Dog's Dream for breakfast. Their cook was Barizheise and made traditional oslov, and while they were dreadful at the more delicate teas, their Airmen's Blend was strong enough to starch a shirt collar. This morning that was what I needed, something to chase away the cobwebs, the dreams, the memory of Evru's eyes.

※

After breakfast I decided to eschew the tram and walked up out of the Airmen's Quarter, cutting across to Bridge Street and climbing up the hill to the Veren'malo, the Old City, and to the hulking government buildings of the Amaleise Court. I had been given an office here, in the Prince Zhaicava Building (in preference to finding space in the cramped underground warren of the Amalo-meire), a box of a room where citizens who required the services of a Witness for the Dead could petition me. There were never very many, hence my relief that the Vigilant Brotherhood was willing to seek me out after hours, as it were, for without them I would have been like a becalmed ship, or a beached whale, with nothing to do but read the three Amalo papers from start to finish and then the imported Barizheise novels in their lurid purple covers that were hawked in the Silkmarket at two zashanei each. I had a row of them, the size and shape and nearly the weight of bricks, lined up along the wall behind my desk.

I had to be in my office and available to petitioners through the morning hours of the Court. After that, I was free to roam the city in pursuit of my docket of petitions. I had the matter of Mer Ur-menezh's sister, for whom I could not witness if I could not find her body, and the morning brought, along with an unsigned letter in the post from someone who certainly needed help, but not any help that I could give them, a larger than usual handful of petitions, two of which were questions for the Municipal Registry of Deaths, one a matter which had to go to the Amalomeire before it could come to me, and the fourth, brought by a very angry young elven woman, involved a disputed will, with each side accusing the other of fraud.

"How long has your grandfather been dead?" I asked.

"Two weeks."

"Then even if his spirit has remained with his body, he will not remember what you want to know."

"You do not know our grandfather," she said darkly. Her gaze lowered for a moment, then returned resolutely to mine. "All we ask, othala, is that you try. It is the . . . the *cleanest* way to end our family dispute."

"Even if what he says is not what you want to hear?"

She shook her head, frowning. "Even that would be better than this endless squabble. Please, othala."

It was not my place to refuse a petitioner. "Yes, then, on the un-derstanding that it may be too late."

"We understand," she said. I hoped the rest of her family would agree.

※

Her name was Alasho Duhalin. Her grandfather had been the Duhalar of Duhalada and Cedharad, one of the biggest im-porting firms in Amalo, with arms in several major cities of the south and east. I knew from long and bitter experience that fights over inheritance had nothing to do with the amounts involved, but I also understood why Min Duhalin was so upset. The longer this fight went on, the longer the employees of Duhalada and Cedharad did not know where they stood. (Mer Cedharad lived in Barizhan and thus could not be relied on for guidance.) Min Duhalin, a good burgher's daughter, was worried about the effects on business and the ploys of the company's rivals.

We took the Vestrano tramline down the hill to the wealthy neighborhoods north of the Mich'maika. By virtue of the fact that we took the tram together, rather than her returning home in her family's private carriage, I knew that Min Duhalin's decision to bring a Witness *vel ama* into the proceedings had either been disputed by or was entirely unknown to her family. It was fashionable among the sons and daughters of the bourgeoisie to take the municipal trams instead of using their families' carriages. The young women, however, usually traveled in pairs.

I asked her, "Does anyone in your family know of your petition?"

She startled guiltily and I had my answer.

"Your family will not thank you," I said in warning.

"At least they'll stop *fighting* about it. Our father and our uncles do not speak together unless it is in argument over Grandfather's will. And our mother has an undiplomatic tongue." That, as I knew from my own childhood, was a true curse among the women of a house, who came together not by their own choice. Min Duhalin sighed and said, "We did not think there was such rancor in our house."

We got off the tram at the Dachen Csaivanat, the deepest well in the north of the world, and walked two blocks north to a house within sight of the city wall. The neighborhood was of an age to have been new when Min Duhalin's grandfather made his fortune, and the brick had aged to a soft pinkish red, meaning that it had been made of local clay. Min Duhalin set her jaw and walked straight up the front steps.

The house steward opened the door before she could, demanding, "Min Alasho, where have you *been*?"

"We have brought a Witness for the Dead," said Min Duhalin, and gestured me inside.

The house steward stared at me as if I were a rain of frogs, and the atrium of the house was suddenly full of people: the three Duhaladeise brothers of whom Min Duhalin had told me, and an assortment of their spouses, their children, and their children's spouses; Min Duhalin had not detailed her siblings and cousins to me, but I found, watching, that the Duhaladeisc family resemblance was extremely strong, and it was easy to tell a blood relation from a spouse. And the one nervous-looking Barizheise lady was clearly someone's wife.

"Alasho," said the eldest of the men (and therefore her father), "what is the meaning of this?"

"We petitioned the Witness *vel ama* to come and speak for Grandfather," said Min Duhalin, whose forthrightness certainly could not be faulted.

As I had expected, her announcement was met with a chorus of horrified and angry voices, protesting that there was no *need* and that she had had no *right*. I thought it unfortunate that her father seemed to be even angrier than his brothers, berating Min Duhalin as one would a small and disobedient child.

Finally, when it was clear that the din was not going to resolve on its own, I stepped forward, finding some sour amusement in how quickly everyone fell silent. They all stared warily at me.

I said, "We have accepted Min Duhalin's petition as reasonable and proper. It is futile to remonstrate with her, and you may be glad it is not within our remit to inquire why no one else thought to do the same as she."

The horrified silence grew a little more horrified.

I said, "We understand that Mer Duhalar was cremated, but that you retain his ashes?"

After a very long pause, the eldest Mer Duhalar still living said, "Yes, that is correct. We cannot scatter the ashes until—Our father specified that his heir was to scatter his ashes."

And without an heir being determined, that meant that nothing could be done with the ashes. They were lucky that both the real and the fraudulent will had specified cremation. If one had specified embalming, the Duhalada—able then to do neither—would have been in a dreadful mess.

I was tempted to say, as I had been tempted before, *The fastest way to get rid of us is to cooperate.* Instead, I said, "We understand that your house is in a very difficult time, and we do not wish to make it more difficult. It will take us only a moment with Mer Duhalar's ashes to know if we can even be of help."

"It is a sensible thing to do," one of the younger brothers said suddenly. "If you will follow us, othala."

I followed him, although my heart was sinking. Either he was bluffing—gambling that I would be unable to speak for his father—or he was innocent of fraud. And if the younger brothers were innocent, for Min Duhalin had told me that the two of them were united behind the second will, then Min Duhalin's father was the one who had presented a false will.

)(

The family shrine was elaborate with marble and gold leaf, the name plaques each carved with the family's wolf signet. The Duhalada's funerary practices—cremating the bodies and scattering the ashes—were considered barbaric in the capital, but it was the best deterrent against ghouls. It was the custom followed by about half of Amalo's citizens, those wealthy enough to be able to afford it. The others buried their dead with the best gravestones they could.

The younger brother indicated his father's box on the altar, surrounded by the michenothas, and then tactfully withdrew.

I picked up the box—cedar and beautifully carved with an intricate pattern of interlocking circles—and said a silent prayer to Ulis, asking only that I should find the truth. I knew better than to ask for the unobtainable.

I began murmuring the prayer of compassion for the dead—such a constant companion that some nights it ran through my dreams—and gently, carefully, opened the lid of the box.

The dead man's signet ring rested among the ashes. I touched it with one finger, being careful to maintain my grip on the box. Contrary to my prediction, I got an immediate and strong sense of Nepena Duhalar, cold and grasping and deeply satisfied that his business would prosper in the hands of his son. His son Pelara.

That was not the name of an eldest son.

I warned my petitioners that they might not like the answers I provided, but I had never had anyone heed my warning.

I closed the box carefully and returned it to its place on the altar. I said the prayer of compassion for the dead once more, bowed to the house gods, and left the shrine.

The younger brother's face tightened, his ears lowering, when he saw my expression, but he led me without speaking back to the atrium, where everyone was still standing in fraught and awkward silence.

"Well?" said the eldest Mer Duhalar. Now that I knew, I could see the bluff, and I felt some reluctant admiration for his refusal to yield.

"Which of you is Pelara Duhalar?" I said.

"We are," said my guide.

I saw Min Duhalin start to frown; she knew she hadn't told me her uncles' names.

"We offer our condolences on your loss, Mer Duhalar," I said. "You are your father's heir."

✕

I left the Duhalada house more than an hour later, exhausted and hungry. There had been, as there always was, a great deal of arguing. No one who had supported the eldest son's claim wanted to believe he had forged his father's will, and I had to reiterate several times that the name the dead man had told me was Pelara, not Nepevis. On the other side, Pelara Duhalar very sensibly got two of the servants to come witness a formal testimony, so that there would be no confusion after I left about what I had said. I told him I would make a deposition, to the same end.

No one said anything about how they were going to deal with

Nepevis Duhalar's dishonesty, but I thought that question would be keeping the younger brothers awake tonight.

Min Duhalin simply disappeared. I hoped she was not blaming herself, but knew she was. How could she not? She had made her decision, as petitioners often did, based on a belief that she knew what the dead would say. She had been wrong, as petitioners often were. In time, she might find comfort in knowing that she had caused the truth to be revealed. Some people did; some people did not.

I could not help; I had no gift for comfort, and myself found the truth no comfort at all, only duty.

I walked back to the Deep Well ostro. Most major shrines in the city were associated with stations, and the Deep Well was no exception; although the station was the size of a wax seal, it did boast a teahouse called the Lady of Rivers, operated by the novices from the shrine's associated csaivatheileian. I bought a sticky bun and a two-cup pot of orchor and sat in a curtained booth for two people.

I drank the orchor black, grateful as I usually was for its bite, but also today grateful for its harshness, like drawing a thick black line between me and the Duhalada. I tried not to think about how many miserable families I had left in my wake, and I did strive to remember, as the Archprelate had said to me, that I did not do anything but what I was *asked* to do. Some days that felt like casuistry, but it was another thick black line like calligraphy on good rag paper.

I took the tram back east to the Dachenostro and changed to the Zulnicho line, which took me straight south to Ulvanensee. Properly, I should have been going to the Ulistheileian to find a panel of three prelates, but after yesterday's conversation with Vernezar, I was, not merely reluctant, but actually opposed to going there. Fortunately, I knew where to find three prelates, and even a fourth to serve as scribe.

Anora had three prelates serving under him, Daibrohar, Erlenar, and Vidrezhen. Daibrohar and Vidrezhen were elves from Zhaö, Erlenar a half goblin from Choharo. Daibrohar and Erlenar were in their first prelacies; Vidrezhen had come from a wealthy benefice in Cairado and said she liked Ulvanensee much better.

I found Anora and two of the three prelates copying register entries to send to the Municipal Registry of Deaths; Erlenar was washing windows. They were all glad of an excuse to do something else, even if it was something as dull as listening to me give a deposition. They'd done this for me before, since it had become clear to me very early in my stay in Amalo that the Ulistheileian was not friendly to me.

Daibrohar settled to be scribe, and I related the incidents of the morning, laying particular stress on the fact that the dead man had remembered his heir's name. And that the name was Pelara, not Nepevis.

"What an unpleasant business," said Anora when I was done.

"Yes," I said. "I'm only grateful that this is the end of my part in it."

Anora made a warding sign and said, "Let us hope so. I will deliver the deposition to the Ulistheileian if thou likest."

"That would be a great kindness," I said.

Anora shrugged. "It's easy enough. They won't obstruct me the way they will thee."

"No," I said, feeling suddenly very tired. "No, they won't."

✕

I took the tram from Ulvanensee back north to the Bridge Street ostro, where I got off and walked to the Reveth'veraltamar at the bend in the Mich'maika where it curved around the Sanctuary of Csaivo. The Reveth'veraltamar was where all the bodies that ended up in the canal washed aground. There was a gate in the wall there, and stairs down to the water. I had a key.

Today I walked down to the water not because I expected to find anything useful, but because one of my duties as a prelate of Ulis was to mourn for the unnamed dead, and to mourn for her meant following the path of her body as clearly as I could. The Reveth'veraltamar was where they'd pulled her out; I sought to remind myself of the gray moss-slimy stones; the slap of the water against the walls of the canal; the smell. The Reveth'veraltamar was an ugly place.

As I was turning to go, something sparkling caught my eye among the stones. I bent and picked up an earring: three clear, faceted glass drops with a broken clasp. There was no guarantee that it belonged to the dead woman in the crypt, but it was not unreasonable as a guess, either. Although inexpensive, it was pretty, and by gaslight the glass might look like diamonds. If I found someone the woman *might* be, the earring would be a way to try for certainty. I tucked it carefully in an inner pocket and climbed back to the city.

I locked the gate behind me.

X

I walked to the municipal ferry dock. In the middle of the day, the ferry was a better way than the tram to get from the middle of town to the Zheimela district. When the manufactories closed at sundown, the opposite would be true, for anyone who wanted something stronger than tea would be going to the bars along the south side of the Mich'maika out toward its eastern end, and so would the prostitutes. And the pickpockets. The ferry was probably how the dead woman had gotten to the place where she died.

Now the ferry passengers were mostly bourgeois families heading to their tiny bungalows along Lake Zheimela's western shore, plus the first few bartenders and servers headed out to clean the bars before they opened. I got several curious looks, although no one was impolite enough to ask my business. I pretended to be too abstracted in my own thoughts to notice.

I left the ferry at the southside docks and walked along the canal, looking for a dock to match the dead woman's memories. The image was stark and vivid in my mind, as the memories of the dead always were, if there was anything left at all. I saw more than the dead woman had. I knew the way the dock jutted into the canal. I knew there were crates stacked along it, but nothing out at the end, nothing that could have sheltered her or provided a weapon or anything. Whether by luck or by plan, her murderer had chosen his spot well.

Hulking warehouses lined the canal here, none of them with

the dock I was seeking. Then a rope-maker's shop. Then the only bar open during the day, the Canalman's Dog, a sprawling establishment—built around an ancient shrine to Osreian—that also operated as a teahouse. The city council had passed legislation that said no teahouse could also be a bar, but it was too late to stop the Canalman's Dog, which had been both for two or three generations at the point the legislation was proposed.

And behind the Canalman's Dog, there was a dock. I recognized it at once.

It was cool and dark inside the Canalman's Dog, and I wandered for some time along its narrow passages before I found the hearth of the teahouse. There, a young goblin man with his hair in the traditional Barizheise braids—although he wore Amaleise embroidered felt slippers—bowed to me and asked how the house could serve me, the traditional Amaleise words. Then, reading my black coat and thick, untidy prelate's plait, he added, "othala," and looked uneasy.

I said, for my calling forbade deception, "I am Thara Celehar, a Witness for the Dead. I'm trying to find the last hours of a young woman who was dragged out of the canal yesterday. A blue-eyed elven woman, probably your own height. Her cuffs were embroidered with flowers." I showed him the drawing that one of the Brotherhood's novices had made of the dead woman, easing the angles subtly so that she appeared alive again. He studied it dutifully, but shook his head.

"She looks like many of our customers, othala," he said apologetically, "but I will ask Csatha the bartender to come talk to you. He may know the lady."

I waited. Csatha was very little older than the goblin boy (who returned to washing teapots at the side of the hearth), but he was elven; he wore his white hair in a thickly braided bun and had enough money for a line of amethyst chip earrings to accent the sweep of his left ear. There was a haze of gold in his gray eyes that suggested Barizheise blood somewhere in his family tree. He looked at the drawing and listened to my description, then said, "She's not one of our regulars, othala, but more than that I couldn't say."

I hadn't expected to have any luck on my first try. I got Csatha to draw me a map of the bars in the immediate area, which he did with quick, certain lines. He smiled as he handed me the map and said, "Good luck, othala. You might try the Golden Tea Light. Most of the iönraioi drink there."

"Iönraio" was the Amaleise word for an unaffiliated prostitute, just as it was the word for a queen-cat in heat, based on the noise she made as she called her toms. It was a good guess at the dead woman's occupation. I still wasn't sure it was correct; she had looked too healthy and too prosperous for the shadowy hand-to-mouth life of an iönraio. But at the moment I had no better guess.

I explored the Zheimela district that afternoon, finding the bars Csatha had marked, along with chandler's shops and greengrocers, secondhand clothing shops, brothels, photographers' studios, an array of pawnbrokers, the district's municipal baths, the livery stable, a shrine to Csaivo (as Amalo's lifeblood was the Zhomaikora and the Mich'maika, so the city was full of shrines to the goddess of rivers). Just before dusk, I found a street cart near the manufactories west of the municipal ferry dock and bought a tobastha for half a zashan. Then, with dusk, the bars opened, and I began working my way through Csatha's map.

It was in the eighth bar, or maybe the seventh, or the tenth, that the half-goblin bartender, in the act of handing the drawing back to me, suddenly frowned and looked at it again. "Oh," he said. "*Her.*"

"You recognize her?"

"She was in here night before last. Overdressed. Never seen her before. One glass of rice wine and she took up a table for two hours. Alone. She wasn't an iönraio, because I saw her turn down more than one man. And then at half past eleven, she got up and walked out." He thought a moment and added, "I think Athris said she was an opera singer."

My ears dropped with astonishment. "She was a what?"

"Hey, Athris!"

One of the servers wiping down tables looked up. "Me?"

"Anybody else here by that name?"

"I guess not." He came to the bar, a delicately pretty elven boy with wide violet eyes.

"You were saying you know who this lady is," the bartender said, and showed Athris the drawing.

"Oh!" His face lit up. "Yes, the lady who was here night before last. That's Arveneän Shelsin. She's the senior mid-soprano at the Vermilion Opera."

"You're sure?"

"Oh, yes. I saw her in *Thormedo* last spring."

"Why are you looking for Min Shelsin, othala?" asked the bartender.

"She was pulled out of the canal yesterday morning," I said, and took no pleasure in the way Athris's face sagged with horror.

"Oh no!" he said. "But how could—"

"That's what I'm trying to find out. Did she talk to you at all?"

"She said once she was waiting," Athris said, "but she didn't say what she was waiting for."

"Was she alone?"

"Oh, yes. She left at half past eleven, and she was as alone as when she came in."

So probably her death did not meet her here. But now I knew her name. I remembered the earring and showed it to him, and he said, "Yes. She had crystal drops lining both ears and a strand of crystal beads in her hair. It was a marvelous effect."

"Thank you," I said. "You have been a great help."

I left the bar wondering who Min Shelsin had been meeting at midnight the night before last. *Where* almost had to be the Canalman's Dog, for why else would someone pick that particular dock to throw her off?

I walked back that way, wondering also why an opera singer from the Veren'malo had come all the way down to the Zheimela to meet whomever her appointment was. It suggested a powerful need for secrecy, and anything that secret was probably also a motive for murder.

The Canalman's Dog was raucous now, people in every room,

Guild prostitutes moving among them, offering cool, alluring looks from under their eyelashes. I started to fight my way toward one of the bars when it occurred to me that the people to ask were the prostitutes. If she had been here, they would have been watching her to be sure she wasn't an iönraio; they would have seen who she met.

I talked to prostitute after prostitute. They were amused and intrigued to be spoken to by a prelate, and they looked at the drawing carefully. But I had to ask several before an elven woman who called herself Haro said, "You know, I *did* see her, night before last. She had crystal in her hair, and she was overdressed."

"Yes," I said. "Was she with anyone?"

Haro bit her lip, thinking. "She was at a table, and, yes, she was with someone, because I remember the stagey way she laughed at something he said. But I'm sorry, othala, I don't remember a thing about him."

"Don't be sorry," I said. "You've been a tremendous help."

She smiled, a sudden, shy smile with no coquette in it, and said, "She wasn't one of us, but I don't think she was an iönraio, either."

Before I could say thank you, or ask another question, Haro's face and body changed, and she was moving away on the arm of a middle-aged goblin man, as graceful and untouchable as a cloud.

✕

In the morning, it was back to the Prince Zhaicava Building and the post and the papers and the wait for petitioners. No one came, and I used the time to write down everything I had learned about the dead woman.

Then, with an hour before noon and no petitioners in sight, I went down the hall to one of the other oddities housed in the Prince Zhaicava Building, the cartographers for the Amalo Municipal Tramline Authority, the clerks and mapmakers in charge of knowing exactly where the tramlines ran and of giving exact and accurate directions to the repair crews. Maps, some complete, some half drawn, some still uninked sketches, covered the walls, and there were filing cabinets full of written directions on how to get from the Prince Zhaicava building to every major landmark in Amalo. I had overheard an argument one day about changing the starting point to the Amal'theileian, as being "more suitable," but Dachensol Orzhimar, the master mapmaker of the Amalo Municipal Tramline Authority, said sharply, "All that would accomplish is that we'd have to add directions from here to the Amal'theileian to the start of every script." And there the matter rested.

The mapmakers were an intense group of young elven men, passionately in love with their work. The clerks were mostly middle-aged elven ladies, efficient and serious and very proud of their abilities. They were also proud of their well-earned reputation for knowing everything that happened in Amalo, since everyone involved in the city or principate bureaucracies (insofar as the two could be separated) came to them when they needed directions to anywhere. It was amazing, Min Talenin had told me, how often the bureaucrats of the court ended up out in the city, inspecting and interviewing and participating in ceremonies.

Min Talenin and Merrem Bechevaran, the elven clerks who had the office to themselves this morning, were pleased to see me. Although I did not gossip, I did ask for their help if I had a case that warranted it. I had asked them about Mer Urmenezh's sister, and now I showed them the drawing of Arveneän Shelsin.

Min Talenin said, eyes widening, "That's the mid-soprano from the Vermilion Opera."

Min Talenin was a good middle-aged bourgeoise elven lady, the daughter of a clockmaker, thrifty and responsible. The only luxury she allowed herself was the opera. If she and Athris in the Zheimela agreed about the woman's identity, it seemed most probable that they were correct.

"Are you sure?" I said, but I knew she was before she said, "Absolutely sure. What happened to her?"

"She was thrown in the canal three nights ago," I said.

"Oh *no*," said Min Talenin. I realized that I could perhaps have phrased it more tactfully.

"Who would want to do such an awful thing?" said Merrem Bechevaran, who was younger than Min Talenin and a widow.

"That's what I'm trying to find out," I said. "I was hoping you could help me. I need directions to the Vermilion Opera."

"Oh, that's easy!" said Min Talenin, brightening. She dug in one of the filing cabinets beside her desk.

Merrem Bechevaran went to the wall and began sorting among the maps. She returned with a map leaf at the same time Min Talenin emerged with a beautifully written sheet of directions.

Merrem Bechevaran spread the map out on her desk and Min Talenin said, pausing occasionally to let me scribble notes in my notebook, "So. Starting from here, you take the Mountain Road northeast until it intersects General Baizhahar Boulevard. It will be a sharp turn backwards, for you want to follow the boulevard northwest. You follow General Baizhahar until you come to the Plaza of the Armistice, where seven streets meet. You'll take Indigo Street, which runs straight north. In one block, it crosses Vermilion Street, and the Opera is on the northeast corner."

Merrem Bechevaran came back from another filing cabinet with a drawing of the Vermilion Opera. It was a massive brick building that clearly would be impossible to miss or mistake.

"Thank you," I said.

"Come and tell us if we are inaccurate," said Min Talenin.

"Of course," I said, made my bows, and departed.

※

After lunch at an inexpensive Barizheise zhoän, I followed Min Talenin's directions. As always, they were as clear as you could ask directions to be, and I found the Vermilion Opera with no difficulty at all.

The Opera was an enormous building, four or five stories tall and covering an entire block. The great arches of the entrance seemed like gaping mouths waiting to swallow me whole.

I told myself sternly not to be ridiculous.

I had never been to the Vermilion Opera before—the ticket prices, even for the cheapest seats, were far beyond my meager budget. I was unprepared for the rich vermilion walls of the lobby and could only be grateful there was no one to see me standing there as stunned as a fish. The lobby was vast and its color, combined with its cavernous vault, intensified my impression of being caught in the jaws of some monstrous beast. I started toward the ticket office at one end of the lobby, uneasily aware of the clacking sound of my shoe heels, and a young half-goblin man, pale eyes in a dark face, appeared suddenly in the ticket window and said, "Can I help you, othala?"

"My name is Thara Celehar," I said, "and I am a Witness for the Dead. I need to speak to someone about a death for which I am witnessing."

He looked both alarmed and uncertain. "I . . . I don't know. Mer Kalmened is not here, and I don't know if . . ." He trailed off, thinking hard. Then an idea came to him, for he said, "I will ask Mer Pel-Thenhior. Excuse me just one moment." He disappeared from the window.

I did not have to wait long before one of the auditorium doors swung open, and another half-goblin man came striding out.

He was several inches taller than I was, though not goblin-bulky, with ash-gray skin and eyes of the luminous gold particular, like the form of his surname, to the Pelanra, the western coast of Barizhan. He had his hair in long Barizheise braids, and there were gold charms hanging from his ears. He was wearing a beautiful fawn-colored suit and an irritated expression. "I am Iäna Pel-Thenhior," he said in a carrying baritone. "What can I do for you?"

"My name is Thara Celehar," I said again. "I am a Witness for the Dead."

His face went through a complicated series of emotions, and he said, not asking, "It's Arveneän."

"Yes," I said.

"Curse it," he said, with a strange mixture of anger and sadness. "I knew something had to be wrong. She might skip a rehearsal, but she'd never skip a performance. I've been waiting for you for two days."

"It has taken us this long to identify her," I said. "She was found in the canal."

"In the *canal*?" His ears showed his genuine surprise. "What in the name of all that's holy was she doing there? Arveneän prided herself on never going south of the city wall, and although that wasn't *strictly* true, she certainly did not venture that far south in the city very often."

"She washed up at the Reveth'veraltamar," I said. "Assuming that our identification is correct—we still need someone who knew her to come see the body."

"Do you?" He grimaced. "I suppose that would be me, then. Just a moment." He disappeared back through the double doors. When he returned, he was scowling, and his expression did not lighten as we rode the tram south to General Parzhadar Square and the Chapterhouse.

The novices on duty at the main doors were accustomed to taking people to view the dead. They led us through the public halls of the Chapterhouse and down the great main staircase of the crypt. At the bottom, Subpraeceptor Volar was on duty, and he led us to the cold room, where the woman's body still lay on the marble slab.

Pel-Thenhior did the dead woman the courtesy of looking closely. He nodded tightly. "That's Arveneän. Goddesses of mercy." He did not seem grief-stricken, precisely, but badly rattled.

"Did you know her well?" I asked.

"I've known Arveneän since we were children," he said absently. "We hated each other." Then he seemed to hear his own words, for his ears twitched violently, making his earrings chime. "Oh dear. Should I not have said that?"

"Did you kill her?"

"No."

"Then you have no reason not to tell the truth, and I appreciate your honesty."

"My mouth always runs half a minute ahead of my mind," he said ruefully. "You said she was found in the canal? What happened?"

"She was murdered," I said.

"Do you know who did it?"

"No," I said, "but to witness for her, I must find out."

)(

We ended up in a teahouse on General Parzhadar Square, drinking a golden orchor that was not as strong as I liked, but also lacked the harshness of the black orchor I drank for preference. Pel-Thenhior laced his liberally with honey and said, "What do you need to know about Arveneän?"

"The last time you saw her?"

"It was on the ninth. We argued about the new opera we're rehearsing and she left with her newest patron, Osmer Borava Coreshar. That was at about six in the evening, since they were just beginning to set the stage for *General Olethazh*."

"And she was last seen alive a little before midnight."

Pel-Thenhior's ears flattened and he said, "That's an awful feeling, knowing that she flounced out of the theater with only six hours to live."

"Obviously, I need to talk to Osmer Coreshar—to all of her patrons. Do you know how I can find them?"

"Her patrons?" I was surprised that he seemed taken aback. "You don't think . . ." Then he caught himself. "Well, of course, there's no reason it couldn't be one of her patrons."

"Murder is no respecter of rank," I said. "But in any event, I need to speak to them, for she might have said things to them that she would not have said to anyone else."

Pel-Thenhior snorted. "I can guarantee that much. Arveneän with her patrons was an Arveneän the rest of us never saw."

"Did she have many?"

"Most certainly. She and Nanavo, our senior principal soprano, sometimes seemed almost as if they were in a competition to see how many young men of means they could bedazzle. Arveneän was not interested in young men without means, even though there were several who would have married her without a blink. But only the wealthy men would do for Arveneän—she wasn't as picky about their age."

"Then what was she doing in the Zheimela after dark?" I said, more bluntly than I had meant to.

His eyes widened. "She was found in the Zheimela?"

"She was found at the Reveth'veraltamar," I said, "but she was thrown off a dock in the Zheimela. I could discern that much from her corpse."

He shook his head slowly, clearly distressed. "But why would she be there? No, I'm sorry, obviously that's the question you're trying to answer. But if you want to talk to her patrons, come to the opera tonight. They'll all be there."

When I hesitated, trying to calculate the price of a ticket to the Vermilion Opera against my finances, he said, "Oh, don't worry about that. You can sit in my box."

"Your box?"

"I'm the principal director of the Vermilion Opera," he said with a tiny mock-bow. "Also the principal composer. I sit in a box by the stage and terrify the singers by taking notes."

"But . . ."

"Those seats are never sold anyway," he said. "I promise you, no one will mind."

"Most people prefer not to associate themselves with those of my calling," I said cautiously.

"Why in the world not? It's not as if it's contagious."

"Some people seem to believe it is."

He dismissed such people with a jingling flick of his ears. "Never mind that. Come with me back to the theater now and I'll make sure the ticket office knows to let you in."

ХК

On the tram ride north, Pel-Thenhior, making up (he said) for previous sullenness, proved to be a lively companion. He told me about the new opera in rehearsal, which was one that he had written, called *Zhelsu*. "It's quite a departure from the usual, but I'm tired of operas about emperors and generals. I wanted to write an opera about ordinary people. Manufactory workers."

"That is certainly different," I said.

He grinned. "Oh, the expression on your face. I get that reaction quite frequently, but it only makes me more certain that this is a thing that needs to be done."

"Needs?"

"Opera is amazing, but it's been doing the same thing over and over again for hundreds of years. I think it could do *other* things, and the only way to find out is to try."

"And thus you've written an opera about manufactory workers."

"Yes!" he said. "And it's coming together beautifully. More so now that Arveneän isn't picking fights and complaining, which, you understand, is—was—what Arveneän did. That reminds me. I have to find Toïno and tell her she's singing Merrem Chovenaran tonight. She won't be happy." He sighed. "And then I have to tell everyone about Arveneän."

I noticed that there was no suggestion of closing the theater that evening and asked him about it.

"We can't afford to," he said unapologetically. "Our ticket revenues are barely ahead of our expenses as it is. And our patron ..." He made a face. "Financial discussions with him are always unpleasant. I don't *think* he'd let the theater fail, but I admit that I'm not sure."

In the lobby of the theater, Pel-Thenhior immediately went to the ticket window and told them I was his guest that evening. He then turned to me and said, "Is there anything else you need from me, othala?"

"Do you know where Min Shelsin lived?"

"As it happens, I do," said Pel-Thenhior. "She lives—lived—not far from me. In Cemchelarna."

"Cemchelarna," I said. On the Zheimela Road between the city wall and the canal, Cemchelarna had been intensely fashionable about five hundred years ago and was now a mix of manufactory workers and artists. I had chosen to live in the Airmen's Quarter for Ulvanensee and for the straight shot up the Zulnicho tramline to the Prince Zhaicava Building, but I could easily have chosen Cemchelarna instead.

Pel-Thenhior thought a moment and then gave me directions as lucid as any cartographer's clerk's: "It's a red clapboard building with a stone foundation, only the clapboard is so old it's faded to pink, and it's directly across from the East Water Works on North Petunia Street. You take the Zheimela Road out the Zheimel'tana to Emperor Belvorsina III Square. The Coribano line will take you that far. Then you turn east on Hawthorne Street. Take the Abandoned Bridge over where the Cemchelarna River used to be, and you'll find yourself in the confluence of five streets. You walk south on North Petunia for three blocks until you see the East Water Works, which is a hulking brick monstrosity you cannot possibly miss."

"That's very clear. Thank you."

His smile was sudden and dazzling. "You are welcome. But now, I am sorry, but I must find Toïno. I'll see you tonight."

He strode away, leaving me for a moment off balance, as if the force of his personality had been holding me upright. Which was a ridiculous notion, and I shook it off, leaving the theater to go in search of Min Shelsin's home.

※

I followed Pel-Thenhior's directions southeast along the Zheimela Road—I walked to save the tram fare—to the Emperor Belvorsina III Square. Then two blocks east on Hawthorne Street until I came to the Abandoned Bridge.

The Abandoned Bridge was badly misnamed, for it had never been abandoned. There were still shops and houses all along its length, and many of the buildings that had been erected over the

buried river had bridges of their own from their upper floors teth-
ered to the wrought-iron railings of the Abandoned Bridge.

I crossed over the bridge, dodging several hawkers and a troupe
of street acrobats, then walked south on North Petunia Street until
I saw the brick bulk of the East Water Works looming among the
two- and three-story clapboard houses, some with shops on their
ground floors. I stopped on the sidewalk in front of the East Water
Works; the building directly across the street, faded clapboard just
as Pel-Thenhior had described, was clearly a boardinghouse, complete with the green-and-silver flag hanging over the porch railing
to indicate an empty room and an elderly elven lady sitting on the
porch with a great mass of patchwork spread out over her lap. Resi-
dent or landlady, she seemed like a good place to start.

She watched me come with bright pale eyes, and the closer I got
the more clearly I realized how truly venerable this lady was. I said,
"Greetings, dachenmaro," as I came up the porch steps.

It amused her. Her eyes almost disappeared into her wrinkles
and she said, "Greetings, othala," in return. "Come sit beside me,
if you don't disdain to keep an old lady company." Her voice was
hoarse but still firm, and she had a strong Amaleise accent of the
sort the comic operas gave to their villains.

"Of course," I said, and took the chair next to hers.

She showed me her quilt, scraps of fabric pieced together into
the pattern called Valmata's Return. She was now stitching the
top and batting and backing together, overlaying Valmata's Return with a pattern called Scorpion Dance—appropriate to the
story of Valmata, who returned from war and poisoned his father
in order to take control of the family estates. They sang the ballad
in Lohaiso.

It was a great deal of aggression for one quilt, but I judged it wis-
est not to say so. Instead, I complimented her on her beautiful tiny
stitching.

She laughed, pleased, and said, "When you've been sewing for
ninety years, othala, your stitching hand will be just as crisp."

"Ninety years is a lot of stitching, dachenmaro," I said.

"Don't I know it!" she said, laughing again. "But I am no one's mother. My name is Rhadeän Nadin."

"I am Thara Celehar," I said.

"What brings you here, Othala Celehar? Are you looking for a room?"

"No," I said. "I've come about Arveneän Shelsin."

"We don't know where she is," Min Nadin said, "as I told the other young man."

Probably someone from the Opera, possibly Pel-Thenhior himself. "No, not that. I'm witnessing for her. She was killed three nights ago."

"We wondered why she did not come home," said Min Nadin bleakly, again using the first-person plural. "You should talk to my niece, who is the landlady. I only know that her name was Arveneän Shelsin, and she was an opera singer with the Vermilion Opera. But truly you should be talking to Vinsu." She raised her voice into an unexpectedly powerful shout: *"Vinsu!"*

Almost immediately, a stout, hen-like elven woman emerged from the house, saying, "Aunt Rhadeän? What's wrong?"

"A prelate has come asking about Min Shelsin," said Min Nadin, nodding at me. "They've found her body."

"Her *body*? Oh no!" She sank into the remaining chair, wide blue eyes on me.

"I'm very sorry," I said. "I am Thara Celehar, a Witness for the Dead. I am trying to witness for Min Shelsin."

"But what *happened* to her? Oh dear, my name is Vinsu Nadaran, and you are welcome to my house, othala. I will tell you anything I can, but I don't know very much about Min Shelsin. Some boarders tell me everything about themselves, but Min Shelsin was very secretive."

That, at least, was not a surprise. I said, "She was found at the Reveth'veraltamar. Someone threw her in the canal."

"Oh *no!*" moaned Merrem Nadaran again.

"I knew that girl was going to come to a bad end," said Min Nadin. "Ambition is one thing, but she was greedy."

"Aunt Rhadeän!"

"Oh hush, Vinsu. I'm ninety seven. Surely that's old enough to be allowed to speak my mind."

Only some of the sects in the city believed that one should never speak ill of the dead. I said, "I'm grateful for any details you can give me, and it would be of tremendous help if I could see her room."

"Oh no," said Merrem Nadaran again, though clearly not in refusal.

Min Nadin sighed.

"I would not take anything," I said.

"Oh, I'm sure you wouldn't," said Merrem Nadaran. "Yes, of course. Just follow me."

The house was spotlessly clean and stretched back from the street farther than I had expected: eight rooms in two rows of four on each floor, plus the staircase at the rear. We climbed to the third floor in silence, and Merrem Nadaran led me to the second room from the front on the north side of the house. The door was locked, but she had a master key.

"I have a rule," she said, "that I don't use this except in emergencies."

I was glad to be ranked as an emergency, but I thought I might offend her if I said so. I asked instead, "Do you know anything about Min Shelsin? Did she have family in Amalo?"

"Not to my knowledge, but she was as close-mouthed as a turtle." Merrem Nadaran opened the door and waved me inside. "All she'd ever talk about was the Opera. She'd been a principal there for three years, and she was puffed up like a turkey cock about it."

The room was of medium size, furnished with a bed, a dresser, and a table by the window with one spindly chair. Everything had the distinctive air of secondhand furniture. As many people did, Min Shelsin had used the top of her dresser as a tiny shrine with five michenothas to represent the gods and a token from the Sanctuary of Csaivo to indicate that she'd made at least one pilgrimage in Amalo. The shrine was the only character the room showed until I opened the door of the closet and was ambushed by a riot of color: red and blue and gold, a vivid splash of fuchsia, green and blazing yellow and purple. And the fabrics were just as wild, silk and taffeta and velvet and all manner of brocades, gauze and lace and ribbons everywhere. I parted the row of lush and brightly colored gowns and saw that the closet made a right-angle turn with another bar full of hanging gowns, just as peacock-bright as the first row.

"How far back does the closet go?"

Merrem Nadaran looked blank for a moment, then made a gesture indicating the width of the room. "All the way to the hall," she said. "All my lodgers appreciate the closets."

Thinking of my own room, I could only nod in agreement.

Min Shelsin's room held nothing more of interest. I thanked Merrem Nadaran for her trouble and left, saying good-bye to Min Nadin on my way.

"Will we see you again, othala?" she asked.

"Very likely." I felt no enthusiasm at the prospect, but that closet was a mystery I knew would nag at me.

"If you come back often enough," she said, "I'll make you a quilt."

⚜

I took the tram to General Parzhadar Square, where the novices on duty at the Chapterhouse thought about refusing me entry and then thought better of it. I knew where to find Azhanharad, for I had been here before, and I made my way through the dark, narrow halls to the tiny room he used as an office. He always looked to me like he was on the verge of bursting out of it, like a bull out of a too-small cage.

"Othala!" he said. "What news?"

"The dead woman is an opera singer named Arveneän Shelsin. She lived in Cemchelarna. She doesn't seem to have had any family in Amalo."

Azhanharad sighed and said, "We don't suppose they knew which sect she followed."

"She had the michenothas in her room," I said, "and a token from the Sanctuary of Csaivo."

"That does narrow it down," Azhanharad said, looking marginally more cheerful. "With any luck we'll be able to bury the poor woman properly."

"It doesn't look like there's anyone who will know if we're wrong," I said, although I knew that was of no more comfort to him than it was to me.

⋊⋉

I returned to the Vermilion Opera that evening, still wearing my black silk coat of office, for I had no other clothes fine enough for a box at the opera—and I was certainly not attending for pleasure.

The staff at the ticket office knew me immediately, and a goblin page boy appeared seemingly out of nowhere to lead me to Pel-Thenhior's box.

The box was in the first tier, almost on the stage—not an angle the stage was meant to be viewed from, but I understood at once why it was ideal for someone who wanted to watch what the singers were doing rather than to watch the story. It was also one of the least fashionable boxes, being farthest from the prince's box at the center back of the auditorium. It was not likely that Prince Orchenis would visit the Vermilion Opera, but the best box in every Amaleise theater was called the prince's box just in case. This evening, the prince's box held two elven couples, all lavishly dressed, with jewels glittering in hair and ears. Town gentry, most likely, who could be unnoticed at the Amal'opera or could be peacocks here—and not have to pay as much for the privilege, either.

After one look out at the rapidly filling auditorium, I retreated to the back corner of the box, where my view was of the flounced and tasseled stage curtain. Less interesting, but it could not look back at me and speculate about who I was. From this vantage point, I could also see the almost invisible door set into the box's opposite wall, and that explained why this of all boxes was the director's box.

I had not been there long before the door opened and Pel-Thenhior—beautifully dressed again, in an evening suit of dark blue and silver brocade with earrings of lapis lazuli—came through. He smiled when he saw me, his ears lifting, and said, "Oh good, you came!"

"Of course," I said.

"I wasn't sure. You seemed a little taken aback."

That was true enough. I gave the easiest answer: "I follow my calling."

"Then come sit down and let us see whom I can find."

I took one of the seats at the front of the box, and Pel-Thenhior sat beside me. He scanned the auditorium with one comprehensive glance and said, "Good house tonight. *The Siege* always draws them in, old warhorse that it is. And there's Mer Dravenezh in the Parzhadeise box as usual."

The soberly dressed Mer Dravenezh looked out of place but also perfectly self-possessed.

"Does his employer not attend?"

"The Marquess Parzhadel is an invalid and never leaves the Parzhadeise compound. But Mer Dravenezh is here most nights. I have never been sure if Parzhadel *sends* him or if use of the Parzhadeise box is one of the perquisites of his job as Parzhadel's secretary. He's probably the most attentive person in the audience, so I hope for his sake he wants to be here."

"You have never asked him?"

"It would be vulgar curiosity, nothing more. I prefer to leave Mer Dravenezh in peace. So. The people you're interested in are going to be across from us and above us. Arveneän was only interested in men who could afford a box."

That was unsurprising; I nodded.

"She aimed as high as she could," Pel-Thenhior said. "She allowed burghers' sons to court her because they have money, but she wanted men like Osmer Elithar"—he nodded across at a fashionably dressed young elven man on the tier above us—"and Dach'osmer Cambeshar, who is sitting in the box on the other side of the prince's from Mer Dravenezh."

I leaned on the railing of our box, and looked over, easily spotting an older elven man, just as fashionably dressed, who was sitting with an elven woman, very beautiful and half his age.

"Yes," said Pel-Thenhior to a question I had not asked. "Dach'osmer Cambeshar is a patron of many beautiful young women. Arveneän wanted badly to oust the others, but she never could. He is far too canny to let her have that kind of power over him. Other men are not so wise."

He nodded at Osmer Elithar again. "She's just about ruined him, for all that he maintains the appearance that she hasn't."

"Is that a reason to kill her, do you think?"

He considered my question carefully, pointing out two more of Min Shelsin's patrons, Osmer Ponichar and Osmer Isthanar, before he said, "It could be. But I'm not sure Osmer Elithar is the man who could do it—not that I think murder is in any way a courageous action."

"No, I understand. Are there any of her patrons you think *could* commit murder?"

"Dach'osmer Cambeshar would order it done and not think twice," he said, "but I simply can't imagine him caring enough about Arveneän to want her dead." He pondered a moment. "The trouble is deciding what makes a man capable of murder. We all might be capable of murder in the right—or wrong—circumstances."

Which was either a neat evasion of my question or a genuine philosophical conundrum. I didn't know him well enough to be able to judge which.

"Perhaps if I rephrase," I said. "Did any of them—other than Osmer Elithar—have reason to want her dead?"

"I don't know that she'd bled any of the others quite as dry," Pel-Thenhior said, "but—"

There was a knock on the door he'd come in by. He cursed in Barizhin and said, "I must go, but I'll be back as soon as I can." He gave me a stern look and added, "And there's no reason for you to hide in the back of the box, either. You are far from the strangest guest I've entertained." In a swirl of startling crimson-lined coattails, he was gone.

I kept my seat, pointing out to myself that in fact no one was looking at me at all, and watched the glittering audience, wondering how many of them were like Osmer Elithar and on the brink of penury.

When the curtain began to rise, I felt a childish thrill out to the tips of my ears, as if I *had* come to the opera for pleasure. I knew the story of the siege of Tekharee; it was the subject of a long poem which I had been required to memorize as a child. The elves on the battlements within, the goblins on the plains without, the failure of the relief efforts, the growing desperation of the elven officers, the deadly patience of the goblins, the final agreement among the elves that rather than watch their wives and children starve, they would kill them and then burn Tekharee to the ground—and then the horror of the goblins as they find the murdered children among the smoldering wreckage. I had seen the opera before, but found myself as absorbed by the terrible dilemma of the garrison of Tekharee as ever. I barely noticed when Pel-Thenhior returned to the box. I did notice that Merrem Elorezho was sung by a goblin woman—who arguably had the best voice in the company. Her duet with Merrem Devatharan (sung by a sweet-faced elven soprano who was probably fifty trying to pass for thirty) filled the auditorium with a twining harmony so exquisite that we all forgot to breathe. Even the scratching of Pel-Thenhior's steel nib stopped.

At the intermission, Pel-Thenhior said, "A couple more of Arveneän's boys came in late. That's Mer Csenivar in the box directly across from us, and Osmer Olchevar is in the box above us."

"Mer Csenivar must be quite wealthy?"

"To attract Arveneän's attention, you mean? Yes, he has a generous allowance from his very wealthy father, but he's also incredibly persistent. If any of her patrons was obsessed with her, he's the one."

The young elven man in the unfashionable box was talking to his companion, another young elven man who was obviously his brother. They had the same shape to their faces and went to the same tailor.

Pel-Thenhior said, "Do you want an introduction to anyone? Not all of them like me, but we certainly know each other."

"No, thank you, although I appreciate your offer. This is not where I want to try to get information out of them."

"I see your point," said Pel-Thenhior, glancing around at the brightly chattering audience. "This is a terrible place to try to have a serious conversation."

"They won't even really see me," I said.

✕

Perhaps because Pel-Thenhior was sitting beside me, furiously scribbling notes, I noticed things about this performance of *The Siege of Tekharee* that I hadn't thought about before: the way that the chorus of the goblin army was swathed in black cloaks and helmets rather than painting their faces, the way the battlements of Tekharee were shown just by a low stone pillar and the acting ability of the officers and wives, who never failed in their pretense that on the other side of that imaginary wall was a fatal drop. The costumes of the officers and wives were magnificent, and I thought of the contents of Min Shelsin's closet.

After the end—the goblin army lamenting in lurid red light the deaths of their enemies—and after the curtain calls, as I was sitting and watching Min Shelsin's patrons collect their belongings and prepare to leave, Pel-Thenhior returned to the box and said, a little breathlessly, "Oh good, you're still here."

"Did you need something from me?"

"More that I was wondering if *you* needed anything from *me*." He gave me an oddly defiant look. "I hated her, but I didn't want her dead. If she was murdered, I want her killer caught. And if you are trying to catch her killer, I want to know how I can help you."

My face must have been as blank as the wall behind me. He said, "If I offend, othala, of course I apologize, but I thought . . ."

"No, no, of course not," I said hastily. "I am in sore need of help, to be honest. I was just surprised."

"Surprised?" he said, surprised in turn. "But does not everyone want killers to be caught and justice to be done?"

"Many people would prefer the whole thing just quietly disappear."

His ears flattened in disapproval. "Such people dishonor their ancestors," he said, the particular phrasing he used telling me—probably without meaning to—that he was a member of a Barizheise sect which included among the gods a figure called the Grandmother of Grandmothers, the Dakh'dakhenmero, who, they believed, watched over the family. Every family's Dakh'dakhenmero figure was different.

"I will gladly accept any help you can offer," I said. "Certainly, I could use *someone*'s help in going through her room."

"Well, there you are," he said. "I can help with that. I knew her probably as well as anyone." He winced. "What a horrible epitaph. For she hated me as much as I hated her."

"Did she have any friends? Or only patrons and, um, colleagues?"

"She was friendly with two of the office clerks. I don't have their names to hand, but I can find out."

I eyed him cautiously. "I will need to talk to everyone."

"Everyone?"

"The only way to find the person who has the piece of information I need is to ask everyone I can find."

"I do not envy you your work," Pel-Thenhior said. "Well, as long as you don't mind it being rather piecemeal, you're welcome to talk to people around rehearsals, when they're not on stage. It's the best way to be sure of finding them. They'll all show up here sooner or later."

"All right," I said. "When can you go with me to her boarding-house?"

"Any morning you like."

"Morning?"

"Afternoons are rehearsals," he said. "I have to be here. Why?"

"Mornings, I must wait for petitioners in an office in the Prince Zhaicava Building."

"That sounds dreary."

Sometimes, I nearly said, but bit my tongue in time.

"Well, I'll come petition you," said Pel-Thenhior. "It feels strange to be taking the place of her family, but they all died in the iärditha epidemic five years ago."

"You are an honorable man."

"Am I? For wanting a murderer to be caught?"

"For being willing to take action. As I said, most people simply want the problem to vanish. The witnessing for a murder victim can be a very painful thing."

He regarded me with his ears at an inquisitive angle. "And yet you continue witnessing."

"It is my calling," I said. "I tried to stop, but that was far worse, a kind of living death. I could not . . ." I trailed off, unable to find the words to explain.

"When I was fifteen," Pel-Thenhior offered, almost shyly, "and my voice changed, I went from being an excellent soprano to being a quite unremarkable baritone. I tried to quit the opera entirely— wounded vanity, mostly—and I could not. I could only try to find another way into the Empress Corivero's garden, if you will forgive a rather overelaborate metaphor. So perhaps I understand a little."

"Music is a calling," I said.

"Not a religious one."

"No, and many prelates would disagree with me. But, to take your metaphor one step further, Ulis is the god of dreams."

His ears dipped in surprise, almost alarm. "I had not made that connection. You are a poet, othala."

I was unsure whether he meant that as a compliment. He might have been unsure as well, for he said briskly, "The Prince Zhaicava Building, you said? I will meet you there at ten," and he was gone like a rabbit down a hole, leaving only the soft click of the door-latch behind him.

ᛉ

Perhaps unsurprisingly, I found myself wakeful. The moon was approaching full, flooding the world with its cold, beautiful light. Some sleepless nights—for this was a problem I was familiar with—I simply lay in bed and thought about whatever puzzle my petitioners had most recently brought; some nights I lit the lamp and reread one of my lurid novels, accepting the expense I was incurring. Often, I went out walking in the local cemeteries—the small ones, the collective and family cemeteries, not the great bleak precinct of Ulvanensee. The paths were as carefully tended as the graves, and the lingering fear of ghouls, more superstition than necessity in a city like Amalo, meant that I did not encounter clandestine lovers or other night wanderers. Since Mer Urmenezh had come with his petition, I had used these walks to look for Min Urmenezhen's grave, with failure after failure to reward me. Tonight was the cemetery Ulchoranee, a small collective in a neighborhood close to my own.

Ulchoranee was laid out in a simple pattern, nothing ambitious or artistic. I walked up and down the rows, reading the gravestones by moonlight, noting that the stone-carving was clear and crisp and the stoneworker had some interesting and recognizable idiosyncrasies in the way he formed his letters. Most collectives had a single stoneworker they patronized, sometimes even entering into a contract to ensure that their gravestones received the promptest attention.

When I found her, I almost walked straight past her, both because I wasn't expecting to see her name and because I had become accustomed to thinking of her as Inshiran Urmenezhen, but her gravestone read INSHIRAN AVELONARAN. Beneath it, there was another inscription, ULANU, a suitable name for a dead child of unknown sex.

I stood stock-still in astonishment for some moments, only now realizing just how much disbelief I had been carrying. I had truly never expected to find her, and I certainly hadn't expected to find her *here.*

"How did you come to Ulchoranee?" I said aloud. In a novel, she would have answered me; in truth, no Witness for the Dead could achieve results without actually touching the corpse they spoke to, and furthermore she had been dead far too long.

She and her unborn child, and I wondered if Mer Urmenezh was right about murder.

Mer Urmenezh, a most respectable bourgeois elven bachelor, had come to me in great distress. He had said that his sister was in her mid-thirties, a lifelong and content spinster, a birdwatcher who spent her spare time (when she was not teaching seven-year-olds the first rudiments of history and mathematics) on Lake Zheimela in an unladylike canoe.

Then, one day, she had met a man.

She came home excited as her brother had never seen her, and her conversation was full of this Croïs Avelonar and what he said and thought for a week. Then, without warning or discussion, she quit her job and eloped, leaving behind a letter that explained nothing, apologized for nothing, and almost seemed to have been written by a stranger.

Mer Urmenezh and his two other sisters (their parents being deceased) assumed sorrowfully that that was the last they would ever hear from Inshiran. But barely six months later, Inshiran wrote to announce her pregnancy. The Urmenada were elated, for they had thought it most likely that none of them would ever marry, being—as Mer Urmenezh said wryly—a family of recluses. Inshiran's child might be their only chance for the family to reach another generation.

They wrote back, assuring Inshiran of her welcome in their house—in fact begging her to visit—but the next thing they received was a brief, brusque letter from Avelonar telling them that Inshiran was dead and buried in the Airmen's Quarter, and that was that.

Except.

Mer Urmenezh was tormented by the timing. Inshiran had just gotten pregnant, she had gotten back in touch with her family—and Mer Urmenezh was convinced, from certain phrases in her letter, that Avelonar had forbidden her to write to them—and then she died. Avelonar did not give a cause of death, nor any kind of explanation; he did not invite them to the funeral (which apparently had already happened by the time he wrote). The letter was so unlike that of a grieving widower that Mer Urmenezh had become convinced that he was in fact Inshiran's murderer.

One of his sisters, he admitted, thought he was deranged.

But Mer Urmenezh had come to me because, if nothing else, he wanted to find Inshiran's body. After that one letter, there had been no further communications from Avelonar, and letters to him had been returned marked UNKNOWN.

I was puzzled by another thing. "Did your sister have any money of her own? Something that would tempt a man like Mer Avelonar into marriage?"

Mer Urmenezh nodded grimly. "Our mother's father—for she was an only child—chose to leave his money to her oldest daughter rather than to her family. Inshiran received a monthly allotment, most of which she contributed to the household, but the money remained under her control."

"And thus when she left, you lost that income."

"Yes."

"What happened to the money at her death?"

"We have no idea. We do not know if she made a will."

"We shall have to find out. It also might help you locate Mer Avelonar. If anything was left to him, the lawyers must have some means of communicating with him."

"You are wise, othala."

"Merely practiced," I said. "His behavior throughout has been that of a man who wants something other than a wife from his marriage."

"He has behaved vilely," said Mer Urmenezh.

"Yes. But our question is, where would he have had her buried?"

"Wherever was cheapest," Mer Urmenezh said bitterly.

"Certainly that seems like a good way to start," I said, and thus I had begun with the poorest cemeteries in the Airmen's Quarter and had worked my way slowly through them.

I had been sure when I reached Ulvanensee, the municipal cemetery, that I would find her there, for municipal burial was cheap. But in their enormous, centuries-old ledgers, where they kept all the names of the dead, Anora and his prelates had no record of burial for anyone named Inshiran, and I wandered the entire width and breadth of the cemetery and did not find a headstone for her. She had not been dead long enough to have been moved to the catacombs, for which I was thankful. At that point, finding her would have been impossible.

But, no, she was not there. She was in Ulchoranee, where Avelonar must have been sure no one would ever think to look for her.

I felt considerable satisfaction to have proved him wrong.

᙭

I spent the first part of the morning in my cold office writing a letter to Mer Urmenezh, informing him of my findings and giving him what advice I could on how to proceed. It was a grim task, but I felt that I had at least performed the duties of my office to the best of my ability. I told him that he should speak to the clerics at the Sanctuary of Csaivo about an autopsy. They might or might not be able to find evidence of murder this long after death—it would depend on how Avelonar had killed her, if he had, and how the body had decayed. But it was necessary that they look.

I had no suggestions about finding Avelonar.

Halfway through the morning, Iäna Pel-Thenhior appeared in the doorway. He was dressed with great elegance, this time in dark green with emerald chip earrings.

I felt intensely shabby, but I set aside my pen and paper and said, "How may we help you, Mer Pel-Thenhior?"

He bowed, echoing my formality, and said, "We have come to petition you to witness for the death of Arveneän Shelsin. And again, to offer our help."

I got up gratefully and said, "Then let us go examine her room."

᙭

W alking across the Abandoned Bridge with Pel-Thenhior was
    a different experience. He seemed to know all the perform-
ers and street philosophers and most of the barrow-men. We actually stopped for several minutes while he haggled with one of them
over a book, a squat duodecimo volume the approximate size of a
half-brick. Pel-Thenhior apologized when he came back, but he was
too pleased with his purchase for me to be irritated.

"It's *The Complete Operas of Pel-Teramed*," he said, as if that
would explain everything. Then he laughed and said, "I beg your
pardon. Pel-Teramed was a southern Barizheise dramatist who
lived about two hundred years ago. There was a fad for his operas
in the elven cities when my grandfather on the Thenhior side was
a boy, so that there are volumes of his operas floating around the
great book—" He paused, searching for a word. "—the great secondhand book market that exists piecemeal across Amalo, one
shop here, another barrow there. But it has taken a long time for the
Complete Operas to circulate to me. Sadly, it's scripts only, or we'd
need a barrow of our own."

"Do you intend to perform one of his operas at the Vermilion
Opera?"

"I doubt it," he said cheerfully. "They're bloodthirsty old things
and full of people swearing revenge over their beloveds' literal
corpses. But now that I *own* it, I can see if perhaps I can adapt something for a more modern sensibility. Or just enjoy them and the
memory of my grandfather telling me the plots when I was little.
That's probably what made me want to write scripts as well as music, come to think of it. Because otherwise I'd be stuck writing music
for other people's stories."

"Do you still perform?"

"I *can*," he said, "but I'll never make a principal singer, and in
any event I'm temperamentally better suited to telling everyone else
what to do." He grinned, inviting me to enjoy the joke at his own
expense, and I was surprised to find myself laughing.

"You don't laugh enough, othala," said Pel-Thenhior. "Is it the
nature of your calling?"

"Not all prelates of Ulis are gloomy by temperament," I said.

"But you are?"

I hesitated, Evru so present in my mind that for a moment I could not speak, and Pel-Thenhior said, "I beg your pardon. I should not have asked that question."

"It is a good question," I said, "but I do not know the answer to it."

His brows drew together, but he said nothing.

I said, picking my way through a morass of truth, "I have been grieving for a long time for someone who was very dear to me. And it is only recently that I have been shown that my calling did not die with them. I suppose I simply got out of the habit."

"That is very sad," said Pel-Thenhior.

I shrugged uneasily. "It is in the past."

"Is it? I think I would argue otherwise, but I do not mean to make you uncomfortable. Let us talk of other things. I mostly talk about opera, which is very boring of me, so you should pick the topic."

"I have no gift for conversation," I said truthfully.

"That's just because you haven't had the right partners. Are you happy here in Amalo or do you miss the court?"

"I hated the court," I said.

Pel-Thenhior's eyebrows went up. "You are frank. Why did you hate it? Most people dream of going to the Untheileneise Court."

"I was there on charity," I said. "Charity grudgingly given and grudgingly accepted. And being a member of my cousin Csoru's household would sour anyone on court life."

He eyed me sidelong. "Rumor has it that you have spoken with the emperor."

"I have."

"What is he like? All we get are the lithographs of the coronation, and they don't do justice to anyone."

"He is about your height and very thin. His skin is darker than yours and his eyes are very pale. In feature, he rather takes after his father." I thought for a moment about how to describe Edrehasivar VII. "He is soft-spoken, patient, honorable."

"Will he be a good emperor, do you think?"

"Yes," I said with conviction. "He is now and he will continue to be."

The house on North Petunia Street was as I had left it, venerable lady on the porch and all. "Othala!" she said. "You are back and you have brought a friend."

"Min Nadin," I said, "this is Iäna Pel-Thenhior, who worked with Min Shelsin at the Vermilion Opera. Mer Pel-Thenhior, this is Min Rhadeän Nadin."

Pel-Thenhior made a formal bow, which pleased Min Nadin greatly. She said, "You must be here about the closet. Vinsu is at her wits' end."

"The closet?" said Pel-Thenhior.

"Min Shelsin's closet is remarkable," I said.

"Go in," said Min Nadin. "Vinsu will only be relieved to see you."

"I am agog," said Pel-Thenhior, and followed me into the house.

Merrem Nadaran emerged from the back, her hands covered in flour, and said, "Oh, othala, you've come back!" Whereas with Min Nadin it had been a greeting, with Merrem Nadaran it was plainly a cry for help. "What am I to do with all those clothes?"

"I have brought someone from the Vermilion Opera," I said, feeling doubly fortunate that Pel-Thenhior was with me, "who may be able to help. This is Iäna Pel-Thenhior. Mer Pel-Thenhior, this is Merrem Vinsu Nadaran."

"Oh dear, and me all over flour. Please go up! I can't leave my baking." She vanished again.

"I am even more agog," said Pel-Thenhior.

We climbed the stairs and found Min Shelsin's room. The door was open and it looked as if Merrem Nadaran was starting to clean out Min Shelsin's things. I crossed the room and opened the closet.

After a moment, Pel-Thenhior said, "I understand Merrem Nadaran's despair."

The great swirl of color seemed even brighter than I remembered. I said, "I thought perhaps Min Shelsin was borrowing her costumes from the theater."

"'Borrowing' is a very kind word, othala, but unfortunately

imprecise. 'Borrowing without permission' would be closer. 'Stealing' would be closer still."

"I was afraid that might be the case."

"I am surprised and a little dismayed that no one ever said anything to me. Here's Ishoru's dress from *Emperor Edretantivar*." He pulled an opulent pearl-white gown off the bar and all but threw it at me. "This is the dress the chorus wore in *The Cavaliers of Zhaö* five years ago. Anmura give me strength, here's the Second Maiden from *The Castle of Shorivee* and the Eldest Rose from *The Dream of the Empress Corivero*. I wonder if she was planning to bring it back for our production this autumn."

"There's another bar behind that one," I said.

Pel-Thenhior made a noise of fury and disappeared into the closet. I laid my armful of finery carefully on the bed.

"She wasn't even *in Calistrana*!" Pel-Thenhior shouted from the depths of the closet. "This is one of Amaö's costumes. The wardrobe staff is going to have hysterics, joy or fury I don't know which."

"Are they *all* stolen gowns?"

"Only the expensive ones," Pel-Thenhior said sourly.

"How could she steal so many costumes and not have anyone notice?"

"If you'd seen the Opera's wardrobe, you wouldn't ask that question. Osreian have mercy on us, is there another bar behind this one? This closet is like a dragon's cave." A pause full of rustling noises. "Yes, but there's nothing stolen on it. Thank goodness. I'm not sure my heart could have taken it." More rustling and Pel-Thenhior emerged from the closet, his braids awry and dust on his coat. "The problem is how I get all of these costumes *back* to the Opera. Arveneän clearly stole them just by wearing them home—*someone* must have known she was doing it, and I rather want to talk to that someone about what they were thinking—but I'm going to have to hire a carter. There's just too many of them to carry without dragging them through the muck of the streets."

"Is there anything else we should look for that she might have stolen—or anything that the Opera can use? You said she had no family, and Merrem Nadaran clearly wants none of it."

"Gloves," Pel-Thenhior said promptly. "We go through gloves at a pace you would not believe—and that's *with* mending them until there's simply nothing left to set a stitch in." After a moment's reflection, he added, "Also petticoats in good repair. I am very pleased with the idea of Arveneän somehow paying the Opera back for this monstrous theft."

"Restitution," I said.

He laughed. "I suppose."

"No, I'm quite serious. As a Witness for the Dead, it is part of my duties to see that the dead both give and receive restitution." I started opening drawers, but was stopped almost immediately by a flock of pawn tickets like sleeping moths. "I think I know where all her jewelry went."

Pel-Thenhior came to see. "Oh dear," he said. "Well, that's beyond our reach."

"Yes," I said grimly. "But perhaps the pawnbrokers will at least let me match the tickets."

"Do you need to?"

"I don't know," I said. "Which means yes."

※

We scavenged through Arveneän Shelsin's room that morning, piling everything that belonged or might be of use to the Vermilion Opera on the bed. Merrem Nadaran was only too pleased to have the proportions of her headache diminished. Aside from the gowns, like the plumage of unimaginable birds, we took gloves, handkerchiefs, petticoats, combs and tashin sticks (many of which were also the property of the Vermilion Opera, recognizable by the tiny letters vo scratched into them with the point of a needle), silk stockings, and shoes.

As we worked, Pel-Thenhior told me more about Min Shelsin in bits and pieces. He talked about her voice, which he said was "excellent but not incomparable. She talked about the Amal'opera, but she could never have been a principal there, and she knew it. And Arveneän *loved* being a principal. I don't think she would ever have forgiven me for giving Zhelsu to Othoro."

"The Opera must have another principal mid-soprano," I said. "It would have been in the papers if you were regularly casting a goblin woman."

"Wouldn't it, though?" Pel-Thenhior said. "Merrem Anshonaran is away to have her first child. She stayed absolutely as late as she could. We will welcome her back."

"Not like Min Shelsin?"

"Not in the least."

A little later, he said, "All singers are gossips—and I frankly include myself in that—but Arveneän enjoyed telling people things that would hurt them. She loved starting fights, although she hated being in fights herself."

"She preferred causing trouble unseen," I said, thinking of one of my parishioners in Aveio.

"Not a bad way of putting it," said Pel-Thenhior, carefully bringing out from the closet's second bar a midnight-blue dress made of velvet and layer after layer of gauze dyed to match. "She hated to be seen for what she was, which was probably why she valued those two little clerks so greatly. They would always think the best of her and she needed that." He laid the blue dress across the bed and stood staring at it absently. "This is a costume from *The Masque of the Night Empress,* which we performed to celebrate Prince Orchenis's wedding. Just before the crash of the *Wisdom of Choharo.* And Arveneän stole it."

"It is a beautiful gown," I said.

"I don't know why I'm surprised," Pel-Thenhior said. "If she'd had any decency, she wouldn't have been stealing from the Opera to start with."

"She might not have meant it to be stealing," I said, a little hesitantly, for I was not sure if I believed my own argument.

"You didn't know Arveneän. This is thousands of muranai's worth

of costumes, and I guarantee she had no intention of ever returning any of them. She never let go of anything. Not a grudge, not a
zashan. She was like a lamprey eel, and to tell you a horrible truth, I
am not sorry that she is dead."

"Are you not afraid I will use that truth against you?"

He stopped and considered me for a moment, then said, "No.
You are honest and you serve Ulis faithfully. If you were merely
looking for a convenient person to blame, you wouldn't have made
it as far as the Vermilion Opera in the first place."

"You are wagering rather a lot on your reading of my character."

"It isn't a wager," said Pel-Thenhior.

※

When we had the contents of Min Shelsin's room organized
into things the Vermilion Opera could use and things it
couldn't, Pel-Thenhior left to hire a carter. I went downstairs to talk
to Min Nadin.

It was not difficult to get her started talking, and I soon had another portrait of Arveneän Shelsin. This one was a good lodger:
quiet, polite, always paid the rent on time. But she wasn't friendly
with anyone, not the other lodgers, not Merrem Nadaran, not Min
Nadin herself. "And we tried," she said, "but Min Shelsin wasn't interested. The only thing you could ever get her to talk about was
opera, and then she wouldn't stop."

I was surprised Min Shelsin hadn't wanted admirers. "What did
she talk about? Her fellow singers or the operas they were performing or . . . ?"

"She *complained* about her fellow singers," Min Nadin said tartly.
"But she really liked to talk about her parts and how difficult they
were—they were always difficult—and if there were any good duets
and the like."

"Did she ever sing?"

"No, and I never asked. She was a conceited child—there was no
need to encourage her."

"She must have practiced," I said. "But not here?"

"Not here," agreed Min Nadin.

Ж

That afternoon, I went back to the Vermilion Opera. This time, the goblin boy in the ticket office said, "Mer Pel-Thenhior says you're to go in," and pointed to the great double doors of the auditorium.

I went through one set of double doors and into the foyer, with staircases up to the balconies and passages leading off on both sides to the boxes on this floor. There was another set of double doors in front of me, and when I pushed open one leaf, I heard a woman singing.

I slipped to one side, letting the door swing silently shut behind me. She was singing, incongruously, about manufactory work, about getting up before dawn and going to bed after dark, about soot and machine grease and how the clothes of a manufactory worker were never clean.

I could see her now, a tall goblin woman, heavy featured and with granite-gray skin, standing alone on the stage. She had been Merrem Elorezho last night, but had had no solos, and that seemed to me to be a terrible pity. Even singing softly, even singing about ugly things, she had the most beautiful voice I had ever heard. Her voice soared, lamenting, turning a discontent that many might call trivial—especially in relation to the likelihood of maiming or death which was also part of a manufactory worker's daily life—into a plangent symbol of all the things a manufactory worker would never earn enough to have, starting with clean clothes.

For a few minutes, I thought she was alone in the auditorium, singing only to the vacant seats and dim gas globes. But then, as her song came to an end, Pel-Thenhior's voice, instantly recognizable, shouted from the floor of the auditorium, "Where's my Chorus of Workers?"

There was a moment's silence, as if no one was there to answer the question, and then an elven man leaned out of the wings and said, "Sorry, Iäna, we've got in a bit of a muddle."

"A muddle? What is there to get muddled over? Othoro"—which he pronounced Barizheise-fashion, with the emphasis on the first syllable—"sings 'cruel clock masters' and the Chorus of Workers enters from both sides of the stage. I'm sure that's what I wrote."

"It's not *that*," said the elven man, in a tone suggesting "that" was exactly what it was.

"Then what in—no, never mind, I'll just come up there." Pel-Thenhior bounded across a plank laid from the floor of the auditorium to the stage as a makeshift stair, and vanished into the wings.

The goblin woman remained where she was, as tranquil as a statue.

I moved cautiously down the aisle to stand by the row where Pel-Thenhior had been sitting, easy to identify because of the stacks of paper holding one seat down.

The goblin woman saw me and called, "Iäna, there's someone here to see you." She squinted at me past the footlights and added, "I think it's a prelate."

"A prelate?" Pel-Thenhior erupted from the wings. He saw me and smiled, saying, "Othala Celehar! Welcome to the madhouse! All right, everyone, give me a moment. Vethet, kindly get your muddle sorted out." He bounded back across the plank and up the aisle. "How would you like to do things, othala? I found out the names of Arveneän's two friends in the offices."

"That will be very helpful. I would like to speak to the company of singers first, though."

"Of course," said Pel-Thenhior.

"How many are there in your company?"

"We do everything by twos: sopranos, mid-sopranos, altos, tenors, baritones, and basses. Then there's the chorus, which is another twenty, and the children's chorus, if you want to count them."

"Children are as observant as anybody," I said.

"True enough. So I guess that's fifty-two all told."

"Do you use them all in every opera?"

"Not hardly," said Pel-Thenhior. "Most operas only use half our principals, in different configurations, and only maybe one in five has a children's choir."

"And how many are in this opera?"

"Eight principals and both choruses. And my junior principals who don't have named parts are singing in the chorus, because I wanted to give as much impression of a busy manufactory as I could."

"Was Min Shelsin the only troublemaker?"

"Tura—Tura Olora, the senior bass—is never satisfied with any-thing, but I wouldn't call him a troublemaker. And Nanavo's a gos-sip, but she doesn't mean any harm by it. Not like Arveneän. So, yes, Arveneän was our only deliberate troublemaker. And there's another horrible epitaph."

"Min Shelsin made her own choices."

"Meaning that if she wanted me to speak well of her, she should have behaved better? Perhaps. Or perhaps I have a malicious tongue." He raised his voice to a ringing shout: "Everyone out on stage!"

They came in ones and twos, then in a rush, and then stragglers. The children came in a long line, holding hands. Almost all of the singers had elven coloring except for the goblin woman—Othoro Vakrezharad, I remembered from last night's program—one man in the chorus, and three of the children.

"All right," said Pel-Thenhior. "First, I think you all already know that Arveneän Shelsin is dead."

A murmur ran through the group, but no one said anything loud enough that I could hear it, and there were no immediate signs that the news was painful to any of them.

"Second," said Pel-Thenhior, "this is Othala Celehar. He wishes to talk to you."

They all stared at me.

I said, "I am a Witness for the Dead. Right now, I am witnessing for Min Shelsin, who was murdered—"

"*Murdered?*" said someone, sounding both shocked and disbe-lieving.

"Someone threw her in the Mich'maika," I said. "Her skull was fractured before she could drown, but it was clear murder either way."

In my memory, a number of my superiors bemoaned my inability to be tactful.

The singers of the Vermilion Opera all looked rather stunned. Then Min Vakrezharad said, "You're the Witness *vel ama*. I have read about you in the papers."

"Yes," I said. "I'm here to try to find out more about Min Shelsin—anything at all that you can tell me."

"She was friends with some of the office clerks," said Min Vakrezharad. "That's all I know, for she disliked me intensely."

"She was envious," said another woman. "Envious of your voice, and then the best mid-soprano role to come along for thirty years and *she* didn't get it. I tell you, Othoro, if *you*'d turned up murdered, we'd all know who did it."

Someone as tactless as me. I made a note of her face.

"She didn't talk to us," said the woman standing next to the tactless one.

"The clerk she was friends with is named Meletho," said a man.

"Meletho Balvedin and Toreän Nochenin," said a woman.

I glanced at Pel-Thenhior, who nodded. Those were the names he had found, too.

They were all looking at me, hoping, as people always did hope in my investigations, that if they gave me someone else's name, I would go away.

I said, "Do you know of anyone who might have wanted to hurt her?"

Silence. Even the tactless woman said nothing.

"These aren't all of your singers, are they?" I asked Pel-Thenhior.

"No, just the ones for this scene and the children's chorus for the entr'acte. And Toïno, who is very kindly helping us with the chorus this afternoon, is Arveneän's understudy."

A tall elven woman blushed scarlet and nodded.

"Is there anything else you can tell me?" I asked the singers. "Anything at all?"

They looked blankly at each other, shaking their heads. Then one of the children said, "You should ask Matron. Matron knows *every-thing.*"

I gave Pel-Thenhior a questioning look, and he said, "We have a woman who minds the children's chorus." He raised his voice to a shout: "Davelo! I need you on stage!"

She was a stout middle-aged goblin lady with a kind face. She listened to the news calmly and said, "What a terrible shame."

Pel-Thenhior said, "I *have* to continue this rehearsal. Davelo, will you talk to Othala Celehar? Tell him everything you know."

"And the children?" said Davelo.

"Can stay on stage if they *sit quietly.*"

The children giggled, obviously knowing better than to be afraid of Pel-Thenhior's ringing voice, but at once sat down, each child the same distance from the child before and after, as if they had rehearsed it.

The goblin woman crossed the plank with less élan than Pel-Thenhior, but her steps were steady and her balance assured. She said, "Good day, othala."

I bowed back.

"I am Davelo Matano," she said. "I will be happy to help you in any way that I can, othala, but let us go out to the lobby, where we will be able to hear ourselves."

At that moment, Pel-Thenhior shouted, "All right, back to the beginning of Zhelsu's aria. Chorus of Workers off stage, Chorus of Ghosts stay put."

I said, "Your suggestion is a good one." I followed Merrem Matano up the aisle and back out into the cavernous lobby. As the door swung shut behind us, she said, "I don't know, really, that I can be of any help to you, othala. I was not an intimate of Min Shelsin."

"I understand," I said. "But I am hoping you will tell me more about . . ." I groped for the words to explain. "About how she fit here." It was the opposite of *stathan,* but there wasn't a word for it, for the connections a person created during their lifetime. By study-ing the connections, you learned a great deal about the person, and

the more I learned about Arveneän Shelsin, the more connections
I traced, the more likely it was that I would be able to find her connection to the person who had killed her.

Merrem Matano seemed to understand something of what I
meant, for she said at once, "Min Shelsin was a troublemaker. For
her, nothing was ever done right. Her part was never big enough,
the other principals were never good enough, her costumes were
never flattering enough . . ." She shook her head. "If she had not
had such a beautiful voice, she would have been dismissed from
the company a dozen times over. Toïno, who has her parts now,
is hardworking and uncomplaining, but she does not have Min
Shelsin's voice. Only Othoro Vakrezharad matched her, and Min
Vakrezharad was never going to get the best parts. Not until Mer
Pel-Thenhior wrote *Zhelsu*."

"How so?"

"Mer Pel-Thenhior wrote an elven opera with a goblin lead," said
Merrem Matano. "That's never been done before. He wrote it for
Min Vakrezharad, although he denies it."

"And Min Shelsin was unhappy?"

She corrected me calmly: "Min Shelsin was *livid*. Tamo was right
that if *Othoro* had been murdered, it would be no great feat to find
her murderer. Min Shelsin became even more of a fault-finder than
usual, and she kept trying to get Mer Pel-Thenhior to increase her
part. They had terrible, yelling arguments in the auditorium, in front
of everyone, which I think is very bad for the children."

"Yes," I said. I wondered, though not out loud, if I had just found
a motive for Arveneän Shelsin's murder.

"She was driving the wardrobe ladies to tears. She hated the
costumes—which, I admit, they are all workers' clothes."

"Dull colors, much mended, and frequently ill-fitting?"

"Yes—and even then the costumes are much better than the
clothes I had as a child."

"My first prelacy was in Lohaiso," I said, and she nodded understanding.

"But Min Shelsin could never be satisfied. She had started

threatening to go to the Marquess Parzhadel—our sponsor—and tell him that Mer Pel-Thenhior was destroying the Vermilion Opera and shouldn't be allowed to stage *Zhelsu* and all such poison, anything she could think of. Mer Pel-Thenhior laughed at her, but she swore she was going to do it."

"Did she?"

"I don't know. Mer Pel-Thenhior said it didn't matter because the marquess already knew all about *Zhelsu*. He wasn't stupid enough to put on such an opera without our sponsor's approval. But Min Shelsin would make trouble if she could. It was her way."

"Did she have friends outside the Opera?"

"She had no *time*. None of the singers does. They are rehearsing four operas, you know."

I hadn't known. "Four?"

"*General Olethazh, The Siege of Tekharee,* and *Seleno* are in performance—the Opera, of course, only performs every third night, but that is still a rigorous schedule—and when *Seleno* closes, *Zhelsu* opens. Then when *General Olethazh* is done, they start performing *The Dream of the Empress Corivero* and when *The Siege of Tekharee* is done, they start *The Hotel Hanaveise*. All year round, it is like this, and the singers only work harder. They have an eitheiavan." She used an upcountry word for a religious calling, which was a startling echo of last night's conversation with Pel-Thenhior. "Some of them have their patrons as well, but by and large they live for the Opera."

I nodded my understanding. "Did Min Shelsin have many patrons?"

"I believe so," Merrem Matano said cautiously, "but I do not know for sure."

"Despite what the children said, I do not expect you to know everything," I said, and got a flicker of a smile in return. "Do you know of any reason someone would want to hurt Min Shelsin?"

"I think we all wanted to slap her at one point or another, but nothing worse than that. I know of no reason someone would want to kill her."

"Thank you," I said.

She hesitated.

"Anything," I said. "Even something very small."

"Duets," said Merrem Matano. "She always preferred her duets with men, and she would be much more likely to confide in a man than in a woman. She was that sort of person."

"Who were her male duet partners?"

"Mer Veralis Telonar, the junior tenor, in *Zhelsu,* and Mer Cebris Pershar, the senior tenor, in *The Siege of Tekharee.* She wasn't in *General Olethazh,* which has no mid-soprano roles, and in *Seleno* she had no duets with a man." She considered a moment, then added, "You will probably have more luck with Mer Telonar. Mer Pershar detested her."

"Thank you. Where might I find the two clerks she was friends with?"

"That's easy," she said. "They'll be upstairs. I'll show you."

✕

The room to which Merrem Matano led me, by a series of what seemed very much like secret passages, was long and lofty, but very narrow. At each of its arched windows was a desk; at each desk was a woman, most of them elven, but there were a few Barizheisoi. They all had their heads bent over their work. After a minute, a woman at the far end of the room got up and walked briskly to where I stood. "Good afternoon. How may I help you, othala?"

I said, "My name is Thara Celehar. I am a Witness for the Dead. I am here because Arveneän Shelsin has been murdered."

She made the ritual warding gesture. "That is distressing news," she said, "but I do not quite understand why it brings you here."

"I have been told that Min Shelsin was friends with two of the clerks here, and I am hoping that they may be able to help me understand Min Shelsin better, so that I may better understand how she came to her death."

Her face had become very still. "What are their names?"

"Meletho Balvedin and Toreän Nochenin. It is no reflection on them, merely that I hope for their help."

She nodded, then turned and called, "Meletho! Toreän! Attend, please!"

Two elven women stood up, nervousness plain on their faces, and joined us by the door. They were both blandly pretty, wearing dark, plain dresses, and without jewelry, save that the taller had a pair of cloisonné bead earrings.

The first woman said, "Minnoi, I am very sorry to tell you that Min Shelsin has been murdered."

"I was praying it wasn't true," said one. "Murdered," the other whispered, as if the word were a weight against which she could not breathe.

"This is Othala Celehar. He is a Witness for the Dead, and he has some questions he wishes to ask you."

Their eyes widened in obvious alarm.

I said, "I do not suspect you of involvement, minnoi. I merely seek a better understanding of Min Shelsin."

"You may leave the room for your discussion," said the first woman, "but I will expect you back promptly when you are done."

"Yes, merrem," they said in soft, ragged unison, and they preceded me out the door.

In the corridor, they looked at me anxiously; one of them was fighting not to cry.

I said, "Which of you is Min Balvedin?"

"That is I," said the slightly taller of the two. By her accent, she came from Zhaö.

"Then you are Min Nochenin," I said to the other, who nodded and swallowed against tears.

"Thank you for talking to me," I said. "Will you tell me about Min Shelsin?"

They complied willingly, and it was quickly apparent that the Arveneän Shelsin they had known had been a completely different person from the one Merrem Matano had described. Their Arveneän was kind and generous. They were awed that she even spoke to them, she being a principal singer and they merely office clerks.

It was hard not to be cynical about the friendship Min Balvedin and Min Nochenin described, for they had clearly worshiped

Arveneän Shelsin, and she did not seem to have been the sort of person who would dislike that. They were uncritical and loyal and perhaps it had been a genuine comfort to her to know that she had people who would always be on her side. Perhaps she had merely enjoyed playing the grand lady in front of these two overawed girls. It did seem that she had treated them well, either out of actual fondness or because she knew better than to drive them away.

When I asked, they admitted that Min Shelsin had patrons. When I asked about names, they said they did not know.

I raised my eyebrows, and Min Balvedin blushed. "She did not talk about them very much."

Min Nochenin said, "She talked about Osmer Ponichar sometimes. She showed us the gifts he gave her."

"Gifts?"

"Jewelry for her to wear in performance," said Min Nochenin. "He gave her a beautiful set of gold and turquoise earrings, and a silver pendant set with a moonstone."

Min Balvedin chimed in, "And a ring that was gold set with amber, and a choker necklace that was silver with garnet drops."

"She had to pawn it, though," Min Nochenin said. "Arveneän was terrible with money."

"Just terrible," said Min Balvedin. "And she'd never let us help. She said she'd rather pawn her jewelry than her friends."

This was completely contrary to everything else I had been told about Arveneän Shelsin, but it was impossible to imagine either of these young women successfully telling a lie.

"Do you know what sect she belonged to?"

Min Nochenin frowned. "I think she said once that she was raised in the Harnavetai, but I don't know if she still practiced."

"Thank you," I said. While not definitive, that was enough to be able to bury her without offense.

Min Balvedin was quick to understand why I asked. "Will there be a funeral? I would like to attend."

"Of course. She will be buried in the municipal cemetery of the

Airmen's Quarter. I will send you word when the date and time have been set. It will be soon."

They nodded solemnly.

"Thank you very much for your help, minnoi," I said. "I think I have taken up enough of your time."

They both glanced involuntarily back at the door.

"If I have more questions, may I come talk to you again?"

"Of course," said Min Nochenin.

"We want to help," said Min Balvedin.

"Thank you, minnoi," I said, and let them return to their work.

※

When I found my way back to the auditorium, I found Pel-Thenhior alone, scribbling madly in his notebook. He looked up at my approach and answered the question he read on my face: "I made them all go rest for half an hour. They're healthier that way and Merrem Matano doesn't glare at me quite so much. Have you had any success?"

"I have heard," I said carefully, "that Min Shelsin was very unhappy about your new opera."

"True," said Pel-Thenhior. "She didn't understand why a goblin girl should get the best role and she said so. Frequently."

"Did she threaten to go to the Marquess Parzhadel about her complaints?"

"Oh, yes," said Pel-Thenhior. "I told her it would be a waste of her breath and Parzhadel's time, but she wasn't listening. No great surprise."

"Did she actually go?"

"I have no idea. If she did, she kept quiet about it, which is exactly what she would do if she didn't get what she wanted."

"Is there a way I can find out for certain?"

"Of course. Parzhadel's secretary—Mer Dravenezh. If you go to the Parzhadeise compound and ask for him, he'll be able to tell you." He cocked his head at me. "Do you suspect me of murdering her to protect my opera?"

I managed neither *no* nor *yes,* only a weak "Perhaps?"

It made him laugh. "I might kill someone over an opera, but it would never be one of my singers. Not even Arveneän. I need them all too badly. To be blindingly insensitive for a moment, this is a very bad time to lose a singer."

I liked him for being willing to say it outright, rather than leaving it to haunt my investigation unsaid and unknowable. "Perhaps you can tell me where you were when she died?"

"Here," Pel-Thenhior said promptly. "We performed *General Olethazh.* It wasn't over before midnight, and I have an auditorium full of people who can attest that I was in my box."

"That is very useful," I said.

"I really didn't kill her," he said, "although I can see why you might think I did."

"They would have remembered you in the Zheimela," I said. "I don't think you were there."

He thought a moment, then took my meaning. "I will have to tell my mother that being gaudy has its uses."

Ж

I went home, shared sardines with the cats that were not mine, meditated, went to bed, and dreamed nothing that I remembered. I woke in the middle of the night, as I sometimes did, and could not remember where I was. I lay awake for several minutes, slowly reasoning it out. This wasn't Lohaiso, where I'd never had a room to myself. It wasn't Aveio—my heart beat more painfully even at the thought—it wasn't my tiny barren room at the Untheileneise Court. Finally I remembered Amalo, remembered that I was in my own room with my own things, few though they were, and was able to fall back to sleep.

When I woke again it was daylight, and I lay for a long time looking at the slivers of sunlight on the wall before I was able to bully myself into getting up.

※

The Parzhadeise compound was in the plains to the northwest of the city, where the nobles had fled as the wealthy merchants began taking over the districts immediately around the Vercn'malo. I made a painful calculation of finances against time and physical fatigue and hired a horse from the municipal livery at the Atta stop on the Kinreho line.

She was a good horse, a pacer from the western plains, and had probably ended up in a livery stable because her owner had been forced to stave off bankruptcy by selling his horses. She carried me smoothly and swiftly from Atta out along the Kinreho Road to a stone wall and a gate with the Parzhadeise crest on it.

The elderly elven gatekeeper came out to see who I was, and I said, "I am hoping to speak to Mer Dravenezh. Is he here?"

"I can see," the gatekeeper said unencouragingly. "Who should I say is calling?"

"My name is Thara Celehar, and I am a Witness for the Dead."

The gatekeeper's expression did not change. He said only, "I will inquire," and vanished.

I waited. I had no means to compel Mer Dravenezh to speak to me, only the hope that either curiosity or conscience would draw him out. As the minutes ticked by, it seemed increasingly unlikely that he would agree to see me. When the gatekeeper finally returned, I fully expected to be told to leave. But instead, the gatekeeper said, "You are welcome in the House Parzhadada, othala. Please enter." He swung one leaf of the gate open, and I led my rented horse inside.

The compound was extensive, but the main house and stables were relatively close to the road. The groom was polite about the livery horse, and Mer Dravenezh was waiting at the door to a covered walkway that led from the stables to the house.

"We are Ema Dravenezh, othala," he said, leading me to a small, austerely appointed room, "and we will help you in any way we can."

Ema Dravenezh was as I remembered from seeing him at the Opera: a young man, with pale elven coloring except for the red-orange fire of his eyes. He was dressed in a sober-colored frogged coat, black trousers, and black, laced boots, and he wore his hair with two plain tortoiseshell combs.

I said, following his use of the formal first, "We are Thara Cele-har, a Witness for the Dead. We have come on behalf of Arveneän Shelsin."

"Min Shelsin has died?" he said with what I thought was genuine shock. "We noted her absence from the stage, but did not imagine it was . . . What happened to her? She had made an appointment to speak to the marquess, and we were quite surprised she did not keep it."

"When was the appointment for?"

"Yesterday."

"She was already dead. Someone threw her in the Mich'maika on the ninth."

He flinched a little and made the ritual warding gesture. "How horrible. But we do not quite understand why you are here."

"Someone was angry enough at Min Shelsin to murder her," I said. "One way to find out who is to find out who *she* was angry at. And we know she was angry."

"She wasn't angry at anyone here," Mer Dravenezh said defensively.

"No, of course not. But she was coming out to talk to the Marquess Parzhadel because she was angry. Did she give you any information?"

"Her note was very brief. Merely a request to talk to the marquess about matters of interest. He said he already knew what she wanted, but that he would see her, that it was the easiest way to head off trouble. But she did not come."

"A note? Did you keep it?"

"We keep all the marquess's correspondence," said Mer Dravenezh.

"Might we see it?"

He gave me a suspicious look, but said, "Yes, of course." He was gone for only a few moments, and returned with a plain cream envelope, which he handed to me.

Min Shelsin's handwriting was well-educated and assured, the ink she used very black. The contents of the note were as Mer Dravenezh had said. The extravagant curls and swoops of her letters gave me a vivid sense of who she had been, how she had faced the world. I handed the note back to Mer Dravenezh.

"The Marquess Parzhadel knew what she wanted. Did anyone else?"

"No one here. The marquess keeps his own counsel. We do not, of course, know to whom Min Shelsin may have spoken."

"Of course not," I said. He was still defensive, as if I had made an accusation. "Had she ever made an appointment with the marquess before?"

"Once," Mer Dravenezh said with plain reluctance.

"Then you saw her? In person, that is, not performing. What did you think of her?"

He looked startled to be asked, but answered reflexively, as all polite elven children are taught to respond to questions, "Overdressed. Overdressed and bourgeois-vulgar."

I thought of Min Shelsin's closet full of stolen dresses.

Mer Dravenezh thought something over, then surprised me by adding to his answer: "She was a woman with the worst kind of temper, for she was vengeful. If you angered her, she would not be satisfied until she had found a way to hurt you. The last time she was here, she was trying to get one of the other singers dismissed."

"How long ago was that?"

"Two years. Maybe a little more. The marquess sent her away and told her she was lucky he didn't dismiss *her*."

I reckoned that my chances of getting in to see the marquess were nonexistent, but I had to try. "Might it be possible for us to see the marquess? We need only a minute of his time."

Mer Dravenezh looked horrified. "The Marquess Parzhadel is a very busy person."

That might or might not be true, but it was a clear sign I was not going to get past Mer Dravenezh. I thanked him for his help and departed.

ᛞ

On the ride back to the livery stable, I tried to assess what I now knew.

On the tenth a body had been pulled out of the canal at the Reveth'veraltamar. Subpraeceptor Azhanharad and I had determined cause and manner of death: no mistaking that this was murder. I knew the dock she had been thrown off of, behind the Canalman's Dog, and I had found places in the Zheimela where she had been the night she died; in one of them I learned she was Arveneän Shelsin, a mid-soprano with the Vermilion Opera. The Opera had provided a wealth of information, including the fact that at the time of her death, Min Shelsin had been furiously angry about the opera in rehearsal and had in fact made an appointment to speak to the Opera's sponsor. An appointment she had not been alive to keep.

But where was the cause of her murder? In the Zheimela district, where her death had found her? Or in the Opera, where she had lived, where she had demanded attention (a conceited child, as Min Nadin had called her)? I would have to ask Pel-Thenhior what kind of salary she commanded, and I wondered if anyone knew how much she had made in gifts and trinkets from her patrons. I wondered if *she* had known.

Arveneän Shelsin had been a troublemaker and a thief, but so bad with money that she had a drawer full of pawn tickets instead of jewelry. She had been infuriated by Pel-Thenhior's new opera, so infuriated that she had genuinely intended to go to the Marquess Parzhadel, even though her previous experience would have suggested it was futile. Did she simply not learn from setbacks? Or had she had some real reason to think that this time Parzhadel would listen? But listen to *what*? Parzhadel already knew about the opera. Was there something else she could tell him, something about Pel-Thenhior or one of the other principal singers, that she might think she could use as leverage?

I turned the idea around in my head as the livery stable horse and I went from the long stone walls with which the nobles of Amalo defined and defended their property, to farmland, interspersed with the occasional smaller compound, to rows of small, neat houses, brightly colored, and then to the city proper, where the municipal livery and the tram station awaited us. But I gained no new insights.

)(

The next afternoon, the Vermilion Opera's auditorium was much busier, not just one woman standing and singing on the stage, but a number of people making entrances and exits; pausing in their singing to argue with Pel-Thenhior; standing just off stage to listen. There was a harried-looking young elven man sitting beside Pel-Thenhior in the auditorium, scribbling notes in a giant bound book that I could just see was full of musical notations.

Pel-Thenhior saw me and smiled, but continued his argument with a barrel-chested elven man whose voice was a deep grumble, like thunder far in the distance. I could not follow their argument at all. I occupied myself in waiting by watching the other singers. Another elven man and an elven woman were currently on stage; the woman was Toïno, who had been given Min Shelsin's roles.

Was *that* a motive for murder? No woman could have hurled Min Shelsin off the dock like that—her memory of it still vivid in my mind—but men could be hired or (looking at the bass singer's massive chest) suborned. However, the young woman's face did not show any pleasure, but only anxiety. I would have to speak to her, but she did not look at all like someone whose schemes had come to fruition.

The other man, presumably one of the tenors, had what my Cele-hadeise grandmother would have called "good" elven features. He was tall, lean, beautifully poised. Most opera singers wore wigs for performance, but this man's hair was long and thick and glossy white, and would clearly take an elaborate court dressing. Not that that would matter for this opera, given what Merrem Matano had said about manufactory workers. I wondered if that bothered him as much as it had bothered Min Shelsin.

Finally, Pel-Thenhior said, "Tura, we could argue all day, but you're not going to win this one. My original phrasing stands." He turned to me and said, "Othala, greetings! How may we help you?" using the first-person plural as if there was no doubt that all the company was equally eager to catch Min Shelsin's killer.

"I need to speak to your principal singers," I said, "as many of them as are here."

"What is this?" said Tura—his last name, I remembered, was Olora—bristling. "Who is this person?"

"This is the Witness for the Dead," said Pel-Thenhior. "He is here because of Arveneän's murder."

Mer Olora's face resembled a stunned carp's, and he did not pro-test further.

"We can do that," Pel-Thenhior said to me, "but first you should come meet a young lady who has a very interesting story."

I followed him into the maze of the Opera—a different route than Merrem Matano's, ending at a set of double doors painted, in beautiful script, with the word WARDROBE.

"I wanted to know how she'd managed to steal so many cos-tumes," Pel-Thenhior explained, "so I started asking. And I found Min Leverin."

The Wardrobe Department was a stunning experience, Min Shel-sin's closet dozens of times over, racks upon racks of elaborate cos-tumes, silk and brocade and velvet, trimmed with lace and pearls and ermine and bullion, in a bewildering array of colors and fashions. Pel-Thenhior grinned at the expression on my face and said, "You do get used to it, but it takes a while. But here. This is Min Leverin."

She was part goblin, with pale gray skin and tip-tilted eyes as red as rubies. And she was distraught. "Mer Pel-Thenhior!" she cried, starting up from the chair where she had been hemming a heavy brocade skirt. "I didn't—"

"Lalo, I told you," Pel-Thenhior said, "you aren't in trouble. The only person I'm angry at is Arveneän."

"But," she started. I could see that she had been crying.

"No," said Pel-Thenhior. "This is Othala Celehar, the Witness for the Dead who is witnessing for Arveneän. I need you to tell him what you told me."

Her gaze turned apprehensively to me. I said, "I seek only the truth, Min Leverin."

It did not appear to comfort her, but she sat down again, dragging the skirt back across her lap and anchoring her needle safely beside her last stitch. She said, "I have been a wardrobe assistant at the Opera for five years. Please, Mer Pel-Thenhior, I don't know what I'll do if—"

"Lalo," said Pel-Thenhior, "I'm not going to dismiss you. Merrem Adalharad has told me you are indispensable."

Her skin showed a blush, but something in what he said seemed to calm her, for she looked back at me and said, "Min Shelsin caught me with one of the milliner's girls."

I knew my ears dropped; I could only hope they both took it as simple surprise. "What did she do?" I said, and was relieved that my voice was calm.

Min Leverin's blush was deepening by the second, but she said, "She made a bargain. She wouldn't tell anyone about me, and I wouldn't tell anyone when she took costumes home."

"Did you know she wasn't bringing them back?"

"Yes," Min Leverin said wretchedly. "But I didn't know what to do. I didn't want to get D—my friend in trouble, and I couldn't afford . . ."

"I understand," I said. "How long has this been going on?"

"Two years," she said.

"What were you going to do when someone noticed?" Pel-Thenhior said. "You must have known it would happen eventually."

"I don't know," said Min Leverin. "Min Shelsin said it wouldn't. She said there's no inventory and nobody knows all the costumes down here. So I just . . ." She shrugged hopelessly. "Hoped."

"Did Min Shelsin come up with her 'bargain' immediately? Or did she have to think about what she was going to do?"

Min Leverin frowned over that question for several moments. "She came to me the next day," she said. "So I suppose she didn't have to think very long."

"Blackmail would come naturally to Arveneän," Pel-Thenhior said.

"Did she ask your friend for anything?" I said. "Or just you?"

"I don't know," Min Leverin said. "We haven't . . . we haven't really spoken since. But I don't think my friend has anything Min Shelsin would have wanted."

"Thank you, Min Leverin," I said. "You have been very helpful."

"You aren't in trouble, Lalo," Pel-Thenhior said. "And your friend isn't in trouble, either. I'm not about to punish anyone for being in love."

Min Leverin put her face in her hands and sobbed.

As we walked back to the auditorium, I asked Pel-Thenhior, "Do you think she was blackmailing anyone else at the Opera?"

"I'm afraid to speculate," he said. "Certainly, we have proof that she wouldn't balk at doing so if there was something she wanted."

"Not a question of whether she *would*, but of whether she *could*. I suppose then the question is whether anyone here had anything she wanted. Aside from the role you wouldn't give her."

"She couldn't blackmail her way into that," Pel-Thenhior said. "No wonder it vexed her so."

I remembered my question about Min Shelsin's salary, and Pel-Thenhior answered without hesitation, "Four thousand muranai a year. She was not the most highly paid of the singers, which galled her, but she was really senior principal in name only—just until Merrem Anshonaran can return from bearing her child."

"Is Min Vakrezharad now senior principal?"

"Yes, although that won't really count until we start rehearsing *The Dream of the Empress Corivero*. Until then, Toïno has the senior principal roles."

"And what do you do about the junior principal mid-soprano?"

"Well, it can't be Toïno," he said with a grimace. "And Merrem Anshonaran can't come back for at least another three months. We'll have to hold auditions, and we'll end up with three principal mid-sopranos where we only need two—although perhaps Amaö will be glad to have someone to share the weight."

"Min Vakrezharad won't go back to the chorus?"

"Not while I'm director here," said Pel-Thenhior.

In the auditorium, people were standing in small groups, some of them practicing harmonies, some of them gossiping. Pel-Thenhior called, "I need all principals on stage, please." Several people on stage turned to face him like sunflowers; others emerged from the wings, all elven in coloring except Min Vakrezharad: four men and four women including Min Shelsin's replacement. She looked nervous; the others merely seemed curious. Pel-Thenhior said, "Merrai and minnoi, if you would be so kind as to give Othala Celehar your cooperation. He is trying to find the person who murdered Arveneän."

Now they all looked nervous, which was normal. Few people had Pel-Thenhior's self-assurance, to look a Witness in the face without flinching.

"Do you want them one at a time or all at once?" said Pel-Thenhior.

"One at a time," I said, although I winced at the thought. But talking to people in a group allowed an individual to avoid saying anything, and with these singers I knew I could not afford it.

I much preferred talking to dead people.

Pel-Thenhior nodded and said, "We shall manage. Come up to

the ticket office where there's somewhere to sit and you can hear yourself think."

I spent the afternoon talking to singers, none of whom had liked Min Shelsin any better than Pel-Thenhior had, but none of whom wanted to admit it. Even Min Vakrezharad, who knew that I already knew of the animosity between her and Min Shelsin, was reluctant to speak frankly about her own feelings. Finally, I said, "I suspect you of nothing, Min Vakrezharad. I am merely trying to learn about Min Shelsin by learning how she affected the people around her."

She looked skeptical, but said, "It is not a secret that I did not like her, nor that she did not like me. Even when we were not in competition—for I never expected to become a principal, no matter how long I remained at the Opera—she acted as if I had threatened her."

"And she was very angry about *Zhelsu*."

"She was. Even though . . . it is not as if there are any *other* principal roles where I would be chosen before her. She could not bear that there should be *any*." She stopped suddenly, looking horrified at herself.

It was not uncommon for people to say more than they meant when talking to a Witness for the Dead. My teacher, Othala Pelovar, had said that it was because we were taught to *listen,* and that once you had learned to listen to the dead, the living posed no challenge. The elderly Witness for the Dead in Lohaiso said that anyone could achieve a similar result simply by keeping their mouth shut and letting people talk. I was never sure which I believed, but I had seen the effect over and over again. I had only had it done to me once since I first became a prelate of Ulis, and that had been by the emperor himself.

I said, "I do not judge. I only seek the truth."

"The truth about Min Shelsin?"

"The truth about her death. Why do you think someone would kill her? Not why someone might *want* to kill her, but why someone would actually *do* it?"

Min Vakrezharad frowned, an alarming goblin scowl, but her face cleared as she caught the distinction I was making. "She ... Arveneän liked secrets. She liked *knowing* things about other people, and it has always seemed to me that this is a very dangerous habit."

"True," I said.

"It was fairly harmless within the company—we all knew better than to confide in her—but I do wonder about her patrons and what one of them might have said to her that he then regretted."

The women also told me about Arveneän Shelsin's patrons, in particular Osmer Coreshar, Osmer Elithar, and especially Osmer Ponichar, who had spent the most money on her and with whom she had had the loudest fights.

"We all pretend not to hear," said Min Lochareth, the senior alto, "but we all *do* hear. We can't help it." She had another suggestion for why someone might want Min Shelsin dead: "She was terribly expensive, you know. She always wanted *more* presents and *more* dinners at Hatharanee, and I don't know that I ever saw a young man successfully extract himself until Arveneän was done with him."

"Was she so captivating?"

"She was delicate," said Min Lochareth, who was not, "and doe-eyed, and I saw the way they all looked at her and the way she looked at them. She *was* that captivating, and she didn't like letting go of anything once she had hold of it. She was an awful person, othala, but even so, no one had any right to kill her."

Toïno Culainin, Min Shelsin's luckless understudy, had probably observed her more closely than anyone, for she had to know her movements on stage as well as her singing part. She said, simply, "Min Shelsin did not notice me."

"But you noticed her."

"I memorized her," said Min Culainin. "I can walk like her. I can gesture like her. But I cannot sing like her, although I do my best. Iäna will be holding auditions for a mid-soprano soon."

"A junior, correct?"

"Yes. Othoro is the senior mid-soprano now, which Min Shelsin would hate. She disliked Othoro very much, because Othoro has the better voice. She disliked Voniän—our junior soprano—for the same reason. She saw herself in competition with *everybody*."

"That sounds a very fatiguing way to live."

"She seemed to thrive on it," said Min Culainin. "Certainly, I never saw her tired or defeated. She lost fight after fight with Iäna, and it never seemed to discourage her in the slightest."

I thought of that appointment with the Marquess Parzhadel that she had not lived to keep. "Was that because of an indomitable nature or just bad judgment?"

Min Culainin almost smiled. "Her judgment was very bad, to be sure. She never seemed aware that other people disliked her quite as intensely as she disliked them. And she was as greedy as a spoiled child."

"Would you say she had enemies among the company?"

"Not *enemies*," Min Culainin said, horrified.

"You said she fought with Mer Pel-Thenhior."

"So does half the company, at one time or another," she said.

"But people disliked Min Shelsin. Who?"

I had trapped her, though I felt no pride in it. "Cebris hated her," she said after a long silence. "And Othoro—but how do you not dislike someone who dislikes you and makes no secret of it?"

"I'm not judging anyone," I said, "just trying to understand her connections with the people she saw and worked with every day."

"I don't suppose any of us *liked* her," Min Culainin said, and then put her hand over her mouth as if she could keep in the already escaped words.

None of them, in other words, had any reason *not* to murder her, except Pel-Thenhior and Min Culainin herself. That was disheartening, both because it made my task as a Witness more difficult and because it was a sign of just how determined Arveneän Shelsin seemed to have been to destroy her own life.

"Thank you, Min Culainin," I said, and she could not hide her relief that I was letting her go.

The men were not as helpful. Cebris Pershar, the senior tenor, was perfectly frank that he had despised Min Shelsin (as Merrem Matano had told me) and tried to know as little about her as possible; the other tenor, the man with "good" elven features, was twitchy with nerves and gave nothing but vague answers. The baritone seemed earnestly desirous of helping, but he knew as little as Mer Pershar. The bass was sullen and grumbling about losing rehearsal time. A thought struck me, and I asked him, "Do you think someone would kill Min Shelsin to sabotage Mer Pel-Thenhior's opera?"

I was expecting, *No, of course not,* and I did not get it. Mer Olora blinked, as if seriously considering the matter, and said slowly, "I don't think so," almost asking it as a question. "The only person *in* the company who hated it that much was Min Shelsin herself, but the question is the other opera houses. They know Pel-Thenhior's come up with something new and scandalous, and they know that means their ticket sales will go down. You might inquire, othala, whether any of them is in particularly desperate financial straits. . . . Although there Arveneän is a strange choice. Her part simply isn't that big."

"I don't know," I said. "I don't know enough about opera."

He looked scandalized. "Well, you may take it from me that Arveneän's death, while regrettable, is no serious impediment to the staging of *Zhelsu.* If it had been *Othoro* . . ."

I noted, as I rode the tram home, what a common refrain that had been. Everyone at the Vermilion Opera seemed to think Othoro should have been the one murdered; I wondered for a moment if I should have warned her to be careful and then remembered that Min Shelsin had died in the Zheimela, which was about as far from the Vermilion Opera as one could get.

And then I wondered if that was deliberate, if Min Shelsin had gone to the Zheimela *because* it was so far, in both the literal and the figurative sense, from the Opera. It occurred to me that if you wanted to meet someone and not have anyone else know about it— especially if you were an opera singer who lived in a boardinghouse and had no privacy—the Zheimela, say, for instance, the warren of the Canalman's Dog, was exactly the place to go.

But who in the world would Arveneän Shelsin want to meet with so much secrecy? That was a question that nothing so far had offered an answer to, and no amount of pondering could provide one.

)(

The morning brought, just before noon, Mer Urmenezh, who looked as if he had slept no better than I. His sister Inshiran's fate was enough to make anybody wakeful.

"Mer Urmenezh," I said, rising.

"Othala," he said, and remembered his manners enough to nod. He always reminded me of a toy clockwork heron one of my wealthy cousins had had, all bones and long legs, the resemblance helped by his long nose and weak chin and the round glinting lenses of his pince-nez. "Thank you for your letter. You have done so much for us already, but we have come to ask if you might do one more thing."

"Of course," I said. "What can we do for you?"

"We have ex . . . exhumed poor Inshiran and had a most uncomfortable conversation with the president of the collective of Ulchoranee, and we did as you suggested and petitioned for an autopsy and . . . and . . ."

"Mer Urmenezh?"

"The Sanctuary answered our petition much more swiftly than we expected. The autopsy is to be this afternoon." His mouth worked for a moment, and then he blurted, "We wondered if you would represent the family."

"Me?" I said, involuntarily abrogating formality in my surprise.

"We just . . ." And then he abrogated formality in turn. "I cannot watch them carve up my little sister. Othala, *please.* I am desperate."

"Of course," I said, responding more to his pain than to his request; then I caught up with myself and added more rationally, "It is within the remit of our office, and we quite understand your reasons. Tell us when and where and we will be honored to represent the Urmenada."

And that was how I ended up attending Inshiran Urmenezhen's autopsy.

)(

The Sanctuary of Csaivo fronting the Mich'maika predated the city of Amalo by at least a thousand years. The elesth trees had grown gigantic the walls and walkways were covered with moss. The outer wall blocked the sounds of the Airmen's Quarter and the canal traffic, so that it was truly a sanctuary. I had gone there often when I first came to Amalo and still walked there from time to time, when the jostling throngs of Amaleisei became too much.

There was a novice waiting just inside the doors of the main building, goblin dark and elven thin. She bowed to me and said, "Are you Othala Celehar?"

"I am."

"Then please follow me. Dach'othala Ulzhavar is waiting in the autopsy chamber."

"Do you see many autopsies here?" I asked, curious. I knew only that they performed them. My calling had not previously brought me to attend one.

"One or two a week," she said as we started down the stairs. She flashed me an apologetic smile. "Not everyone wants to go to a Witness for the Dead for their answers."

"There are many answers I cannot give," I said.

The lower floor of the Sanctuary was lit by gas globes. The massive stonework and the nearness of the canal made it cool and somewhat damp. The floor was tiled in mosaics of the sigils of healing, which mitigated the intimidating aspect of the ancient stones. The hallway led to a vaulted room with a colonnade of arches that were both lovely and utilitarian, as they made the open expanse possible, and with a gas globe on each pillar, there was a surprising amount of light—surprising until I looked up and saw the collector at the apex of the vault. In the middle of the room, beneath the collector, there was a slab-topped table, on which lay an object wrapped in a shroud. Standing beside the table was a middle-aged elven man in the green robes of a cleric of Csaivo, although I was insensibly heartened to see that beneath them, where he'd kilted the long skirts up to get them out of his way, he wore prosaic trousers and a worker's heavy boots.

He looked up at our approach and smiled. "You must be Othala Celehar. I am Csenaia Ulzhavar."

I bowed and said, "Thank you for letting me attend, dach'othala."

"About the lady on the slab. Can you tell me about her?"

"She is Inshiran Urmenezhen, also known as Inshiran Avelonaran," I said, and explained the story of seduction and betrayal. Ulzhavar listened carefully, frowning.

"That is all very interesting," he said when I had finished, "and I certainly understand why her family wants her autopsied at this late date. Normally, I would have to tell them that there's most likely no point, but this young lady is well preserved. Remarkably so."

"Her brother is convinced she was murdered," I said.

"Well, let's see if we can find out," said Ulzhavar. "Denevis!"

A novice came out of the colonnade at the far end of the vault, where I saw there was a row of massive chests of drawers against the wall. He was elven and probably fifteen or sixteen, nearly ready to be sent out as a junior cleric.

He bowed to me. Ulzhavar said, "Denevis is my apprentice. He'll be helping today so that you don't have to . . . although I imagine you're not very squeamish?"

"No," I said, answering his wry smile with my own. "I am not."

"Speaking of which, do you want to try her before we start?"

"It's been too long," I said, but I did step up to the table and touch Inshiran's forehead, noting that Ulzhavar was right: she was in remarkably good condition for a woman who had been buried for six months or more.

As expected, there was nothing of the spirit left. I shook my head and stepped back.

"Ah well," said Ulzhavar. "It was worth trying. Denevis, you can get the cart now."

Denevis ran back to the end of the vault and returned pushing a wheeled cart. As he got closer, I saw the autopsy instruments—the scalpels, the bone saw, and all the rest—laid out neatly on a green cloth.

"Many people need some warning," said Ulzhavar.

"I think Mer Urmenezh was right not to attend," I said. "He is already distraught over what happened to his sister."

"Watching this will not help," Ulzhavar agreed. "All right, Denevis. Tell me where we start."

I watched while the two clerics worked their way down Inshiran Urmenezhen's body, examining brain, lungs, heart . . . Ulzhavar spent quite some time looking at her hands. I followed enough of their conversation to know that there was something unusual in what they were finding, but could puzzle out no more than that before Ulzhavar said, "Dear goddess, look at her liver." He turned to me and said, "Well, it's perfectly clear what killed her. This poor woman has practically been pickled in calonvar."

"*Calonvar?*"

"It's a slow poison," said Ulzhavar with a grimace. "He could have stretched her suffering out for weeks. The vomiting, the scaly patches on the hands—"

I remembered something else. "Was she pregnant?"

"Yes," said Denevis.

"She might have thought it was nothing more than the early sickness. Until it killed her."

"The poor woman," said Ulzhavar. "What did you say the husband's name is?"

"Croïs Avelonar." Another horrible thought struck me. "Although who's to say that's his real name?"

"It most likely isn't," Ulzhavar said grimly. "He cut the sheep out of the flock *far* too effectively for this to be his first time."

I nodded. Their calling, like mine, would inevitably bring them in contact with men who were widowed multiple times, women who buried one family member after another, husbands and children and siblings and parents all dying from enteric fever, which poisons like calonvar mimicked so closely. Sometimes one could take one's suspicions to a Witness who would listen; oftentimes, though, the poisoner moved away to find a new hunting ground. In a city like Amalo, Avelonar wouldn't even have to move very far, just far enough to find new neighbors, a new cleric, a new prelate, and he could start the cycle all over again.

"Mer Urmenezh never even met him," I said. "We have nothing but a name he probably isn't using."

"Ah, but now we know he's out there," said Ulzhavar. "I can tell all the clerics to be on the lookout for similar cases."

"Do you think you'll have any results?"

"Perhaps," he said. "I admit it is not as simple as I made it sound."

"Still," I said, "I thank you for letting me attend the autopsy. At least I will be able to tell Mer Urmenezh something definitive."

"Yes," Ulzhavar said. "It will be of no comfort, but perhaps it will allow him to rest."

"Perhaps," I said sadly, for rest was what Mer Urmenezh most desperately needed and what he would not give himself. "But I doubt it."

)(

Outside the Sanctuary's main gates, I found Mer Urmenezh pacing back and forth to the detriment and irritation of the passersby. He stopped when he saw me.

"Othala?"

"She was murdered with calonvar," I said, and his eyes welled with tears.

"I *knew* it," he said, clearly not to me. Then, recollecting himself, he took out his handkerchief and wiped his eyes, then his pincenez, then said, "Thank you, othala. You have done considerably more than your office demands."

I said, "The Master of the Mortuary is going to have the clerics of the city watch for similar cases. He thinks this cannot be the first time the man has done this, and it almost certainly will not be the last."

"Goddesses of mercy," said Mer Urmenezh, as if doubting such beings existed.

"All the clerics of the city will be looking for him now, and we do not think he is cunning enough to elude them."

"We suppose that's true." He squared his shoulders. "We must go give this news to our sisters. We bury Inshiran this evening. Will you come?"

"Of course," I said.

"Thank you again, othala. The House Urmenada will remember your kindness." He bowed deeply and left.

I watched him go and tried not to think about Croïs Avelonar, out there somewhere in the city looking for his next victim.

By now he might have found her.

※

The Urmenada belonged to one of the city's collective cemeteries, where a number of families, bourgeois and town gentry, pooled their money in order to avoid the municipal cemeteries. Their prelate was an intense young elven woman, Othalo Bershanaran. Her husband, a broad-shouldered elven man who wore his hair in a braided club as the manufactory workers did in Lohaiso, was the cemetery sexton. It was not an uncommon arrangement for married female prelates.

There were not many mourners. Mer Urmenezh and his sisters, some cousins, some tired-looking elven women, whom I guessed to be Min Urmenezhen's fellow teachers. Several of them had been crying, as had the sisters. As had Mer Urmenezh.

Seeing no reason to spare expense, Mer Urmenezh had paid for a sunset funeral, and Othalo Bershanaran had been a prelate long enough to judge the timing of the ceremony; she said the last words of the Ul'izheve, the final blessing, just as the last bright sliver of the sun vanished below the horizon. I offered a small prayer of my own that Min Urmenezhen might finally be left at rest.

At the gravesite, Mer Bershanar and his assistant placed the new headstone, with the names of both Min Urmenezhen and her unborn child—and I wondered how greatly it must have rankled Mer Urmenezh to be forced to use the name the child's father had picked—and Othalo Bershanaran said an older, little-used blessing, the one that prayed for the dead child to stay sleeping in its dead mother's womb.

I went home, shared sardines among the waiting cats, and went to bed early, although I did not sleep until late.

※

I n the morning, there was a courier waiting outside my office. I recognized his colors immediately as being those of the Prince of Thu-Athamar; whatever Prince Orchenis wanted to see me about, it was too urgent to wait for the post. I developed a cold hard knot in the pit of my stomach.

"Othala Celehar," he said, bowing. "We bring you a message from His Highness Prince Orchenis."

"Thank you," I said, taking the letter, and broke the seal.

To Thara Celehar, prelate of Ulis and Witness for the Dead, greetings,
It has come to our attention that you are involved in the inheri-
tance question of the House Duhalada. We would speak with
you on this matter and request your immediate presence.
                                                    With all good will,
                                                    Orchenis Clunethar

And the prince's personal signet of a swan was at the bottom, in case I had had any doubt that the message actually came from him.

"Immediate?" I said.

"Those are our instructions," said the courier.

"All right," I said, and kept my hands away from my hair.

I was grateful that it was only a few minutes' walk from the Prince Zhaicava Building to the Amal'theileian. The courier took me in a back entrance and along the servants' hallways. I could not decide if that was a good sign or a very bad one, and the courier said nothing.

Prince Orchenis had two audience rooms, besides the throne room that was only used for the most formal occasions. I had been presented to him in the Azalea Room, which was a beautiful room full of light and the glowing soft azalea pink of the walls. The courier took me to the other audience room, the Cinnabar Room, which was smaller, dark paneled, with cinnabar tiles flanking the fireplace. It, too, was a beautiful room, but far more intimidating.

Prince Orchenis, elven pale, tall, thin, and with a permanent frown line engraved between his eyebrows, was standing by the fireplace, his hands clasped behind his back. He was wearing silver-on-gray brocade and was jeweled with diamonds. His secretary, an elven man old enough to be Prince Orchenis's father, was seated discreetly in the corner by the door. The room was otherwise empty, and the cold knot in my stomach got tighter. This was not a casual interview.

"Othala Celehar," said Prince Orchenis. "We trust we have not inconvenienced you."

"Of course not," I said, as I was obliged to, regardless of truth. "We are pleased to attend upon Your Highness. How may we be of service?"

Prince Orchenis's permanent frown made him very difficult to read, although I did at least know he was not as ill-tempered as he looked. He said, "We have had a most disturbing meeting with Mer Nepevis Duhalar." He stopped and for a moment seemed to find it impossible to continue. "He has suggested the possibility of fraud."

I bit down hard on the inner surface of my lower lip, a reflex I had learned as a novice after several blistering punishments for blurting out what I was actually thinking in response to a question. It was enough to keep me from simply accusing Mer Duhalar of fraud in turn. There was no point to that—if the solution were that simple, the matter would never have reached the prince. Instead, I said cautiously, "That is a very serious accusation. Did he explain why he felt we had committed fraud?"

"He alleges," Prince Orchenis said, choosing his words carefully, "that you are in the pay of his brother Pelara in a plot to take over the company."

I stared at the prince. "Why should we do such a thing?"

"The prelates of Ulis and the Witnesses *vel ama* are notoriously poor," Prince Orchenis said. To my disbelief and horror I saw that he was actually blushing, and the cold knot in my stomach knew what he was going to say before he got the words out: "There are also allegations of . . . misconduct."

My heartbeat roared in my ears, and for a moment I truly thought that I was going to faint. I had learned the breathing meditations in Lohaiso and I called on the simplest of them, steadying my breath until my heartbeat calmed and I could say in a level voice, "Your Highness, you must know that we would never do such a thing."

Prince Orchenis's frown had deepened, and he was looking past me instead of meeting my eyes. "It is not a matter of our personal beliefs, othala. Mer Nepevis Duhalar is an influential voice in our government, and we cannot simply ignore his allegations. And he has already threatened to go to the papers."

"What about the allegations that *he* is a fraud? Can you ignore *them*?"

And then I cursed myself for saying exactly the thing I had sworn I wouldn't.

Prince Orchenis did look at me now, a level and disapproving stare. "We have asked the Amalomaza to look into the matter of the documents. That is not what is at issue here. We are considering *your* actions, othala. For it is entirely possible that *both* Duhaladeise brothers are frauds. Pelara's claim is legitimate only upon your testimony."

"But if they're both frauds, where is the genuine will?" I protested.

"Destroyed," Prince Orchenis said, so curtly that I understood he had had such cases come before him. "The Duhalada have surrendered the entire matter to our judgment. We have not, as yet, said anything to the Amal'othala."

"He will have heard," I said bleakly.

"Of course," said Prince Orchenis. "But he will not take notice until he has to."

Prince Orchenis knew the Amal'othala better than I did; I would trust his judgment on that front. But that left me trying to prove a negative to the Prince of Thu-Athamar.

My head was full of Evru. Our love had been "misconduct," and I knew there were prelates who still thought I should have been barred for life, although the Archprelate disagreed. But in the end I had remained true to my calling, and whether I had thereby betrayed Evru was also a matter of opinion.

I said, "Your Highness, we have committed no fraud. We have not betrayed our calling. Tell us how we may prove it to you."

The prince said, "Mer Nepevis Duhalar demands that you submit to trial by ordeal."

"The Amal'othala will definitely take notice of that," I said.

"*If* we concur," said Prince Orchenis, "the Amal'othala will be obliged to take notice of a great many things. But we have no belief in trial by ordeal. Nor, we think, does Nepevis Duhalar." He eyed me for a few moments, then said, "However, we think it would be wise if you were . . . unavailable for a few days, and we would ask of you a favor."

"A favor?" I said, terrified, infuriated, and now also baffled.

"We are receiving reports of a ghoul in Tanvero. The local othas'ala seems to be incapable of action, and although the Ulineise prelates in the area are devoted to their parishes, none of them can speak to the dead."

"You want us to go to Tanvero," I said blankly. Tanvero was a mining town high in the Mervarnens—at least two days' journey from Amalo and those two days not comfortable ones.

"You know as well as we do," Prince Orchenis said, "the problem with ghouls is that they don't stay satisfied with dead meat."

I did know. Ghouls, the plague of the northlands, had been a frequent problem in Aveio, where the graveyards far exceeded the reach of any single prelate. And Prince Orchenis was right; sooner or later every ghoul turned from the dead to the living. During the tenure of the prelate in Aveio before me, an entire family had been found, mostly eaten, in one of the far-outlying farmhouses. The reason the othas'ala of Aveio had tolerated me as long as he had was that I was capable of quieting a ghoul by myself. I couldn't stop them rising, but I could halt their progress before their hunger drove them to living victims. I could listen for their names and have them reburied during daylight with a proper stone. It was repulsive work, for ghouls clothed themselves in the bodies they ate, but there was a grisly sort of satisfaction to it as well.

Unlike proving a negative, this was something I could do. But I had other obligations.

"We are witnessing for two women," I said.

"They are dead," Prince Orchenis said bluntly. "The dead are patient."

"Very well," I said. "When would you have us leave?"

)(

Prince Orchenis was more thoughtful than I had expected. His secretary had found me a place with a caravan taking dry goods to Tanvero. The caravan masters were glad to have me; they had heard about the ghoul and were understandably nervous. They were leaving at first light the next morning, so that I was able to attend Arveneän Shelsin's funeral, which had finally been arranged for noon. Min Balvedin and Min Nochenin were there in shabby, much-dyed black dresses they had most probably borrowed from friends or cousins. Pel-Thenhior was there like an austere and elegant shadow. No one else came.

The municipal ulimeire of the Airmen's Quarter was a dreary building, soot-stained red brick on the outside and yellowed, cracking plaster on the inside. Anora, goblin-boned, tall and heavyset, and goblin dark except for his pale, nearsighted eyes, said the service for Min Shelsin with simple sincerity.

I watched Min Shelsin's assembled mourners, Subpraeceptor Azhanharad looming behind them like a louring storm. I couldn't imagine Min Nochenin or Min Balvedin as murderers, and while I thought Pel-Thenhior capable of murder, I did not think he had murdered Min Shelsin. For all that she hated *Zhelsu*, she clearly hadn't intended to threaten not to perform, and beyond that—itself an empty threat—she seemed to have had only the power to exasperate him, not to drive him into a killing rage. And an elaborate, coldly thought-out plan to hire her murder was even more ridiculous. He had wanted her alive and singing.

After the funeral service was complete, I managed to catch Pel-Thenhior for a moment to tell him I was going to be gone for a few days, but that I was not abandoning the investigation.

"I did not know yours was a traveling position," said Pel-Thenhior, frowning in perplexity.

That in itself was a slightly vexed question. I said, "There are reports of a ghoul in Tanvero, and the most effective way to deal with a ghoul is to get a Witness for the Dead."

Pel-Thenhior still looked troubled. "Isn't that, I don't know, awfully dangerous?"

It was kind of him to be worried, and an unfamiliar position for me to be in. "It's not as bad as it sounds," I said. "Ghouls are very slow, and it usually takes two or three months for them to transition to attacking the living."

"Your idea of reassurance could use a little work," Pel-Thenhior said, but he looked like he wanted to laugh.

"I've dealt with ghouls before. I'll be fine."

"That was better. May I expect to see you at the Opera when you return?"

"Of course," I said. "I have to talk to your principal soprano, if nothing else."

"Excellent," said Pel-Thenhior, and bowed farewell.

The same conversation with Azhanharad—who also needed to

know why I would be disappearing for most of a week—went quite differently. Azhanharad listened, frowning, and said, "We have heard nothing of a ghoul from our chapter in Tanvero."

"We hardly think Prince Orchenis is lying to us," I said sharply.

"No, of course not," said Azhanharad. "We merely wonder how reliable his sources are. You may end up traveling all that way for nothing."

"The best outcome with a ghoul," said I.

Azhanharad scowled. "A ghoul is not something to be taken lightly."

"We take ghouls and the duty they represent very seriously," I said, bowing, and we parted miffed on both sides.

I talked briefly to Anora, who echoed the other exhortations to be careful.

"I will be," I said. "I don't know why everyone is so convinced I won't be."

"It doesn't take a very long acquaintance with thee to see that thou dost not value thine own life," said Anora. "I understand their concern perfectly."

"Anora!"

"I do not mean that thou'rt careless, Thara, for thou art not. And thou wouldst never endanger another soul. But thou carest not whether thou wilt live or die. I fear for thee."

"Thou needst not," I said. The blush was scalding in my face. "I have no desire to be eaten by a ghoul. I promise thee I will be careful."

Anora gave me a dubious look over his spectacles, which as always had slid to the end of his nose. "See that thou art. And come see me when thou returnest. I should like to hear about this ghoul."

"I will," I promised. "Let us hope that my story is very boring."

Anora smiled. "I admit to a fondness for boring stories. Be safe, Thara."

꘎

I packed as lightly as I could for a trip into the mountains. After considerable thought, I left my silk coat of office hanging in its place by the door. Travel was going to be rough, and there was no telling what hunting this ghoul might entail.

Well before dawn, I joined the train of Oshenar and Puledra's dry goods caravan to Tanvero. The caravan guards, goblins all, were flatteringly pleased to see me. They, too, had heard about the ghoul. They asked me if I preferred to ride on horseback or in a wagon, and I was torn, knowing that I was not horseman enough for two days' ride in bad terrain, but also knowing that the wagons' progress would be slow and bone-jarring. Honesty forced me into the wagons, where I at least was able to find some cushioning among the bolts of cloth.

The wagon driver was a middle-aged woman named Csano, who promised she'd give me as smooth a journey as possible. She talked cheerfully and inconsequentially about her family, mostly her married daughter and her daughter's two small sons. She sounded far more like a family friend than a doting grandmother, but she was a good storyteller. She said when I asked that she had taken over the wagon when her husband died, "and that was when my daughters were only a little older than my grandsons are now. I was fortunate that my sisters were unmarried and were willing to join my household."

"You haven't remarried?"

"I don't have the time," said Csano. "And time is what it would take to find a man who wouldn't try to assume that my wagon and my money belonged to him. No, I thank you, I prefer to be Widow Tolinbaran and keep control of my house."

"Did your son-in-law marry in, then?" I said, surprised. That was something that happened occasionally among the noble houses, but not to my knowledge among the working people of Amalo.

"He was a foundling," said Csano. "He had to marry in if he was going to marry at all."

Foundlings were far less uncommon in Amalo, but they were usually taken in as servants, not as husbands.

"It was the scandal of the neighborhood," Csano said, laughing, and proceeded to tell me stories of her daughter's wedding until I almost felt that I had been there.

The roads to Tanvero were every bit as bad as I had expected. In the hotel that night, a tiny establishment that existed only because it was halfway between Amalo and Tanvero, I lay in bed and swore I could feel every separate bone throbbing. I was sharing the bed with a caravan guard named Suru. He was from one of the coastal cities far to the south, and his Ethuverazhin, while better than my Barizhin, wasn't very good. But he was good-natured and apologized for taking up so much of the bed. I said that at six-foot-seven, there wasn't much he could do about it, and he laughed.

In truth, there was something pleasant about having another body in the bed. It evoked old, dim memories of comfort. And Suru did not snore. I did not sleep well or deeply, but it was better than no sleep at all.

Csano waved me back to her wagon in the morning. I settled among the big bolts of calico as best I could and listened with a pleasure I couldn't define to Csano's stories of her sisters and her two unmarried daughters, one of whom, it turned out, was a member of the chorus for the Parav'opera in the city's westernmost district, Paravi. It took only a question to get Csano telling her daughter Soviro's stories about the Parav'opera.

The Parav'opera did not have a house composer, and I began to understand why Pel-Thenhior was given so much leeway. He was a valuable commodity, especially since he had produced successful operas before (two of them, as I had learned from the Vermilion Opera's singers: *The Empress of Ravens* and *The Zolshenada*), and if he chose to go elsewhere, he would be welcomed.

"How many opera companies have composers? Successful composers, I mean."

"I have no idea, othala. You should talk to Soviro. She knows more about opera in Amalo than any three people. She's learning the music for as many operas as she can. She says if she ever wants to do better than the Parav'opera, she needs to be prepared."

"*Does* she want to do better?"

"She has her eye on the Amal'opera, but there's nothing she can do about it until there's an opening, which she says doesn't happen very often, and then you've got all the opera singers in Amalo vying for that one spot. I'm not sure what kind of chance she has, to be honest, but I'm not going to tell her not to try."

She went on, but for a few moments, I barely heard her. Min Shelsin had wanted a place at the Amal'opera. Pel-Thenhior didn't think she had a chance, but what if someone else thought differently? What if some other singer thought Min Shelsin was competition that needed to be eliminated?

Therefore they decoyed her down to the Mich'maika and threw her in the canal? That seemed overelaborate—unless the competitor was a singer at the Prince Orchena Opera, the new opera theater built in honor of Prince Orchenis's father (and already being shortened to the Orchen'opera). It was on the northern shore of the lake, where the wealthy bourgeoisie and the lesser nobility had their summer houses, and it was making the area around it extremely fashionable. A mid-soprano there might well be able to persuade Min Shelsin to a meeting on the south bank of the canal.

But a meeting alone with a mid-soprano was not a meeting that was going to end with Min Shelsin dying in the Mich'maika. I thought again about hired help or a co-conspirator, but it suddenly seemed too far-fetched—this hypothetical mid-soprano hiring someone to kill Min Shelsin for being competition for an even more hypothetical position with the Amal'opera—and my theory collapsed like a gelatin mold disturbed too soon.

☾

In the late afternoon, we reached Tanvero, where a delegation of concerned citizens waited, having been informed by courier that Prince Orchenis was sending me. Like most of the people of the Mervarnens, they were of mixed heritage, some of their ancestors being the elves native to the mountains and some of them the goblins who had come north to prospect for gold and had stayed when they found the trade in furs. Their skin ranged in color from black to white, and their eyes were all hues from gray to brilliant crimson. They were all very frightened.

They had brought rolls stuffed with cheese and a jug of cider, and they did not mind my eating while we talked. I was too hungry to balk at being ill-mannered, for I found it impossible to eat while the wagon was moving, and breakfast had been at dawn.

The mayor, tall and stout, ash-gray with muddy brownish-red eyes, said, "Othala, we thank you for coming. The letter from His Highness says you have experience of ghouls?"

"Yes," I said. "Our previous prelacy was in the plains to the west, where ghouls are very common. How long has this one been walking, do you know?"

They glanced at each other, and finally a matron, dark-skinned and light-eyed like Anora, said, "It's at least two months since Keveris started finding disturbed graves."

"At least?" I said.

The othas'ala, elderly, elven, somewhat stooped, and wringing his hands in distress, said, "We have discovered that our cemetery caretaker has been delinquent in his duties."

"Blind stinking drunk," said one of the other citizens, only just audibly.

"Thus," said the othas'ala, ignoring the interruption, "we cannot be sure how long it was before he thought to notify anyone."

"We trust something has been done about this situation," I said, ice starting to crawl up my spine. The longer a ghoul was allowed to continue feeding, the likelier it was to start attacking the living, but also the stronger it became and the harder it was to find its name and thus quiet it.

"Oh yes," said the mayor. "We have a new caretaker."

"Good. Have there been any instances of this ghoul attacking people?"

There was an exchange of uneasy glances. "Not that we *know* of," said the mayor, and I disliked his emphasis on *know*. "But there are many outlying homesteads and trappers' camps, and we have no way of checking on all of them."

"So that it could have," I said.

No one answered.

The ice around my spine was getting thicker. "Is it *likely*?"

An elderly elven citizen, who hadn't spoken before, cleared his throat. "As best we can tell, the ghoul comes from Irmezharharee," and he pointed roughly east. "There are any number of trappers who work the forests east of Tanvero, so I think we must say that if the creature *has* developed a taste for living flesh, it would have found easy targets."

"Osmer Thilmerezh is a historian," the mayor said, although he did not sound entirely happy about it.

Osmer Thilmerezh made a dismissive noise and said, "Osmer Thilmerezh is an exile who has taken up history to keep from perishing of boredom. But that's beside the point. Othala Celehar's question is, *how dangerous do we believe this ghoul to be?* Unfortunately, I believe the answer is, *quite*."

"We don't know that!" the mayor said, as if uncertainty made things better.

Osmer Thilmerezh merely rolled his eyes.

"Has it been seen?" I asked. "Any sightings at all?"

"Keveris *says* he saw it," said the matron.

"Keveris would say anything to prove he isn't a drunkard," said the othas'ala with unexpected venom.

"No one has gone looking for it," said Osmer Thilmerezh. "We sent a message to Amalo instead."

"Athru—the new caretaker—has found its leavings," said the mayor.

"May we speak to Athru?" I said.

All of them except Osmer Thilmerezh looked surprised, but the mayor said, "Of course. He's working in the Clenverada Mining Company Cemetery today."

"How many cemeteries does Tanvero have?" I said.

"Too many," said Osmer Thilmerezh. "Too many mining accidents—although Irmezharharee was originally for plague victims."

That was a cheerful thought. I said, "Might someone take us to the Clenverada Mining Company Cemetery?"

There was a strange, unhappy silence.

I said cautiously, "Unless there is something else you think we need to know?"

This time, the silence seemed almost guilty. Finally, the matron said, "The Ulineise prelate of Tanvero, Othala Perchenzar, argued very vehemently against sending a message of distress to Amalo."

"Does he not believe the ghoul is a problem?" I asked incredulously.

"No, it's not that," the matron said, but then seemed unable to explain further.

Osmer Thilmerezh said, "He believes we have no need for outside help."

"Is he a Witness for the Dead?"

"No," said Osmer Thilmerezh.

"Then . . ."

"He has a book," said Osmer Thilmerezh. "The author claims that anyone can quiet a ghoul."

That seemed an almost suicidal belief, and I had to bite my lip to keep from saying so.

"We cannot find Othala Perchenzar," said the mayor, "and we are very much afraid that he is attempting to prove his theory."

I censored my reaction carefully. These poor people already knew Othala Perchenzar was an idiot; there was no need for me to say so. I said, "Well, there's very little damage he can do before sundown, and we think the more important thing is to find and quiet the ghoul. If he succeeds, we will congratulate him."

"There's no chance he's right, though, is there?" said the matron.

"We do not believe so," I said apologetically. "Unless his book can teach him another way to find a ghoul's name."

"No," said Osmer Thilmerezh. "For we looked at it, when he was making his arguments. It is specious nonsense."

"So we feared," I said. Then, more briskly, "We would speak to Athru first."

The mayor nodded and gestured to the two young goblin men talking to the caravan master. One of them came over, and the mayor tasked him with taking me to the Clenverada Mining Company Cemetery to find Athru.

"Of course," the young man said.

The cemetery was a brisk ten-minute walk from the town square. The young goblin man, whose name was Tana, proved to have better sources of information than those who had greeted me. He knew two people who *had* seen the ghoul. "Only at a distance, mind you."

"That's the best way to see a ghoul," I said, making him laugh. "Was it still in Irmezharharee?"

"No," said Tana. "It has traveled south, for they saw it in the Old Town Cemetery along the South Road."

"The *Old* Town Cemetery?"

"They didn't plan for Tanvero to grow as much as it has, and the space in the old cemetery was used up almost fifty years ago."

"Do people still tend the graves?"

"Oh yes," said Tana. "Othala Perchenzar is most emphatic about that."

"Good," I said, and was relieved that the missing prelate showed at least some sparks of intelligence.

The Clenverada Mining Company Cemetery was laid out in a neat grid with square, identical gravestones. We found Athru, elven white with goblin red eyes, weeding one of the paths that split the cemetery into quarters. He was profoundly grateful to learn that I was the Witness for the Dead and willingly told me all he knew about the ghoul.

It wasn't a great deal. Athru had found disturbed graves in Irmezharharee, and he confirmed, his expression pained, that the graves' occupants had definitely been mauled by something—something he knew was two-legged, for it left footprints in the freshly disturbed dirt.

He didn't know of any trouble in other cemeteries, but his work took him in a counterclockwise circle around the center of Tanvero, first north of Irmezharharee, then west, while if my information was correct, the ghoul had headed south.

I asked him about what lay to the south of the city; he named several cemeteries and added, "Most of the farms are to the south."

I remembered the isolated farms I had seen from Csano's wagon.

I had another question: "How long do you think this ghoul has been awake?"

Athru hesitated.

"I don't care about Keveris," I said.

"I would think three months. It is strong enough to push aside a slab stone. I suspect, othala, that it did not rise in Irmezharharee, but in one of the tiny trappers' cemeteries further east—the cemeteries that the town of Tanvero doesn't even know about, much less maintain. Many trappers, too, are Vikhelneisei, and believe that their names are known to the gods and therefore they cannot become ghouls."

I nodded wearily. The Vikhelneisei were uniformly hostile to Witnesses for the Dead, believing that our work was nothing but profanation. "The grave might not have had a headstone at all."

Athru said, "It is possible, othala."

"Thank you," I said, and he looked like he wanted to pat me on the shoulder.

Athru walked back to town with us and told me more about the cemeteries of Tanvero, from the ornate New Cemetery to the tiny family cemeteries that might hold no more than two or three graves. "Osmer Thilmerezh will tell you that this region has a long history of religious independence."

"Stubborn as mules," Tana said cheerfully.

"So we've never had a single, unified ulimeire," Athru continued. "It makes Othala Perchenzar mad as fire, and he condemns Othala Dathenchar and Othala Monmara as vagabonds."

"That's a harsh word," I said, surprised. It implied that they were frauds, without either a genuine calling or a mandate from the Archprelate.

"Othala Perchenzar is very harsh," Athru said feelingly.

"The mayor thinks he has gone to try to quiet the ghoul," I said.

Neither Athru nor Tana seemed shocked by this idea. Athru said, "He has been saying there is no need for a Witness for the Dead to anyone who will listen. He and Mer Halvernarad nearly came to blows."

"I would have paid to see it," Tana said. "Mer Halvernarad is the president of the Blacksmiths' Guild."

"I am glad no one listened to Othala Perchenzar," I said.

"Othala Perchenzar has never seen a ghoul—or what's left when one finds a living victim," Athru said. "I have, when I was a boy in Mesivo, which was a logging camp about twenty miles north of here." He shuddered. "We were all Vikhelneisei until that."

"Vikhelno wrote far to the south, where there are no ghouls," I said. "He could afford to call them folktales to suit his anticlericalism. But I am always surprised at how popular his teachings are in the north."

"You would think people would know better," said Tana.

Osmer Thilmerezh was still sitting in the town square when we reached it. I could not judge his age well enough to tell if he might have been exiled by Edrehasivar's grandfather, Varevesena, but most likely he was another victim of Varenechibel IV, who was popularly reputed to exile anyone who annoyed him.

Osmer Thilmerezh waved, and I went to join him on the steps of the stolid brick town hall.

"Othala Celehar," he said, "what can we do to help you?"

It was nice to have someone ask. I said, "It seems likely that the ghoul is somewhere south of Tanvero. We need a powerful lantern and it would help to have a couple of strong men with shovels. We'll want to bury it where it falls."

Tana, who had followed me over, said, "Vera and Valta would help willingly."

"They assist Athru in digging graves," said Osmer Thilmerezh. "That's a good idea, Tana. Will you go ask them?"

"Of course," said Tana, and loped off.

Osmer Thilmerezh said, "South is an unfortunate direction."

"So we understand from Athru and Tana. We are hoping that it has not yet tired of carrion meat."

"Why does that happen, othala? Do you know?"

I shook my head. "We wish that we did. But none of our teachers could offer a reason, only warnings that it becomes twice as difficult to quiet a ghoul after it has killed." Anticipating his next question, I added, "We have never had to deal with a ghoul that has killed, although we have quieted half a dozen."

"Gracious," said Osmer Thilmerezh.

"The northern plains seem to breed them," I said. "We know of Ulineise prelates who tried to turn their parishioners to different funerary practices, simply because of the incidence of ghouls, but we have not heard that any of them had been successful. Everyone believes that *their* cemetery will never fall into disrepair."

"That's why Tanvero has a cemetery caretaker," Osmer Thilmerezh said, somewhat wryly. "And really it's been a remarkably effective precaution. This is the first ghoul in the forty years we have been here."

Definitely Varenechibel, then. I did not ask him what he had done to be exiled to Tanvero; it could be a very sensitive subject, even decades later, and I was a new acquaintance, not a friend of intimate enough standing for such a confidence.

Instead, I asked him to tell me what lay along the South Road.

He was still engaged in that disquisition when Tana returned with two massive goblin men, each with a shovel and a lantern. One of them had a coil of rope slung over his shoulder, which was the only way to tell them apart.

"This is Vera and this is Valta," said Osmer Thilmerezh. Valta was the one carrying the rope. "Gentlemen, this is Othala Celehar, who requires your help."

They both nodded, and Vera said, using the plural, "Tell us what you need, othala."

I explained the situation again. They listened carefully, and Valta asked, sounding not at all alarmed, "Will the ghoul attack us?"

It was a fair question. "I will ask you to wait on the road until I have quieted it," I promised. "But should it somehow get past me, it will be very slow. And a shovel is an excellent weapon."

The twins considered this, then nodded. Valta said, "If we leave now, othala, we will have at least some daylight left along the South Road."

"All right," I said, and Osmer Thilmerezh said a very old luck charm.

The twins set a less punishing pace than I had expected, being kind to the lowlander. But it still wasn't long before we reached the south gate and were out in the farmlands.

"We should check the Old Town Cemetery," I said. "Tana said it was seen there, and maybe it won't have gone farther yet."

That was most likely a forlorn hope, but the twins agreed that it was a sensible place to start. We reached the Old Town Cemetery just before the twins had to stop to kindle their lanterns. I could understand, looking at it, with the road on one side and a steep hill rising up on the other (and on the other side of the road a deep rainwater gully), how the town had run out of room. I still found myself uneasy at the thought of any cemetery being abandoned, even with a caretaker, but that was my own experience of Aveio and how quickly a ghoul could rise in untended ground.

Here, all seemed peaceful. We didn't even find signs of the ghoul's passage until we came to the graves farthest from the road, where there had clearly been some digging, and there were old bones scattered, as if the ghoul had not found what it was looking for.

That was a foolish fancy, I told myself sternly. It was a ghoul. It hadn't the brain to look for anything. But it was hard to rid myself of the idea that it might have ceased to be satisfied with dead victims, might be planning—not *planning*, Celehar, stop being absurd—might be drawn toward the living.

"Tell Athru," I said to the twins, and they nodded, grotesque bobbing shadows in the lantern light. Ghoul-disturbed earth became rapidly likely to spawn ghouls itself.

We continued south, watching for the warm lights of the farmhouses as we went. The next cemetery along the South Road was a family one, but before we reached it, one of the twins stopped and said, "Where's Sherzar's house?"

"We're not to it yet," said the other.

"But we should be. We passed the Reclavada and the Parsinada on the left, and the Obrevada on the right—Sherzar should be right here."

There was a pause while Valta—the rope visible across his chest in the lantern light—recalculated his twin's reckoning. Then he said, "Maybe he's saving money by going to bed with the sun."

"Sherzar? The man all but bankrupts himself buying candles in the winter." They both sounded uneasy.

It wasn't yet dark enough that the landscape was completely invisible, and after a moment, Valta said, "There's the beech copse. If he had a candle lit, we would see it."

We were all nervous now. I said, "I think we had best investigate. We can apologize if he was asleep."

"Yes," said Valta, not happily, and led the way past the beech copse, and down a narrow, rutted path. After about twenty yards, a house became visible, very small but squarely built, and entirely dark. Another three yards and we could see the door was open.

Valta muttered a prayer under his breath and called, "Sherzar! Sherzar, are you there?"

There was no answer; I did not think Valta expected one.

I said, "You can stay here if you'll give me one of the lanterns."

"No, I thank you, othala," said Vera. "I think we would be much wiser to stay with you."

"Yes," said Valta.

"All right," I said, though truthfully I myself had no desire to divide our forces.

When I reached the doorway, I knew it was too late for Sherzar. The thick reek of stale blood was like being struck in the face.

Vera went inside first, then me, then Valta. Vera said, "Goddesses of mercy," in a choked voice. Valta stepped back outside and was quietly sick.

The ghoul had torn Sherzar to pieces. Some of the pieces had been gnawed on, and blood was everywhere: pooled on the floor, streaked across the walls, spattered on the ceiling. There were bloody handprints here and there, clearly Sherzar's.

At least we did not have to search to be sure the ghoul was not there. Sherzar's house had only two rooms; neither was cluttered enough with furniture to offer any hiding places—if a ghoul were bright enough to hide, which it wasn't. I reminded myself again that the ghoul was no longer elf or goblin. It was only dead, hungry meat.

I said the prayer of compassion for the dead and offered a silent apology to Sherzar that we could not stop long enough for more. "All right," I said. "We have to follow it from here. There should be enough of a blood trail at least to start us in the right direction."

"Yes," said Vera, still choked, but he recovered when we were back in the open air, and Valta was already casting around for traces. It took only a very little searching to find the ghoul's path, paralleling the road but apparently careful to stay off it, which was not a good sign.

"Be alert," I said to the twins. "This one has been risen long enough to develop some very rudimentary cunning."

"Keveris should have reported it sooner," said Valta.

"Much sooner," said Vera.

"Be glad it's only one ghoul," I said. "From what Athru and Osmer Thilmerezh told me, it could easily have been more."

Two of us walked on the road while the third followed the ghoul's trail. We traded off regularly, and we hadn't gone more than a mile, the moon now starting to rise, before Valta, beside me on the road, said, "There's the Clestenada cemetery. I can see the fancy fence."

"All right," I said. "Assuming it can't figure out the gate—"

"The gate's open."

Vera came out of the ditch, and we ran for the gate of the Clestenada cemetery.

We were too late again.

It was immediately obvious that the ghoul had not opened the gate—also that Othala Perchenzar's book had not been protection enough against a real ghoul.

"He must have tried to lay a trap for it and ended up trapped himself," I said, my own voice shaking. "And now the ghoul has killed twice."

The twins said nothing, and I said, trying to get my thoughts to

move forward, not to remain stuck on the grisly mess of the Clestenada cemetery, "Tell Athru to watch these graves particularly. The
dirt has been saturated with blood, and I've been told that wakes
ghouls more certainly than anything else."

"We will have to bury Othala Perchenzar," said Valta.

"And Sherzar," said Vera.

"Get someone to pay for proper gravestones," I said. "Maybe the
town of Tanvero. And maybe they should think about hiring a second caretaker." I stopped, scrubbed my face with both hands. My
thoughts were moving, certainly, but in no useful direction.

I centered myself, told the twins to start searching around the
perimeter of the graveyard for the ghoul's trail, then moved forward to the corpse. I said the prayer of compassion for the dead and
a second prayer, specific to prelates of Ulis. It was as I was turning
away from the terrible remains of Othala Perchenzar that I realized
two things. First, that the Clestenada cemetery, with its elaborate
fence, did in fact make a perfect trap. Second, that this ghoul was
smart enough to figure that out.

It was blocking the gate.

It did not have a face, only a mouth, and its teeth seemed to be
made of bones. I never saw its body clearly, only impressions of
blood and bone, fat and raw meat. I wasn't sure that there was any
proper body at all; the ghoul clothed itself in meat, but it clothed
itself badly. One thing I had always been told about ghouls—one
thing I had seen for myself a number of times—was not true about
this one. It was not slow.

It was not lightning-fast, but it was far faster than any other
ghoul I had seen, fast enough that I almost didn't dodge in time
when it rushed at me.

I scrambled out of the way and ran immediately for the gate, for
it took only seconds to understand that I had to get out of the killing
pen the ghoul had found and already used successfully once.

But the ghoul had reasoned that out, too. Even as I bumped hard
into the gatepost, its clawing rib-fingered hands clamped on my
shoulders. I had only enough time to grab the gatepost with both

hands before the ghoul started dragging me backwards toward the jagged bone teeth of its maw.

Wherever they were in the darkness, the twins had the wits to extinguish their lanterns.

I ripped myself free of the ghoul's hold and fell hard on the blood-soaked ground. Before I could pick myself up, I felt the ghoul's hand close around my ankle, and it started to drag me back. I cast desperately for the ghoul's name. The process was the same as with any dead body, and the ghoul might be cunning and fast, but it did not have a living mind. It had only hunger and rage and there at the center, almost unsalvageable, was its name.

"Hiriän!" I gasped, grabbing frantically at the gatepost again. "Hiriän Balamaran, I know your name!" The ghoul had been a woman. I didn't know why I was surprised.

It made a noise, a sort of roaring, sawing sound that I could not imagine how it had produced.

"Vera!" I shouted. "Valta! Say the name! Hiriän Balamaran!"

"Hiriän Balamaran!" a twin shouted from the left, and for the first time I felt the ghoul's grip loosen.

"Hiriän Balamaran!" I shouted again. "I know your name! I know your death!" Hiriän Balamaran—who in truth had nothing to do with the ghoul except that it had started with her body—had died in childbirth. She had started bleeding, and there had been no midwife to help her, only her trapper husband. They barely had time to realize something was wrong before Hiriän was dead.

"Hiriän Balamaran!" shouted the other twin from the other side of the cemetery. That actually distracted the ghoul; I felt its grip loosen a little, as if it couldn't decide whether to drag me in or to go after this other target.

"Hiriän," I said, trying to soften my voice. "Hiriän, you have been wrongly woken from your sleep. You must rest again. Hiriän, let the darkness take you."

The ghoul roared again, but I could feel its grip weakening. This was an old ritual, although it was usually recited over the grave *after* the ghoul had been quieted. I said again, "Hiriän, you have been wrongly woken from your sleep. You must rest again." The twins were still shouting "Hiriän Balamaran!" in turn, and as I said, "Hiriän, let the darkness take you," I felt one of its rib-fingers fall off. "Hiriän, you have been wrongly woken from your sleep." The ghoul let go of me entirely, and I scrambled madly out of the cemetery. "You must rest again," I said with all the conviction I had, and, craning over my shoulder, I saw the ghoul's indistinct shape, half out the gate, slump to the ground.

The twins let out a ragged cheer.

"Hiriän Balamaran," I said, "let the darkness take you," and the ghoul collapsed into a pile of rotting meat.

There was perfect silence for a moment—not even insects singing— and then both twins cried, "Othala! Othala, are you hurt?"

I wasn't sure of the answer. I felt filthy, as if I, too, were made of rotting meat, and both shoulders burned and throbbed with pain from the ghoul's grip. "I don't think anything's broken," I managed as I got to my feet; by then the twins had found me by the light of their relit lanterns.

"You're bleeding, othala," said Vera.

I looked down and saw blood oozing through my torn shirt and waistcoat and coat—long parallel rents that marked the touch of the ghoul's hands. My trousers were stained with a vile mixture of mud and blood, and the ghoul had pulled off one shoe.

"Well, that's the ruination of this coat," I said wearily. "But come. We must bury this carcass."

"We will dig," Vera said firmly.

I should have argued, but I was too grateful to them to try. Also, I realized as I watched, I would only have gotten in their way. They dug neatly and swiftly, their shovels never colliding, and when the grave was deep enough, they carefully transferred the foul pile of bones and body parts into the earth, returning my shoe to me when they found it. It was in no worse condition than my trousers, and I put it back on.

The twins filled in the grave as quickly as they had dug it, and by then I had found a stick and wrote HIRIÄN BALAMARAN in careful letters across the freshly turned soil. I said the prayer of compassion for the dead and added a prayer for rest traditionally said over the graves of ghouls, and then we started the long walk back to town.

※

Tanvero had two clerics of Csaivo; I did not ask why the twins took me to one instead of the other. He was a tall elven man, rather stooped, with an abrupt manner and quick-moving hands. He seemed unfazed by the information that my injuries were from a ghoul, merely muttering, "I'd best clean those out thoroughly then." He washed the gashes on my shoulders and left ankle out with something that smelled like marigolds and stung like hornets. I gripped the edge of his examining table and tried to maintain a decent composure.

Coralezh raised an eyebrow and said, "No one will think less of you if you scream."

"That's good to know," I said.

When he had cleaned the gashes, he smeared them gently with an ointment that smelled of camellias and said, "They've stopped bleeding already, so I don't think I need bandage them, but you will need a shirt."

"Yes," I said ruefully. Mine was essentially torn to ribbons, and if I'd wanted the bloodstains to come out, I shouldn't have delayed to bury the ghoul.

"Not to worry," Coralezh said. "I have a kind of secondhand exchange in the back here. Sometimes patients come, like you, and need clothes. Sometimes they come, and they will never need their clothes again."

I had no objection to wearing the clothes of the dead. Coralezh disappeared for a moment, and came back with a plain calico shirt that proved to be only a little bit too big.

"It will do," I said, and put it on.

He offered me a pair of trousers, which were fine once I'd rolled up the cuffs.

"Unfortunately," said Coralezh, "I have no waistcoats that will fit you, and the only coat back there that I think you could wear is mustard yellow. Do you want it?"

I hesitated. On the one hand, I had no wish to look like a barbarian wandering the streets of Tanvero in my shirtsleeves. On the other hand, I was expected, as a prelate of Ulis, to maintain a suitable palette in my clothes, and mustard yellow was not by any stretch of the imagination suitable. My own coat, the black one with gray embroidery of which I had been particularly fond, was ruined.

"Let me try it," I said finally.

It was both bright yellow and quite fashionable, with the off-center line of frogs down the front and the braid in looping patterns at the cuffs. It fit perfectly. And I really couldn't go out in my shirtsleeves.

"That's a terrible color on you," Coralezh observed.

"I will remember not to wear it again. Thank you for your help."

"My calling," Coralezh said with a shrug. "Make a pilgrimage to the Sanctuary for the people of Tanvero and any debt you may owe me will be cleared."

"I will do so."

"Thank you, othala." We bowed to each other over folded hands, and I departed.

ꙮ

It was dawn before I was able to sleep, on a bed that Valta's wife Sanaro had made up for me in their winter storeroom, and my dreams were strange and restless. I was fairly sure I did not dream Valta saying sternly to someone, "No, you do not need Othala Celehar to bury Othala Perchenzar. Is Othala Monmara ill?"

Someone else said, "But Othala Perchenzar hated Othala Monmara."

"Then he shouldn't have gone out and gotten himself killed by a ghoul," said Valta. "Leave poor Othala Celehar in peace."

I wanted to protest that I was perfectly capable of performing a funeral service on two hours' sleep—I had done so before—but by the time I remembered how to form the words, I was asleep again.

I woke up later and emerged from the storeroom to find Vera and Valta playing cards at the kitchen table, while Valta's elven wife worked around them on a meal that turned out to be supper, their wide-eyed infant watching everything from the sling against Sanaro's shoulder. "Othala!" she said, smiling welcome. "Are you well?"

"I am, thank you," I said. "I hope I am not putting you out?"

"Of course not," she said, lying staunchly as she was bound to do, just as I was bound to ask.

"Othala," said Vera, "we have seen Sherzar and Othala Perchenzar safely buried in the New Town Cemetery, and Athru promises he will keep an eye on the graves."

"They will have gravestones by next week," said Valta.

I nodded. "Does anyone know anything about Hiriän Balamaran?"

"Osmer Thilmerezh did not recognize the name," said Vera.

Valta added, "But he himself says he knows very little about the trappers and the independent miners who choose not to live in town."

"Then we have no way of determining where her grave was or whether her husband was too much Vikhelneise for a marker," I said. "Or whether there are other graves."

"Everyone will be racking their memories," said Vera, "and someone must know something."

"Yes," I said, thinking now of Arveneän and Inshiran as well as Hiriän. "Someone must know something."

Vera hesitated, then said, "Othas'ala Deprena is going to ask you to stay."

"I beg your pardon?" I thought I had misheard him.

"To replace Othala Perchenzar."

"That's a question for the Archprelate," I said stiffly.

"The othas'ala said the Archprelate won't interfere with an agreement that's already in place," said Valta.

I was dubious about that proposition, but said only, "My calling is not in Tanvero, and truthfully I am not much more politic than Othala Perchenzar was."

"The othas'ala thinks that because you quieted the ghoul, people will be more likely to accept you," said Vera.

"That's a terrible basis for a prelacy," I said. "Unless the othas'ala expects there to be a ghoul every year or so—people forget quickly."

"*We* won't," said Vera with a shudder.

"Don't go making Othala Celehar think you want him to stay against his calling," said Sanaro.

"No, of course not," said Vera.

"We just wanted to warn you, othala," said Valta.

"I appreciate it," I said.

They went back to their card game, a northern variant of pakh'palar whose rules I could not follow. I sat and thought about the irony: this was the first time an othas'ala had ever *wanted* me to stay. The othas'ala in Lohaiso had barely noticed me. The othas'ala in Aveio had hated me long before I disgraced myself. The Amal'othala in Amalo had no use for me. I did not share Othas'ala Deprena's delusion that I was the solution to his problem. With Vikhelno's teaching so prevalent in his parish, he needed a strong and charismatic prelate, which I was not.

Sanaro said, "Move aside, boys. Supper is ready."

Valta and Vera both moved with considerable promptness, and Sanaro set a pot of barley and beans and vegetables on the trivet sitting in the middle of the table. She produced a ladle and a stack of bowls and said, "Help yourselves. Othala, will you join us?"

"Yes, thank you," I said, for I was starving. Valta ladled me a generous bowlful.

There was not a great deal of conversation over supper, which suited me very well. We were nearly done when Vera said, "Othala, is there a way to tell if a grave is . . ."

"If a ghoul is getting ready to rise?" Valta finished.

"Not that I know of," I said. "Untended graves are a danger, and graves without a legible stone are the worst. But there aren't any *signs* of a ghoul waking—at least, not any reliable ones. Some Ulineise Witnesses claim they can feel the ghoul in the ground, but they're not really any more accurate than you'll be if you look at the headstone and make a good guess."

The twins looked a little daunted. That was good; it might keep them from doing something stupid. If I closed my eyes, I knew I would see the mauled remains of Othala Perchenzar.

Sanaro said, "There are many cemeteries around Tanvero, othala, as I'm sure you have noticed, and Athru is only one man. What would you suggest?"

"Make a list of all the cemeteries you know about," I said promptly. "Get Osmer Thilmerezh to help. Ask the trappers and the miners. Then you need a roster of volunteers. Make sure every cemetery is being checked regularly and weeded and properly maintained. Make the town pay for repairing and replacing gravestones. It isn't a matter anyone can afford to be stingy about."

Sanaro nodded. "My grandmother used to say that if you get one ghoul, you know you'll get more. Like a disease."

There was a horrid thought. "Not quite that bad," I said. "It's more that where one grave has fallen into disrepair, there are likely to be more. And of course a ghoul's victims *are* more likely to be ghouls in turn. But a legible stone and a properly maintained grave will keep them down."

"Well, that's some comfort," said Sanaro. "A contagion, we could do nothing about. Weeding, even a child can help with."

"That is very true," I said.

There was a knock at the door. Valta answered it and said with some surprise, "Osmer Thilmerezh! Come in, please, you honor our house."

"Oh, nonsense, Valta," said Osmer Thilmerezh. "We have come to speak to Othala Celehar, if that is possible."

Valta, Vera, and Sanaro all looked at me. I stood up and said, "What may we do for you, Osmer Thilmerezh?"

Osmer Thilmerezh hesitated—the first sign of uncertainty I had seen in him.

"The storeroom will be private," said Sanaro.

"Thank you," said Osmer Thilmerezh. "Privacy is desirable." He followed me to the storeroom, where I lit the lamp before shutting the door.

"What may we do for you?" I asked again.

Osmer Thilmerezh said, "We would ask you to bear a message."

"A message?"

Osmer Thilmerezh looked even more uncomfortable. "We are a stranger to the young lady, and we fear she would merely discard the letter if we were to send it through the post."

I stared at him, and he blushed as delicately as any elven maiden. "She is our granddaughter, but we never knew her mother because we were exiled before she was born, and *her* mother wanted nothing to do with us. She married another man, and Veliso was raised as his child. We kept track of her as best we could, and we thought when she married an airman and moved to Amalo that we might have the chance to write to her. But she died in childbirth with her daughter Amiru. Amiru is nineteen now and old enough to be told the truth and decide for herself. We are determined not to let this second chance elude us."

It took me some time to find the words to answer this remarkable story. Finally, I said, "We will carry a letter. And we will vouch that you are a real person and not, as best we can judge, a liar. But—"

"That is all we ask!" Osmer Thilmerezh said quickly. "We could not reasonably ask more. We mean the child no harm. She is the only family we have left, and we should like to know her. That is all."

"We will bear your letter," I said, and he beamed at me.

"Splendid! Truly, we cannot thank you enough. Here." It was a fat document, carefully sealed, and as I watched, he wrapped it in oilskin and tied it with a long leather lace.

"You will not forget?" he asked.

"We will not," I said, choosing to take the question as a sign of his anxiety rather than as an insult. Almost reluctantly, he handed me the packet, which I stowed carefully in the inside pocket of the terrible mustard-yellow coat, where it barely fit.

"Thank you, othala," said Osmer Thilmerezh. "You relieve us of a great burden of indecision."

In the kitchen, everyone was trying to look as though they weren't curious in the slightest. Osmer Thilmerezh wished us all a good evening and departed.

"It is Osmer Thilmerezh's business, not mine," I said into the hopeful silence. "Now, I need to find the caravan master—at least, I trust they haven't departed already?"

"Tomorrow morning," said Vera. "I can take you, othala. Valta has a little one to put to bed."

Sanaro, nursing the still wide-eyed infant, laughed and said, "The little one would rather go run around the streets with you. I dread the day she learns to walk."

"She will be a terror like her mother," said Valta.

"Thank you for your hospitality," I said formally to them both.

"We could do no less," said Sanaro, which I recognized as a formal Barizheise phrase.

"Our house is open to you, othala," said Valta. "I do not like to think about how many people would have died if you had not come."

"It is my calling," I said, as Coralezh had said to me.

)(

Tanvero had no street lights. I was possibly still a little rattled by the ghoul, for I found myself following Vera so closely that I was almost treading on his heels, but he only laughed when I tried to apologize.

There were two hotels in town, one patronized by caravan masters and one patronized by guards and drivers. Vera took me to Elsanesmee, where the caravan masters stayed, and said, "If you need anything, othala, ask for me. Valta and I do repairs for most of the buildings in town, so everyone knows us."

"Thank you," I said. "It is kind of you."

He looked at me oddly, then smiled and said, "If you come to Tanvero again, I hope it is not for ghouls."

Inside Elsanesmee, I was recognized immediately and disconcertingly as the prelate who had quieted the ghoul. The desk clerk offered me a chair behind the desk (which I was glad to take, for I was still fatigued) and a boy was sent running to fetch Mer Malhanar. I was intensely uncomfortable, especially as I knew I was being watched from the servants' corridor that ran behind the desk and under the main staircase. The mustard-yellow coat felt like a blazing torch.

Mer Malhanar appeared with what I supposed was flattering promptness and professed himself delighted to see that I was well and capable of returning to Amalo in the morning. He seemed nervous in my presence, and I suppressed the ridiculous urge to reassure him that I had not torn the ghoul apart with my bare hands. He was also delighted to find me a bed for the night, and I was equally pleased with the tiny single room up under the eaves. It was intended for a merchant's edocharis, but even if there was some subtle insult intended—which I felt confident there was not—I did not care. The door had a lock and the bed could be slept upon and Mer Malhanar had my valise sent up so that I was able to change into my nightshirt and sleep in comfort.

Despite my half prediction to myself, insomnia did not plague me, and if I dreamed, I did not remember them in the morning.

)(

At dawn, when I walked to the town square, the caravan wagons and mule teams were there. So was the mayor of Tanvero.

"Othala Celehar!" he cried, seizing both my hands before I knew what he was doing. "We cannot tell you how grateful we are!"

"We follow our calling," I said.

"You have saved Tanvero!" the mayor said.

That was an exaggeration, although certainly the town would need to build a crematorium in a dreadful hurry.

"Can we not convince you to stay? Othas'ala Deprena—who is with a sick parishioner this morning, or he would be here, too—would welcome you, and the whole town would be grateful."

"We are not suited to the ulimeire of a small town," I said, and managed to get my hands back. "But we thank you for the invitation."

"Then can we not do something else to thank you? Anything? We would be glad to give you a better coat."

My face burned, but I was about to say yes when Csano yelled, "Othala! If you're coming, you'd better come now!" I realized the wagons at the head of the train were starting to move.

"Thank you very much for the offer," I said to the mayor, then turned and ran for the wagon, mustard-yellow coat and all.

※

When we reached the Glassmarket, there was another of Prince Orchenis's couriers waiting for me. I recognized two of the three elven men standing beside him: Goronezh of the *Amalo Arbiter* and Thurizar of the *Evening Standard*. The third had to be a newspaperman for the *Herald of Amalo*.

I liked Goronezh and Thurizar well enough—they didn't go out of their way to cast me in a bad light, neither as a fraud nor as a halfwit, and although Goronezh in particular was cynical about the inner politics of the Amalomeire, they were both respectful of the gods.

This new man was younger, fox-faced, and wore his hair in a sleek knot at the nape of his neck. He made me intensely aware of the mustard-yellow coat.

In the chaos of unloading, I barely managed to shout good-bye to Csano before I was being unsmilingly helped in a two-wheeled carriage, the courier climbing in after me.

The newspapermen were shouting questions:

"Othala Celehar, did you find a ghoul?"
"Othala Celehar, is it true that the prince threatened to throw you out of Amalo?"
"Othala Celehar, is there any truth to the rumors about the Duhalada will?"

It was a good thing I was already sitting down. If the newspapermen knew about the Duhalada, the Amal'othala either did or very soon would. And if it was in the papers, he would be obliged to notice it whether he wanted to or not. I had a terrible feeling about the reason Prince Orchenis needed to see me so urgently. I pulled myself together to protest to the courier, "I can't go before Prince Orchenis like this!" The mustard-yellow coat was practically flaunting disrespect, both for the prince and for my calling.

The courier barely glanced at me. "The prince will not be offended."

That cold, hard knot in my stomach got worse.

I was taken to the Cinnabar Room again, where Prince Orchenis and his secretary were waiting. Prince Orchenis's frown was even deeper, and I bowed to him with my heart pounding and my hands ice-cold.

The prince said, "The Amal'othala has been forced to take notice."

My knees nearly buckled; it was the thing I had most feared. "How?"

"Mer Nepevis Duhalar," Prince Orchenis said with the precision of distaste, "in his panic to avoid the judgment of fraud, which he must know is inevitable at this point, took his concerns directly to the Amalomeire." Even more dourly, he added, "And then the newspapers got hold of it."

My heartbeat pounded frantically against my ribs, and my ears were down flat. It took an effort to ask, "What has gotten in the newspapers?"

"So far, only that there is some irregularity with Nepena Duhalar's will and that you spoke to Mer Duhalar on his sons' behalf. They haven't printed any of the more scurrilous rumors yet."

That was not terrible, although also not good. "What has the Amal'othala said?"

"He is most displeased, and he does not like any better than we do being dictated to by Mer Duhalar. Still, as you have observed, it is impossible to prove a negative."

"We swear," I said through numb lips, "we had never met *any* of the Duhalada before that day."

"Not the point," said Prince Orchenis, "although in all fairness we must admit we believe you. The Amal'othala says that, as you have been accused of profaning your calling, it must be Ulis who proclaims your guilt or innocence."

Incredulity made my voice squeak and break: "Trial by ordeal?"

"Trial by ordeal," agreed Prince Orchenis. "It is the only way."

He would not say that at the Untheileneise Court, but I caught myself before I said anything so obvious and so foolish. I realized my hands were shaking, hopefully not so that Prince Orchenis would notice.

"What is the ordeal of Amalo?" I said.

"That," said Prince Orchenis, "is up to the Amal'othala."

⚬

I insisted and was grudgingly allowed to return to my apartment long enough to change my coat. I left the dreadful mustard-yellow coat in a heap on the floor. I chose a waistcoat and then put on my coat of office. Once properly dressed for an audience with the Amal'othala, I joined the courier in the two-wheeled carriage for the drive south to the Amalomeire where it was carved into the living rock of Osreian's Spur. We left the prince's carriage at the foot of the stairs and climbed endless switchbacks, damp with the nearness of the Zhomaikora. The trick, as I knew from my only other audience with the Amal'othala, was never to look down and never to look back, even when one stopped to rest in one of the elaborately carved, copper-roofed turrets.

Finally, we reached the top of the cliff, where two somber-faced canons were waiting for us. One went one way with the courier; the other bowed to me and said, "Come this way, othala, please."

I followed her through the grounds of the Amalomeire. Unlike other palaces and prelacies I had seen, the Amalomeire had no trees, no flowers, just the stark rock out of which the palace was carved. We entered the Amalomeire from its roof.

Inside, it was a true warren, millennia old, the stone beneath our feet worn smooth and convex with the passage of thousands upon thousands of feet. Everywhere there were elaborate stone lattices, carved to look like vines or lace. We passed canons and novices in the halls, all of whom seemed to know who I was; I saw fear in the quick glances they gave me, as if the Amal'othala's disapproval was contagious. I wanted to ask my guide how many people the Amal'othala sentenced to trial by ordeal, but I didn't trust my voice and I wasn't sure she would answer me. I saw Othalo Zanarin in hushed colloquy with two canons, doubtless pursuing some matter on behalf of Dach'othala Vernezar. She glanced up as we passed, but stared straight through me.

The Amal'othala was at devotions in his private chapel. I sat on the bench carved into the rock while the canon stood in front of me as if she were blocking any attempt at escape.

The Amal'othala was an elven man of excellent lineage (a cousin of Prince Orchenis, though not on the house side). He was short and rather stout, and although his eyes were weak, he refused to wear spectacles, making his canons serve as his eyes instead. He dressed always in the bullion-stiff robes of his office (unlike the Archprelate, who wore his robes of office only when strictly necessary, most times being content with a canon's frock coat), and his elaborately dressed and jeweled hair was almost certainly a wig.

When he came out of the othasmeire, he looked at me blankly for a moment, then scowled. "Celehar," he said. "We have not been hearing good things about you."

"It is not true, Holiness," I said, hearing desperation leak into my voice.

"That's as may be," said the Amal'othala, "when we have Mer Duhalar telling everyone who will listen that you are a fraud."

"Holiness, you must know—"

"Oh, do be quiet, Celehar. What *we* know is not the question. It is all the people who have trusted you. Those are the people who will doubt and who must be given proof. That is the purpose of a trial by ordeal."

Horribly, I understood his reasoning, and I could not argue with it. My petitioners needed to trust me, or what good was it to speak to the dead? A trial by ordeal would naturally be in all the newspapers. If I passed it, Mer Duhalar would be silenced.

If I passed it.

"Traditionally," the Amal'othala said, "the trial by ordeal has been a concoction of asteliär."

Women wore asteliär in their hair to rebuff an importunate suitor. If the dose was small enough, a person might survive swallowing the distillate of its flowers, but only after days of vomiting. And it would be terribly easy for the dose to be just that fraction too large.

"However," said the Amal'othala, "we do not approve of the use of asteliär. It is far too crude. We prefer a trial that in fact involves the favor of Ulis."

I did not know whether to be encouraged or dismayed. Before I had to decide, he continued, "We set your trial, Thara Celehar, as a pilgrimage tonight to the top of the Hill of Werewolves, there to stay until dawn."

"They say the dead walk the Hill of Werewolves," I said, uncertain if I had understood the Amal'othala's intention correctly.

"Oh yes," said the Amal'othala. "It's quite true. But that shouldn't bother a true Witness for the Dead."

"And the wolves?"

"Are a folktale," the Amal'othala said with serene confidence. "People don't turn into wolves, Celehar. Don't be ridiculous."

"And you think Mer Duhalar will agree this is a sufficient trial?"

He gave me a stern, undecipherable look. "There was a man who failed, about five years ago, one of those frauds who claim Ulis's direct blessing without even having been so much as a novice. He was found at the foot of the hill in the morning, weeping uncontrollably and with his clothing torn to rags. It is a sufficient trial."

I wanted to argue several points. I said the only thing I could: "Thank you, Holiness."

☽

I was kept in the Amalomeire all afternoon—the Amal'othala suggested that I might like to practice my devotions, and even without the command semi-hidden in the suggestion, I decided he was right. I was glad to retreat to the Amalomeire's chapel to Ulis, dark and quiet and deep in the rock of Osreian's Spur.

The chapel was itself a relic of a much older tradition in the worship of Ulis, in which one had to earn the honor of worshiping Ulis in a sacred space; the chapel could only be reached by descending a long, dark shaft, a natural chimney made into a ladder by means of handholds and footholds carved out of the rock. Such chapels were not uncommon, and there were still ascetics who spent their devotional hours in desolate places, carving ladders in rock, providing such chapels for those who felt they had to go even farther out of their way before Ulis would listen to them. For my part, I no longer believed it mattered whether Ulis listened to me. What was important was that I had to listen to him.

It took me a few moments after I had reached the floor of the chapel to quiet my heart rate and breathing. The tall lanterns burned steadily in their sconces, carved elaborately with night creatures like bats and cougars. It was the job of one of the junior canons to climb down here every day at sunset and refill the lanterns and trim their wicks. In theory, they never went out, but sometimes the canon might have to make the climb by the light of only one lantern. Very occasionally, they might get halfway down and discover that there was no light at all in the chapel. That was not considered an excuse to turn back and was why the job was given to a canon rather than a novice.

There was no altar; the space itself, hollowed from the great weight of the rock, was altar enough. I did not kneel, not wanting the bruises on my shins and kneecaps, but stood barefoot in the center of the chamber, between the two lanterns and in front of the shaft leading up to the kitchens, and did my best to quiet my mind so that I might hear Ulis if he was inclined to speak to me waking. Thus far in my experience, he had spoken to me only in dreams, but that might only mean I had not been listening carefully enough.

I moved through the Devotion of the Moon—appropriate to any

nighttime undertaking—trying to let go of any thoughts besides the long-familiar prayers, a task which was significantly harder than usual. Every time I dragged myself away from wondering about the Hill of Werewolves, I found myself thinking about Mer Duhalar and the rumors he was spreading. How had he known? For he couldn't have hit upon the scandal at random. Had it been talked about in Amalo? Surely not—Aveio was far away and isolated, and the Duhalada was not one of its houses. But he could not have known simply by looking at me that I had once had an affair with a married man.

Here, I caught myself and returned my attention to the Devotion of the Moon. But the next time my mind wandered, it picked up right where it had left off. He *could not* have known. Even the fact that I was marnis was not visible on my face or clothes. If it had been, I would have suffered even more greatly as a novice, and the othas'ala of Aveio would never have let me stay long enough to prove that I could quiet ghouls. But then I remembered I was well known in Amalo for having caught the Curneisei who had killed the emperor. Who was to say what stories had not trickled north from the Untheileneise Court? Who was to say the whole city did not know my past?

Here, I caught myself again, leading my mind like a wayward child back to the prayers of the devotions. But within minutes, my mind went back to the Hill of Werewolves and the stories I had heard about it.

The dead walked there at night, but it was also a place of disappearances: a child runs ahead of his nurse on a twisting path and can never later be found; a young man is dared to spend the night there alone and is never seen again; a gardener, long accustomed to tending the public lawns at the foot of the hill, fails to return home one night. . . . And that was without even considering the stories of werewolves, the hulking half-elven monsters that guarded a fabulous treasure and that were said to go hunting in the streets around the hill on moonless nights. I had heard many different stories to account for them and the treasure they guarded—a curse, an ancient people driven underground by the advent of elves, even an experiment by a university student gone terribly wrong. I had never been able to decide how much or how many of the stories to believe, but I found I remembered every one.

I returned my vagrant attention to the Devotion of the Moon, knowing it would not stay there.

By the time the canon came climbing down the shaft like a blot of shadows, I was glad to see him. He bowed to me nervously, opened a hidden cupboard, and began to refill the lamps. I stayed a moment longer, trying to find some tiny measure of tranquility, then climbed back up to the kitchens, where another canon was waiting for me.

"Othala Celehar," she said, bowing. "We are Canon Varlenin. The Amal'othala has assigned us to witness your trial."

"Surely His Holiness does not intend you to accompany us," I said, a little horrified.

"No, not that. Here," she said, and pointed me to where someone had thoughtfully left some cold chicken and generously buttered sourdough bread that would do very well as dinner. "We are to wait at the gate to the Hill of Werewolves with the key. There is only one gate."

I ate quickly and drank two cups of water from the kitchen spigot.

"We regret that you are in for a long and uncomfortable night," I said to Canon Varlenin as I put on my shoes.

She was too well bred to shrug and too well trained to smile. She said, "It is no matter. Please follow me, for the Amal'othala wishes your trial to begin at moonrise."

I followed her back up through the Amalomeire, buzzing with canons and novices and prelates like a wasps' nest. The climb down the face of Osreian's Spur was, if anything, worse than the climb up, since it was harder to avoid the dizzying view; I stared grimly at Canon Varlenin's back and did not fall, despite the puddles and slick stair-treads that said it had rained, and heavily, while I was too deep in the rock to hear it.

Another two-wheeler, this one marked with the Amal'othala's signet, and we rattled across Amalo in fine style and at top speed. The

Hill of Werewolves was in the northern corner of the Veren'malo, and I wasn't sure we could make it by moonrise. Our driver, though, by consistently choosing less-traveled roads—and with a preternatural ability to predict and avoid road blockages—delivered us to the gate before the first sliver of the moon rose over the horizon.

Canon Varlenin got out of the two-wheeler with me and unlocked the gate. "We will wait," she said. "The Amal'othala has instructed us to open the gate at dawn."

"We understand," I said, trying not to sound as grim as I felt. None of this situation was Canon Varlenin's fault. "Wait. Let us leave this with you." I shrugged out of my coat of office; it was too valuable to wear for climbing a great stone hill in the middle of the night.

"Of course," said Canon Varlenin, accepting the coat and folding it neatly across her arm.

I walked through the gate, and she closed it behind me. "Good luck, othala," she said, softly enough that we could both pretend she hadn't.

〤

The land around the Hill of Werewolves was a public park, beautifully laid out and beautifully maintained. Despite the stories, the Werewolf Gardens were in fact a very popular promenade, although people were careful to go in pairs and everyone left well before dusk.

I shivered and wished for the terrible mustard-yellow coat.

The Amal'othala had specified the top of the hill, and I knew there was an ancient ulimeire up there, where once the soldiers of the Warlord of Amalo had received their burials. Some stories said that those soldiers were the dead who walked, although I had never heard a story that explained why.

The moon was near full and provided plenty of light, at least down here on the public paths. My first task was to find the path to the top of the hill. I walked the long curves of the public pathways, looking for breaks in the ornamental hedges that ringed the hill like fortifications. I thought at first that there was no break, that I was going to have to force my way through the hedge, but then my eye was caught by a trickery of shadow, and I saw that the gardeners had done their best to both leave the way to the path open—for people made pilgrimages to the Ulimeire of Werewolves and it was illegal to block a pilgrim's path—and to hide it so that no one not actively seeking it should stumble across it. I slipped through the opening and started up the hill.

The path, paved in ancient flagstones, meandered a good deal; I resisted the impulse to try to take a shortcut, even in places where it looked reasonable. I was halfway up the hill before I encountered the first ghost.

Ghosts were not as common as folktales and novels would have had one believe. In fact, it was surpassingly rare to have a spirit of the dead who could be seen by laypersons; I had never encountered one before, although I had seen a few walking spirits. But this was a ghost. I knew it as such, and I could never have mistaken it for anything else.

It was clearly a man who had died in war. He was streaked and spattered with blood, and he wore the leather kilt of the ancient Amaleise soldiers. He was staring at his bare and empty hands and screaming soundlessly as he walked along the path. It seemed to be the same path I was using. I got out of the way, crawlingly certain that I did not want him to touch me—and that was a feeling I had never had about the dead before, not once in my entire life.

He walked past without registering my presence; I told myself it was much too early in the evening to become hysterical and continued up the path.

The next ghost was crouched in the middle of the path. He was covered in blood because his entrails were falling out against the desperate pressure of his hands. He might have been screaming, too; I never saw his face. I edged past him, almost shuddering with the conviction that he was going to reach out and catch my ankle, even though it was readily apparent that he was preoccupied—and that was if he could even sense my presence, which was a question I had never thought to ask before and had no answer to.

The next two ghosts were not directly on the path, but in a stand of trees off to the right. They were locked in combat, trading tremendous blows with their short swords. Both were badly wounded, but neither seemed to have noticed; I saw nothing but hatred on their faces, animal snarls that made them look almost like twins.

I got past them only to be confronted by another pair, a soldier dragging a Ulineise prelate. The soldier looked identical to the others I had seen, but he was clearly the enemy; he had what had to be an excruciating grip in the prelate's hair and was jerking him along the path as if he were tugging the lead rope of a recalcitrant donkey. The prelate, scrabbling to keep off his knees, was pleading with the soldier—I could see his desperate expression and his mouth moving although I could not make sense of the words—but it had no effect. I stayed frozen a moment too long, and the soldier dragged the prelate directly through me.

I lurched off the path and was violently sick in the bushes. I stayed there for some time, gasping for breath, before I wiped my face with my handkerchief and got to my feet. It took an intense effort to make myself regain the path, and my heart was hammering when I did.

The path was empty of ghosts.

I proceeded gingerly, as if the earth might open and swallow me with my next step. I knew I was being ridiculous, but it was simply beyond my capacity to stride confidently ahead as if there were no ghosts at all. And anyway, I said bleakly to myself, I had all night.

I traversed two switchbacks and found myself at the foot of a set of stairs carved into the hill. The stairs were very steep and the treads very narrow, so that the effect was almost more like a ladder than a flight of stairs. The middle of each step was deeply bowed, which did not make them easier to climb.

I struggled up the stairs, cursing the slick soles of my shoes. Even court shoes as plain as mine, with no tooling and buckles instead of ribbons or laces, were not meant for this sort of exercise (which was precisely why I had taken them off before descending to the chapel in the Amalomeire). Once I nearly fell and had to clutch at the stairs, scraping my palms raw. Between fear and exertion, I was panting by the time I achieved the top.

I had gone no more than five steps from the stairs when I was suddenly surrounded by ghosts. There were dozens of them—or perhaps it was more accurate to say that there was one ghost and that the ghost of a battle. Everywhere I looked men were killing each other. The fighting was terrible, made worse, much worse, by the complete silence. I did not wonder at the man who had been found weeping at the foot of the hill.

I certainly preferred this trial to asteliär and it was by any fair measure an ordeal. But the Amal'othala was wrong. These ghosts had nothing to do with my calling or the favor of Ulis. Anyone could see them and no one could talk to them, and whether one made it through the night without going to pieces was purely a matter of courage and steady nerve. The ghosts were caught in their repeated motions, this same agony played out over and over again. Or perhaps the Amal'othala was more subtle than I thought, and the trial was not *getting* to the ulimeire, but staying there the entire night, surrounded by death and unable to do anything about it, unable either to ease the suffering these men had gone through or to stop the endless performance of their deaths.

I watched the path, not looking up, and only twice had to stop to avoid walking through a ghost. Much as I tried not to notice anything about them, I saw that both sides wore the same style of armor, so that there was no way even to guess at the identity of the aggressor. My knowledge of the history of Amalo was not sufficient to provide any clues, and I had no idea what victory would mean— *had meant*—for either side.

I reminded myself that whatever this battle had been about, and whoever had won, it had happened centuries ago. I could not change what had happened, could not stop the brutal slaughter surrounding me.

I watched my feet and presently came to another set of stairs, these broad and shallow and curving in a slow spiral toward—I dared a glance up—the top of the Hill of Werewolves.

I was too exhausted to run, but I climbed the stairs as fast as I could.

The ulimeire that had stood at the summit of the hill was in ruins; the ghostly battle going on around me was probably why. It had been round and almost as small as a chapel. If there had ever been an altar, it had been torn down so thoroughly that no trace of it remained. There was just the rocky, mostly barren crest of the hill and a circle of stumps where the columns had been. It would have been a desolate place even in daylight, even without the ghost of a dying man lying across the threshold.

I slowly skirted the perimeter—unable to convince myself that it was safe to cross the open space—looking for the pilgrim's cache, where the tokens of pilgrimage would be kept. It wasn't uncommon for the cache to be concealed as a last station on the pilgrim's journey; usually I would have enjoyed the challenge, but tonight I kept turning to look at the ghosts, as if they might be reaching for me, even though I knew full well the idea was ridiculous.

I found the cache finally by tripping over it—a short, square pillar with a hollowed-out top. The tokens were square glazed tiles painted with the sigil of Ulis in his aspect as the god of dreams, which I found perhaps inappropriately gentle for this grim hilltop. I chose a tile and put it carefully in my inside waistcoat pocket.

Now all I had to do was to get through the rest of the night without going mad.

Ж

When I reached the gate at dawn, the canon was not the only one waiting for me. The newspapermen were there, Goronezh, Thurizar, and the new man, and not only was I in my shirtsleeves, but I was also muddy from head to foot and, having lost its ribbon sometime in the night, my braid had completely unraveled. I looked, no doubt, like the Wood Man's Child from *Ischanhadra*.

Canon Varlenin opened the gate, wide-eyed.

"Good morning, canon," I said wearily.

"Good morning, othala," she said. "These gentlemen wish to hear about your experiences on the Hill of Werewolves."

No doubt they did. I said, "Gentlemen, we regret to disoblige you, but we must speak to the Amal'othala before we speak to anyone else."

"That's Othala Celehar for you," Thurizar said to the new man. "You'll never meet better court manners, not even from Prince Orchenis."

That was a lie, but Thurizar was an inveterate exaggerator, always the man to go to if you wanted a story twisted away from the truth. I did not trust the things I read in the *Evening Standard*.

"Can't you tell us anything?" Goronezh said plaintively. "We got up at the very breaking point of dawn for you, othala."

"We cannot prevent you from doing foolish things, Mer Goronezh," I said, and surprised all three of them into a yelp of laughter.

"Othala Celehar," said the third man, "my name is Vicenalar, from the *Herald of Amalo*. Is it true that there are ghosts on the Hill of Werewolves?"

I was sorely tempted to say yes, but the Amal'othala was already annoyed enough with me. I said, "We cannot speak to you now," and followed Canon Varlenin to the two-wheeler.

As we rattled away in the carriage, Canon Varlenin said, "A messenger came just before midnight, summoning us to the palace."

"Us?" I said, for she had used the plural.

"We are your witness," she said. "Do you have a token?"

I showed her the tile I had chosen. She smiled, her ears tilting up, and said, "Very good, othala. Thank you."

And then, on a belated thought, I said, "We are hardly presentable for the palace."

"It matters not," said Canon Varlenin.

Rather desperately, I finger-combed my hair, finding twigs and dried bits of mud. The Wood Man's Child, indeed. Without a ribbon, there was no use in braiding my hair, but at least I only looked like a madman, not like a frenzied cstheneisa.

When we got out of the two-wheeler in one of the palace's small side yards, Canon Varlenin helped me brush the dried mud off my trousers and held my coat of office so that I could put it on.

She knew her way around the Amal'theileian and led me swiftly and surely to the Azalea Room, where aside from Prince Orchenis and his secretary, the Amal'othala, two canons, Dach'othala Vernezar, Othalo Zanarin, and several members of the House Duhalada were waiting. I very nearly balked on the threshold. I had expected to report to the Amal'othala; I had been resigned to report to Prince Orchenis as well. And I supposed it was reasonable to report to Vernezar. But the Duhalada were another matter entirely.

It was already too late; Prince Orchenis had seen me. I followed Canon Varlenin into the Azalea Room, bowed to the Amal'othala, bowed to Vernezar, bowed to Prince Orchenis, tried to pretend the Duhalada weren't there.

"Well, Celehar," the Amal'othala said. He sounded irritated; I could only hope it wasn't at me—or at least wasn't *especially* at me.

I took the tile out of my pocket and handed it to one of the canons, who gave it to the Amal'othala. He examined it closely, probably enjoying the tension in the room, then gave it to the canon, who handed it back to me. The Amal'othala said, "It is sufficient. Othala Celehar has passed the trial."

I felt my ears lift fractionally and only then realized how flat they'd been.

There wasn't anything as loud as a murmur from the Duhalada, only a sort of whisper of breath. Prince Orchenis said, "We hope you are at last satisfied, Mer Duhalar. Or will you now accuse the Amal'othala of fraud?"

The man addressed, who I thought was Nepevis Duhalar's eldest son, said, "No, of course not. We see that we were wrong. We apologize to Othala Celehar."

I wanted, very badly, to lose my temper.

I wanted to scream at them for doing something so thoughtlessly malicious. I wanted to howl about the invasion of my private life. Above all, I wanted to tell them exactly what I'd gone through, both in Tanvero and in Amalo, as a result.

I said levelly, "The apology is accepted."

Prince Orchenis's ears seemed dubious, but he said, "Then we trust this will settle the matter. Furthermore, now that it has been ascertained that Othala Celehar is not a fraud, we expect Nepevis Duhalar to present himself to the Judiciary for judgment. Tomorrow."

The Duhaladeise spokesman winced, but said, "Of course, Your Highness."

"Very well." Prince Orchenis stood, said, "Celehar, we would speak to you in private," and swept out of the room.

I followed him obediently. In truth, I was grateful to get away from the Amal'othala, who still looked like irritation searching for a target. And I had no wish to speak to Vernezar or Zanarin.

I followed with his secretary in Prince Orchenis's wake to the Cinnabar Room, where the prince sat and said, "Be seated, Celehar. You look exhausted."

I sat down and wondered what I'd do when I had to stand up again. "It was not a restful night, Your Highness."

"Then it is true that the Hill of Werewolves is a place of ghosts?"

"Very true."

"Is there anything to be done? Can they be quieted as ghouls are quieted?"

I was surprised that the prince was asking—rather than, for instance, the Amal'othala—but could only tell the truth: "There's nothing to quiet. They aren't spirits, or even remnants of spirits. They're just . . ." I struggled to find the right word, remembering my own unreasoning horror of them. ". . . they're memories. Terrible memories."

"But who is doing the remembering?" said Prince Orchenis.

I shook my head. "The land? The clouds? We do not know."

Prince Orchenis sighed. "We had hoped that you, as a Witness for the Dead, would have some insight that had eluded us."

Many people had hoped the same. I had disappointed most of them.

"We regret that we do not. But we know of nothing that can be done to clear a place of ghosts."

"Ah well," said Prince Orchenis. "The massacre of the Wolves of Anmura will just have to continue to play out. The city's nightmare, we suppose."

"Is that what's happening?"

"Yes. One of our ancestors' less creditable moments. When the mysteries of Anmura were proscribed two thousand years ago, the Warlord of Amalo used it as an excuse to loot and burn the Wolves' compound on the Hill of Werewolves, then killed everyone they found."

I reflexively made a warding gesture I had learned as a child. No wonder it had been so difficult to tell one side from the other.

I knew the mysteries of Anmura had been proscribed for good reason. They had become greedy and corrupt, arrogantly assuming themselves above the rule of the emperor, above the rule of the Archprelate. And there were darker stories, as there always were in such cases. When the Archprelate Vinvedris revoked his protection, the Amaleise prince was not the only one who had responded with violence. The Anmureisei had been filling up that ledger book for decades.

But still I thought of the Ulineise prelate being dragged to what was surely his death, and shuddered.

Prince Orchenis said, "We have kept you too long, Othala Celehar. You must be exhausted."

I could hardly deny it.

"Our driver will take you to your apartment," said Prince Orchenis.

The prince's carriage would stand out in my neighborhood like a black horse in the snow, but I wanted to go home too badly to care. I said, "Thank you, Your Highness," and the interview was over.

But Vernezar and Zanarin were waiting for me in the hall with Canon Varlenin.

"Let us walk with you," said Vernezar, falling in beside me. "You need not stay, Varlenin."

She hesitated, but he outranked her. She bowed and left; I hoped the Amal'othala wouldn't be too angry at her.

"How may we serve you, dach'othala?" I said wearily.

"It's interesting that you ask that question *now*, Othala Celehar," said Vernezar. "Shouldn't you have asked it several days ago?"

I offered up a brief hopeless prayer to Osreian, goddess of earthquakes. "We were not aware that we had to get permission from you to leave the city."

The silence was ugly. Zanarin said, "Do you claim that you out-rank the Ulisothala?"

"We make no such claim, Othalo Zanarin," I said. "But our mandate is from the Archprelate, not—"

"Not Prince Orchenis," Vernezar said.

"We did not think we had the right to refuse the Prince of Thu-Athamar," I said.

"And you did not think to consult us?"

"Would you have advised us to defy the prince?"

Of course, Vernezar wouldn't have. We all three knew that.

Zanarin said, "It would have been a welcome gesture of *respect*."

"But surely our comings and goings are of no interest to you, dach'othala," I said. "It has never been our impression that we are much in your thoughts."

There was a pause, while Vernezar failed to deny the indifference bordering on hostility with which the Ulistheileian had greeted my arrival in Amalo. "We would have liked some warning," he said thinly, and I thought we were finally coming to the heart of the matter, "before the Amal'othala demanded to know what you were doing to upset the Duhalada so greatly."

That was a completely different matter. "That has nothing to do with the Ulistheileian," I said. "We accepted a valid petition from a valid petitioner, as is our calling and our purpose. You have no authority over our work as a Witness for the Dead."

Zanarin's breath hissed in.

"Well," Vernezar said with the briskness of anger. "We suppose that answers the question of your rank quite definitively."

"It can only mean you have none," said Zanarin.

"You are not a member of our hierarchy," Vernezar said, "and we will tell the Amal'othala so." He turned and stalked off.

Zanarin lingered only long enough to say, "We hope you do not re-gret this," before she followed him, but I knew she was lying. That was exactly what she hoped, and if she could make it happen, she would.

ХѴ

I changed my mind. Instead of going straight home, I had the driver take me to Ulvanensee so that I could talk to Anora. He was pleased to see me but said, "Thou lookst dreadful, Thara. What hast thou been doing?"

I gave him the best summary I could, which made him scowl. "The Amal'othala should know better. Thou'rt no fraud, with no need of proving it. No fraud could do what thou dost."

"It's better this way," I said, although his defense warmed me. "No arguing."

"The House Duhalada should not be arguing with the Amalomeire," said Anora. "I am surprised at the Amal'othala for countenancing it."

"To support me, he would have to have believed me innocent," I said, more bitterly than I intended.

Anora looked at me over his spectacles. "Perhaps I am old-fashioned to feel that it is the duty of an othas'ala to support his prelates until such time as there is *evidence* of their guilt brought to him. And, no, rumors bruited about by a man with every reason to wish thee discredited do not constitute evidence. They constitute *gossip.*"

"Thou'rt fierce," I said.

"I, too, am one of the Amal'othala's prelates," said Anora. "His treatment of thee is surely a presagement of how I may expect to be treated."

"Thou art no vexation to him," I said.

"Is that how we are to measure probity?" Anora said in great mock-surprise.

"Thou know'st that was not my meaning."

"No, *thy* meaning was that there is no reason the Amal'othala *should* defend thee," Anora said. "But thou hast done nothing wrong, Thara. Thou shouldst be able to have confidence that thine othas'ala will champion thee."

"But the Amal'othala—"

"*Is* thine othas'ala, even if he seems disposed to forget it."

I said nothing.

"But I do not mean to browbeat thee," said Anora. "For it remains no fault of thine. And I am glad thou'rt safe."

"I thank thee," I said. I had no one else to be grateful for my safety.

"I admit, I am *not* surprised that Vernezar turned on thee," he said.

"I have been a burr under his saddle since I came here," I agreed. "It is in some ways a relief to be cast out of the Ulistheileian once and for all."

"It leaves thee woefully unprotected."

"Vernezar was no protection," I said. "No, though I would not have wished it, I do not regret it, either."

"And what wilt thou do now? Wilt finally write to the Archprelate? *He* will champion thee."

"No," I said. "This is nothing to trouble the Archprelate with."

Anora gave me a dubious look. "Someday thou wilt judge something worth troubling the Archprelate. I only hope thou wilt not be dead first—eaten by ghouls, for example."

I said nothing. We'd had this argument before, and neither of us enjoyed it.

"I said I would not browbeat thee," Anora said apologetically. "May I suggest that thou shouldst get some sleep?"

⋊⋉

It was a good suggestion, but ill-timed. I knew that if I slept now, I would find it all the harder to sleep tonight, and would wake the next morning in even greater exhaustion. I had followed that cycle before and knew better than to follow it again. That day I walked.

I walked south for several blocks before my mind cleared enough to tell me what I wanted to do. I had been on one pilgrimage in the night; let me make another pilgrimage in the day.

South and west of the city, along the River Road, there was a sanctuary of Orshan, where they kept a corn maze in the old way, with a great procession to celebrate when they harvested the corn, which then went to the city's poor. It was too late in the season for corn, of course, but the maze was marked out by the weight of thousands and thousands of feet, plodding, dancing, marching, and it was permissible to walk the corn maze even when the corn was not there.

I followed the River Road out of the city, walking through quiet bourgeois neighborhoods, rows of shops, a strip of competing dance halls and gambling houses, though nothing to compare with the Zheimela, and then more houses, poorer, shabbier, and then out into the farmers' fields.

The Sanctuary of Orshan was not far out of the city, not anymore, as the city slyly edged closer every year, but it was still peaceful, a low rambling building, always looking surprised when it produced a second story. The man at the door was sitting on the porch steps, whittling a block of wood into an Orshalvero, a doll given to farmers' daughters to hold them close to Orshan as they grew.

He looked up, a thickset middle-aged man at least half goblin, and smiled at me. "Can I be of help, othala?"

I'd begged a ribbon for my hair from Anora, so that at least I looked marginally respectable again. I said, "I wish to walk the corn maze in search of the blessing of Orshan's wisdom."

"Of course," he said, getting up. The block of wood he left where it was; the knife he put carefully into a sheath at his belt. "I am Brother Cenethis."

All of Orshan's prelates named themselves in this way, renouncing their houses for the family they made for themselves, or some such rhetoric. It always made me slightly uncomfortable.

I said, "I am Thara Celehar, a Witness for the Dead."

The friendliness of his expression did not change at all. He said, "Be welcome here, Othala Celehar. You know, of course, that the maze currently has only the memory of corn."

"Yes," I said, though I knew my ears flicked at the word "memory."

He led me through the sanctuary—itself a maze of white-walled rooms with braided rugs—and out onto another porch that looked out over the cornfields in the sanctuary's care. "Follow the path," he said, and surely it was only my tiredness that made the connection with the path of the night before. "You are welcome to spend as long in the maze as you like, though we would ask that you come back by sundown."

"Of course," I said.

"And you will be welcome to share our evening meal," Brother Cenethis said.

"You are very kind," I said.

He smiled at me. "To Orshan, we are all brothers. I hope the maze brings you what you seek."

He went back into the building—and I was thankful that he wasn't disposed to watch—and I followed the path, a slow, lovely meandering trail that brought me eventually to the edge of a cornfield, where it became the path marked out in pebbles of the corn maze itself.

I had walked Ulineise mazes, but I knew the corn maze was a different thing. Outside under the vivid blue sky, for one—Ulineise mazes were always underground. And in an Orshaneise maze, no one could become lost, which was even more unlike the Ulineise mazes. Novices got lost all the time; frequently a junior prelate had to be sent in to get them out again. My ears burned at the memory of some of the things those junior prelates had said.

In the summer, of course, the experience of walking the corn maze would be very different, and I had always avoided it. But now I needed to walk to stay wakeful, and I needed wisdom, if Orshan cared to offer any. And in these empty fields, if it became too much or too wrong, I could always simply walk back to the sanctuary. It was plainly visible and there was nothing to stop me.

"Fear not, Celehar," I muttered to myself, "and walk the maze."

I set my foot carefully over the perimeter of the cornfield and began walking, following the line of milky white pebbles and the broader path of bare flat earth.

I walked slowly, knowing that hurrying was considered an affront to Orshan. And I did not need to get through this quickly. The white line of pebbles twisted and curled, and I followed it doggedly, even though I had to stop periodically to look at the cornfields around me until I stopped feeling dizzy. I didn't know any of the Orshaneise meditations, but after a while I found I was saying an old

Ulineise prayer under my breath, a prayer that asked for quiet—for peace and for silence—and itself twisted and turned around the line *strength in tranquility and tranquility in strength*. I'd always understood "strength in tranquility" and taken "tranquility in strength" to mean that if one was strong, one could make the tranquility one needed. But now, twisting and turning through the corn maze, I began to see it differently, that "tranquility in strength" meant having the strength to keep one's tranquility of mind, no matter what the world brought. It meant being tranquil—peaceful—even when one was strong, not bullying or picking fights. It meant, I thought with a flash of asperity, not being irritated with one's prelates for things they had not done and could not help.

I would never be able to bring myself to say it to anyone, but I knew the Amal'othala had been wrong to call a trial by ordeal.

I came to the center of the maze, where the pebbles made a cross, and over the cross was a four-legged bowl containing a great heap of the milky white pebbles. I chose one carefully and put it in my pocket alongside the tile from the Hill of Werewolves.

And then I began carefully to follow the pebbles along the twisting path out of the maze. A glance at the sky told me Brother Cenethis had judged correctly. I should be stepping out of the maze again around sundown.

)(

D inner with the Orshaneisei was a strange combination of my memories of family dinners among the Velverada and my memories of the long, echoing refectory in which we ate at the sanctuary where I had undergone my novitiate. The tables were long, and people sat on benches, handing platters of food down the row and each taking what he or she needed, but the conversation was general, sometimes loud, and frequently punctuated by laughter.

Strength in tranquility and tranquility in strength, I said to myself and did my best with the conversation along my part of the table. Although I was guarding my tongue, the elven woman next to me managed to box me into the admission that I had not slept the night before.

"Does that happen to you often?" she said.

Thankfully, no, I thought, imagining for a second having to go back routinely to the Hill of Werewolves at night. "I rarely sleep well," I said instead.

"Goodness," she said. "I'm no Csaiveiso, but I've often found that warm milk before bed helps me sleep."

"Don't listen to that milk nonsense," the goblin man across the table said cheerfully. "My father swore by brandy."

And then somehow the whole table was offering remedies for insomnia, a bewildering array of things I'd tried and things I'd never heard of. The man across the table laughed at the look on my face. "Welcome to Orshaneise hospitality," he said.

The others laughed, too.

"But we do hope you sleep well tonight," said the woman next to me, and somehow I was sure it was true.

X

The walk back from the Orshaneise sanctuary to my building seemed endless, but when at last I could drag myself into bed, I did sleep well. In the morning, after meditating, I went to my office in Prince Zhaicava. The newspapermen, Goronezh, Thurizar, and Vicenalar, were there waiting for me.

"Good morning, gentlemen," I said, as placidly as I could. *Strength in tranquility and tranquility in strength.*

"Good morning, othala," said Goronezh.

"Now will you tell us about the Hill of Werewolves?" said Vicenalar.

"And the ghoul," said Thurizar.

"Oh, definitely the ghoul," Goronezh agreed.

"We will tell you what we can," I said, "as long as you agree to print it without . . . inflation."

"We never inflate," said Thurizar, who was the worst of the lot.

"We are seekers after truth," Goronezh said solemnly.

"Besides," said Vicenalar, "we have a feeling your story will not need exaggeration to appeal to our readers."

"That is most likely true," said Goronezh. "Come on, othala. Tell us what happened."

"We will do our best," I said, unlocking my office. "Come in, please. We regret that there is only one chair."

"Seniority," said Thurizar, and claimed it.

"That's all right," said Goronezh. "We stand around for a living."

"Your story, othala, please," said Vicenalar.

I told them as best I could about the ghoul of Tanvero, although I could not find words that truly expressed its grotesque and terrifying presence. Thurizar wanted me to show them the gashes in my shoulders, but I refused. The Hill of Werewolves was no easier to convey, although there at least I could tell them about the Wolves of Anmura and what happened to them that left their ghosts so indelibly printed on the hill.

The newspapermen were there, asking their prodding questions, for an hour and a half. When they were finally gone, I read my post, read the papers—cringing at every mention of the Duhalada and feeling more and more exposed as the articles discussed my success at the trial by ordeal and went into horrible detail about the reasons for it. None of them was vulgar enough to say it directly, but there really weren't very many ways to get that allegation of "misconduct" wrong.

At noon, I went to the public baths, where no one looked at me twice. Afterwards I went to the Hanevo Tree for the indulgence of a plate of steamed buns.

Then back to my apartment, where I changed my coat for the dark green one with the mostly picked-out embroidery of verashme blossoms, swept the floor, and turned to my next responsibility: delivering Osmer Thilmerezh's letter. He had written the address on the

outside of his package, and I unwrapped the oilskin to read it carefully:

MIN AMIRU CHONHADRIN
GENERAL TARAVAR STREET
3rd house west from the corner with Summer Street, north

I recognized General Taravar as being a street near the Amal-
Athamareise Airship Works; the stop at which one got off, if one
was visiting the company, was in fact Taravar Ostro. That was a
good starting point.

On my way to the tram stop, I took the mustard-yellow coat to
Estorezh's secondhand clothing shop. I had no use for it as it was,
and I suspected that it would not dye well. That mustard yellow
looked all too likely to streak through even the best black dye—and
the best would cost me more than the coat was worth. But Estorezh
would take it and no doubt sell it, and in return, although he did
not currently have any frock coats that fit me, I could procure a
shirt and trousers to replace the ones ruined in Tanvero, plus, as it
turned out, another set of smallclothes to replace the set so threadbare I was embarrassed to give them to Merrem Aichenaran, who
did my laundry. I also bought five new handkerchiefs and re-
strained myself from wondering whose signet had been picked out
of them.

I left my purchases to be picked up on my return and headed for
the tram stop to start on this errand I had perhaps unwisely agreed
to undertake.

I rode the tram south to Taravar Ostro and began looking for
Summer Street. This not being an official matter, it would have
been incorrect to consult the cartographers' office. And in any
event, Summer Street was not difficult to find. The first hawker I
approached was able to tell me it was only three blocks west.

The problem was that it wasn't houses along General Taravar.
It was workers' barracks. The third building from the corner was
identical to its neighbors on either side, and there was no way to tell

which room belonged to Min Chonhadrin, except by asking for her, and she might not thank me for the gossip that would spread like fire in dry grass.

There was no good option. I took a deep breath and started knocking on doors.

It took me five doors to find someone at home, but that young elven woman, a filing clerk, was able to tell me that Min Chonhadrin was fifth floor back. I climbed the central staircase, narrow and twisting, to the fifth floor, where the landing had two doors, one to the front, one to the back. The back half of the building, which had eight rooms around a lightwell, seemed deserted. I knocked on the door nearest me, and a young elven woman answered. She had dressed her white hair in cable-thick braids around her head. She wore airmen's trousers tucked into heavy boots, and a patterned calico shirt under a laced leather vest.

"Min Chonhadrin?" I said.

Her eyebrows went up. "Yes. How can I help you, othala?"

"I have a letter for you," I said, and offered her the package.

She looked at it dubiously. "I don't understand."

"It is not my business and not my story to tell," I said. "I will answer your questions to the best of my ability, but please read the letter first."

The same dubious expression was directed at me. "You don't *look* like a prank."

"I swear that it is not a prank."

"Well, all right. Come in and sit down and I'll read your letter."

"Not *my* letter," I protested, but feebly, and I sat where she directed me, one of two chairs at a small table. Chonhadrin sat in the other, broke the seal on Osmer Thilmerezh's letter, and began reading. I noticed that she kept her nails brutally short and that her knuckles were dark with engine oil.

She read quickly, surprise shifting into a baffled frown. "What *is* this?" she said. "Who is this man claiming my grandfather is not my grandfather?"

"I expect he has told you more in the letter than I know," I said.

"He is an exile living in Tanvero and serving—semi-officially, as it seems—as its historian. I know no more than that."

"You agreed to bear his letter," she said.

"He asked me."

"Do you think what he says is true?"

"I am certain that he is not lying," I said. "Only you know whether he has found the right person."

Her scowl deepened. "What am I supposed to do? My grandfather is still alive."

"You need not do anything. It is Osmer Thilmerezh's hope that you will write back to him. But it changes nothing about your childhood and the people who raised you."

"Except that they were lying to me," she said bitterly.

I had no answer to that. "I am sorry," I said.

"You have no reason to be sorry, othala. You have done a kindness for an old man, but that does not make you responsible for the results."

"Doesn't it?" I said. "I knew what the letter contained."

"You certainly had no right *not* to deliver it," she said, almost indignantly.

"I suppose not," I said.

"I'll forgive you for the one," she pointed out. "I wouldn't for the other."

"I am glad of your forgiveness," I said truthfully.

"Properly," she said, "I should thank you."

"You need not. I was glad to do Osmer Thilmerezh the favor."

"You are a very bad liar," she said, amused. "But if you do not wish to be thanked, I shall refrain."

"Doing this thing for Osmer Thilmerezh involved no hardship," I said, being this time more careful of the truth.

"You are a good man, othala," said Chonhadrin. "Will you give me your name?"

"Of course," I said, for I should have done so to begin with. "I am Thara Celehar, a Witness for the Dead."

"The new Witness? The one who—"

"Yes," I said without waiting to find out what she had heard. "I am."

"Then I am honored that you have judged this small story worth your time. If you do not wish to be thanked personally, is there something I can do to thank Ulis for this kindness?"

She had quite a turn of phrase on her for an ashenin, an airship girl. And her question was a fair one.

I was groping for a suitable answer when the explosion happened.

It rattled the windows in their frames, and Chonhadrin and I both grabbed at the table. "Merciful goddesses," she said, "that came from the A3 Works. Othala, will you come with me? There may be people there who . . ."

"Yes," I said. "I'll come."

A3 was what the airmen called the Amal-Athamareise Ashenavo Trincsiva, and indeed I could think of nowhere else such an explosion could have come from. I followed Chonhadrin out and down the stairs and through a tangled snarl of alleyways with other people coming to their doors and saying, "Was that . . . ?"

To which Chonhadrin replied breathlessly, "Yes, it must have been, please come help!"

As we drew closer to the airship works, the air got steadily smokier. I said, "Something's on fire."

"Well, it would almost have to be," Chonhadrin said, and coughed. "Considering that the entire compound is made of metal scaffolding and flammable materials and nothing else."

When we reached the gates of the compound (flung wide open with no guards in sight), it became painfully easy to see where we were going. The thick plume of smoke was rising from a building much like a barn, only bigger. I knew it to be the main hangar, where the Empire line of airships were built.

"It must be the *Excellence of Umvino,*" Chonhadrin gasped, and set off again, this time at a dead run toward the point where the smoke was thickest. I followed her. Near the hangar, we found men frantically organizing bucket lines. Chonhadrin joined them immediately. I saw a goblin man lying on the ground and went to him.

He was terribly burned, and there was no doubt he was dying. "Othala," he whispered, panting with pain.

"I'm here." I would have taken his hand, but both his hands were raw with burns. I put my hand on his shoulder instead. I began to say the prayers of hope for the dying. I kept saying them, carefully, attentively, as his breathing grew more and more labored and eventually stopped.

I sat back on my heels and looked around. The bucket lines had been joined by people making teams to go in and search for those trapped but still alive. There were other people laying the wounded and the dead in rows on the ground. Already there were more than a dozen.

I said the prayer of compassion for the dead and the prayers of hope for the dying over and over, dozens of times, while people in agony clutched at my hands, sobbing; while people near them screamed, for there is no pain like the pain of burns; while other people lay still and silent as their bodies began to cool. Bits of information floated around me, being denied, being confirmed, and gradually as I worked, I began to piece together the story of the disaster.

They were "floating" the *Excellence of Umvino*, which was what one did to an airship before one launched her, and something had happened. Someone had been careless or clumsy or horsing around—and since that someone was now among the burned and mangled dead, some people were speculating freely while others were unwilling to speculate at all. But it was terribly simple to ignite eisonsar. And surely no one could deliberately wish on themselves such a terrible death.

Surely this was an accident.

The explosion had started fires in at least three different places. Many people not instantly killed by the explosion had been trapped by the fire. Some of them had been rescued and lay, now, sobbing on the muddy ground, but some could not be saved. Sometimes when I came to one of the dead, I would recognize them, for I had worked among the airmen for a time. Sometimes when I came to one of the dead, the widow would already be kneeling by the body, and then I had to do my best to be of comfort, although the idea seemed nonsensical surrounded by the dying in the choking gloom of the fire still destroying the *Excellence of Umvino*.

Finally, hours later, a voice at my elbow said, "Othala?"

I looked around. Chonhadrin, covered in soot from head to toe and with an ugly scorched patch on one sleeve, was regarding me with some anxiety in her bloodshot eyes. I wondered how many tries it had taken for her to get my attention.

"Min Chonhadrin," I said.

"Come have a cup of tea," she said. "You need to rest."

At first the words seemed incomprehensible, but she waited and finally the sense of what she was saying reached me. "All right," I said. There were other prelates of Ulis working up and down the rows, and a number of Csaiveise clerics, although I could not remember when they had come; I could be spared for a few minutes.

I followed Chonhadrin away from the lines of the wounded, across the open quadrangle that would usually make the A3 compound seem airy and pleasant, but that was now rapidly becoming a bog, to a long, low building that I recognized once we were inside as the A3 Trincsiva teahouse. It was called the Red Ruby Fox after something in a mountain folktale, and was itself quite pleasant when not filled with the smell of burning and death. It was crowded, though not quite to the point of discomfort.

I sat at the only small square table that was empty and watched Chonhadrin get two cups of tea from the young goblin woman minding the giant samovars. Chonhadrin came back to the table and said, "I apologize for the tea. It's what they call their A3 Blend, meaning that it's made out of the leftover bits and pieces of all their other teas, I wouldn't ordinarily touch it."

The tea was bitingly bitter and tasted like the dregs of an old woman's tea cabinet. But it was hot and strong, and at the moment that was all it seemed reasonable to ask for.

We were silent for a long time, Chonhadrin no more inclined

than I was to talk about the disaster of the *Excellence of Umvino,*
wrecked before she ever left the ground. Around us, people were
either silent or all but babbling, depending on how tragedy took them.
Finally, Chonhadrin said, "How many people do you think . . . ?"

"How many people would have been in the hangar?"

"Lots of people will come by for a floating," she said, and swallowed hard. "And all the people who were just working. A couple
hundred?"

"At least half of them are dead," I said, and wished I could say
it gently. "And probably half of those who are left will be dead by
morning."

"Goddesses of mercy," she said. "Have you seen many disasters,
othala?"

"There was a manufactory fire when I was in my first prelacy. It
was worse than this." She looked like she wanted to argue; I said,
"No one got out."

It was almost as if I'd spoken a cue in an opera; an elven Ulineise
novice came up to our table, his shaved scalp streaked with the same
soot that covered Chonhadrin and me. He clasped his hands and nodded politely and said, "Pardon, othala, but are you Thara Celehar?"

"We are," I said.

"Would you come with us? Othalo Zanarin has need of a Witness for the Dead."

That boded ill. I said, "Of course," gulped the last of my tea, and
said, "Thank you, Min Chonhadrin."

"I don't at all know what for," she said, "but you're welcome."

The novice and I went back outside, where matters had not im-
proved. He led me to an area quite near the still burning hangar,
where Zanarin was standing over a line of bodies so burned they
were almost unrecognizable as bodies.

"Othalo," I said.

She gave me a cold, dismissive look. "We think one of these men
caused the explosion," she said. "We need to know what happened."

"Does it matter?" I said. "It was a terrible accident. Surely that is
enough."

She glared at me. "We had heard that you were inclined to take your duties lightly, Mer Celehar, but it is one thing to be told and quite another to see for oneself."

She was all but daring me to take offense at her rudeness, but I knew she wanted to make me start the argument about rank again—an argument she could then sanctimoniously chide me for starting in the face of a tragedy like this one. "Very well," I said. "We will try."

I knelt down in the mud, trying futilely not to breathe in the scent of burned flesh, began the prayer of compassion for the dead, and touched the forehead of the first man in the line.

A second later, I all but fell down scrambling back away from him and the memories of his death. "It's too close," I said, and disliked the hitch in my own voice. "He's only been dead a matter of hours. It's too close."

Othalo Zanarin stared at me, her mouth a close, flat line and her eyes bright with disgust or anger or disbelief. I realized, with the detachment of a lunatic, that my hair was coming out of its braid, as it always did; between that and the mud and soot on my shabby clothes and the way I was crouched there, trembling, I thought I must *look* like a lunatic, newly escaped from the Csaiveise hospice in the Tenemora district.

I stood up, got out my handkerchief, which was already streaked with soot and blood, and began carefully cleaning the dead man off my fingers. "We are sorry," I said to Othalo Zanarin, "but we cannot help you."

"Cannot?" she said. "*Will* not, more like. We expected very little from you, Mer Celehar, but we certainly did not expect that you would run away like a cowardly little boy."

I kept my attention on my handkerchief until I was sure I would not yell at her. Then I looked up, meeting the bright hatred in her eyes, and said, "It was foolish of us to try. Now, our duty lies with those who are not yet dead, and we think yours does as well."

I went back to the rows of the wounded, where there were more Csaiveise clerics working. One of them said, "Othala, you come in good time. Will you help me here?"

"Yes," I said, and knelt down beside him. Where Othalo Zanarin went, I neither knew nor cared.

)(

I made it home, lurching like a drunk with exhaustion, sometime well after midnight but before the sky started to lighten toward dawn. I did not try to sleep, but folded down in front of my michenmeire and prayed. I prayed for the dead and for the living. I prayed for the acceptance of death and grief. I even selfishly asked Ulis to guard me against the dreams I knew I would have, old dreams of the Carlinar Manufactory fire, new dreams of the *Excellence of Umvino*. I did not expect Ulis to answer this prayer—he never had before and I knew what my masters from my novitiate would have said about personal weaknesses—but I still felt better for having asked.

At dawn I went to the public baths to wash the soot and smoke and stench of death out of my hair. Then I went to the Hanevo Tree and ordered the strongest tea they had, a kolveris that could be used to strip paint. I even, though reluctantly, managed to eat a scone. Thus fortified, I went to the Prince Zhaicava Building and my cold office and my post and the howling chaos of the newspapers.

Goronezh had found me, sometime after I left Zanarin. He was covered in soot and one hand was wrapped in a rough bandage; he had not been there *merely* to ask questions. I liked him better for it, and when he said, "Othala, what happened here?" I noticed that he wasn't holding his notebook, pencil poised for my answer. He was just asking.

I said, "Nobody knows for sure, but I think it was an accident. Eisonsar is dreadfully easy to detonate."

"Then this could happen to any airship? Blessed goddesses, how horrible." And then he affirmed my good opinion of him by asking, "Othala, do you need any help here?"

I did not, but I had no difficulty in pointing him to someone who did.

The *Arbiter*'s story on the *Excellence of Umvino* was the most rational of the three, although all of them were laced through with the wildest of speculations. Everyone was thinking of the *Wisdom of Choharo* and the Curneisei and, like Zanarin, looking for evidence that this was more of the same.

But it wasn't. The Curneisei—even if there were any of them left who knew how to build their exploding devices—wouldn't have set one of them to kill *only* workers. They would have had a target, and there weren't any in that hangar. Just people, many of whom were probably Curneisei themselves.

All three papers printed lurid stories, better suited to cheap novels than real life, about me "taming" the Hill of Werewolves (stories I could only pray that no one believed), but none of them was on the front page, and I could hope that readers would overlook them.

My morning brought two petitioners I could not help. It was not *conversations* that I had with the dead; it was a fading series of images of the things they had valued in life. I could form a question. *Where is the will?* was the most common, but I had heard everything from *Who is the baby's father?* to *What are we to do about Grandmama?* But anything more complicated than that—any time more than a week or two after the death—and I was useless. At noon, because I had no better answer, I went home, and there I found a letter waiting for me in the post.

It was addressed to THARA CELEHAR in a crisp, impatient hand, and the first thing I did when I opened it was to look at the bottom for the signature.

Ediro Zanarin.

My hands went cold, and I reluctantly began to read the letter. It was brief, as crisp and impatient as her handwriting. It said that the bodies from the *Excellence of Umvino* had been laid out in the Amal-Athamareise Ashenavo Trincsiva's Second Production Hangar, where she required my presence as soon as I received this letter. Her authority, shown by her signet, came not from the Ulistheileian, but from the Amalomeire. Unless I wanted to try to argue that the Amalomeire had no authority over me—an argument I would never win—I had to comply. I remembered seeing her in the Amalomeire, and now I wondered if she had been there on her own business, not on Vernezar's. Certainly, she had gained the Amal'othala's favor in some manner—and persuaded him that this investigation was necessary.

I took the tram south again to the A3 Works stop. From there, it wasn't difficult to find the Second Production Hangar—it loomed over the surrounding buildings like a captive moon—and as I got closer I saw signs of some of the same grim activity as yesterday. At the incongruously small door in the side wall of the hangar, a nervous Ulineise novice stopped me. I showed him Othalo Zanarin's letter, and he immediately and with some alarm directed me to the far end of the hangar, where Othalo Zanarin was arguing with one of the judicial Witnesses *vel ama* about jurisdiction.

It was a very long walk, although I knew it could have been worse. The hangar wasn't quite half full of bodies, making this a smaller disaster than some I had seen in Lohaiso (so much smaller than the Carlinar fire), and every corpse had been laid out cleanly and wrapped in linen so that the terrible evidence of burning was hidden as one passed. But there were still too many of them, and the linen could do nothing about the smell.

As I started between the rows of bodies, Zanarin looked around and saw me, and she and the judicial Witness watched in silence as I approached them.

I had lived in my cousin Csoru's household and had survived audiences with the emperor. I was proof against efforts to stare me out of countenance. Also, I realized as I came closer that I knew the judicial Witness, Zhodeän Parmorin, and respected her, which made me feel that it might not be two against one after all.

"Mer Celehar," said Zanarin. "We appreciate your presence."

"Othalo Zanarin," I said. "We have come as asked."

Her close-set eyes were hard granite gray. She said, "The Amal'othala insists that you truly speak with the dead, and if that is true, we have need of your skills."

"The Amal'othala is right," said Witness Parmorin, and they glared at each other, ears flat against their skulls.

Witness Parmorin turned to me, bowing slightly, and said,

"Othala Celehar, we are the Witness for the *Excellence of Umvino.* We will help your investigation in any way we can."

"*Our* investigation," said Zanarin.

"We do not entirely understand," I said hastily, "what you are investigating. The *Excellence of Umvino*'s destruction surely does not need—"

"You persist in the belief it was an accident," Zanarin said.

"Othala Celehar is most likely correct," Parmorin said.

"You can't know that yet," said Zanarin.

"Not for certain, but we know how airship accidents happen," said Parmorin. "This is not the first airship we have witnessed for."

That was an awful thought. "Have you found anything to suggest it *wasn't* an accident?"

"No," said Parmorin.

"Your investigation is hardly complete," said Zanarin.

"Which is why we are continuing to investigate," Parmorin said. "But we do not think it is necessary for the Amalomeire to send a Witness for the Dead unless we find something that suggests one of the dead might have answers."

"We have no wish to intrude on your investigation, Witness Parmorin," I said, since it was clear Zanarin was doing exactly that.

Zanarin turned on me, as fast and sharp as a snake striking and with such cold, scornful anger that I nearly went back a pace. "We would have thought that you of all people would understand the necessity of investigating such 'accidents.'"

I could hear envy, that gnawing rat, in her voice; she was one of the many who thought that a disgraced prelate was not a suitable person to uncover Varenechibel's murderers. I had seen that look repeatedly when I first came to Amalo—I believed it was the root of Subpraeceptor Azhanharad's dislike of me—but it never failed to dismay me.

I stammered a little, but managed to regroup. "But . . . but surely it would make more sense to wait for the results of Witness Parmorin's investigation?"

Zanarin said, "You are assuming that the evidence will be something Witness Parmorin can find."

Behind her, Parmorin was glaring cold murder, but said nothing.

"Come," Zanarin said impatiently. "We have a great deal of work to do."

※

Zanarin stood over me all afternoon as we moved up and down the rows of linen-wrapped bodies. She insisted that we stop at each one, that we interrogate each body with the same questions— and I supposed, under a drearily pounding headache, that I might have admired her persistence were it not that Parmorin and I had both told her it would be better to wait, and she refused to believe it. She refused to believe anything that contradicted the idea that the explosion had been deliberate and purposeful, and perhaps more importantly, that she could find answers where Parmorin could not.

I could guess why. Zanarin was ambitious—that much was plain to be seen—and she had made a bold move in going over Vernezar's head to seek power directly from the Amal'othala. If she was to keep that power, she had to make this investigation worthwhile. And to make this investigation worthwhile, she had to find evidence of malice. She had in fact placed herself in an ugly bind, for if we did not find evidence of malice (and I thought it almost certain we would not), she would have alienated *both* the Amal'othala *and* Dach'othala Vernezar, and her power would have crumbled to nothing like ashes in her hands.

I was grateful when Parmorin came over to argue with her and I could rest for a moment. I paid little heed to their argument—for I knew already the sides and rhetoric—merely stood and tried not to think of the horrible deaths these poor workers had died. The smell of burned flesh was in my hair and clothes, and I knew it would follow me into my dreams, if I could sleep at all.

Zanarin and Parmorin's voices were rising. I shook my head sharply and said, "We gain nothing by arguing."

"We are not arguing," Parmorin said hotly. "Othalo Zanarin is questioning our scholarship."

Something only a fool or a zealot would do. By the cold scowl on Zanarin's face, she was no fool. "We do not question your scholarship," she said. "We question the scope of your investigation."

"You are chasing shadows, and so our report will say."

"You will look a fool when the truth emerges," Zanarin said, openly scornful, and Parmorin began to turn a slow, deep, brick red. "We will not turn aside so lightly."

"Othalo Zanarin—" I started, but she talked right over me.

"We will examine *every body* and we will find the truth your witnessing cannot."

Every body? We were less than halfway done, if that was her goal.

"You will find nothing," said Parmorin, turned on her heel, and walked away.

"Othalo Zanarin," I said again, more forcefully. "The Witness is right. If she finds no evidence of malice, we will not find any in this endless questioning."

She turned her scowl on me. "We are well aware of your opinion. We do not share it. We think there is every likelihood that one of these corpses holds an answer that Witness Parmorin's wreckage does not." Her mouth crimped, although I could hardly call it a smile. "We progress more slowly than we had anticipated. Come down here, and we will question these bodies before nightfall."

I was so relieved that she intended to stop at sundown that I followed her willingly, although I faltered a little when I saw she was walking toward the row of bodies that were most badly burned, the ones that had been closest to the explosions. The ones she had tried to make me read when they were still smoldering from the fire.

"Come," Zanarin said impatiently, and I knelt down beside the first body in the row.

But all I could get from any of those seven blackened, twisted bodies was death. Nothing before the explosion, nothing to answer Zanarin's question. "He doesn't know," I said again and again. "It's no use asking, othalo. The answer isn't there."

From the expression on her face, I was afraid she did not believe me, but at least she did not accuse me to my face of lying. Instead,

she said with false patience, "It is late. We should stop for the night."
And try again tomorrow, was the implied threat, but I was so grateful for the word "stop" that I did not care.

I fled from her—I could call it nothing else—down the length of
the hangar and past the novice still standing guard at the door. I did
not see Chonhadrin until she said, "Othala Celehar?"

I stopped and stared at her. "Min Chonhadrin? Were you looking
for me?"

"I was," she said, "but they wouldn't let me in the hangar. Do you
have a moment?"

"Of course," I said reflexively, as I would have said to any parishioner who asked to speak to me.

"I was wondering," she said, but then stopped, frowning, and her
ears dipped. "Are you all right? You look . . ."

"I'm fine," I said. "I have . . . a headache."

"Headache" was a kind word for a sensation like someone pounding roofing nails into the left side of my skull, one after the other.

"You need tea," said Chonhadrin decisively. "Come. We will go to
my teahouse and have proper tea, and when was the last time you ate?"

"This morning," I said, and my stomach lurched at the thought
of food. "But, Min Chonhadrin—"

"Everyone just calls me Chonhadrin," she said. "Comes with being an ashenin."

"You may call me Celehar," I said. I would be glad not to have to
listen for a title, for "mer" or "othala" (or the "osmer" I was techni-
cally entitled to, or had been before I was disowned). Just a name.

"Celehar," she said. "Come. The Pearl Dragon isn't far, and their
aikanaro is very good."

Aikanaro was not a tea I usually drank, but its gingery bite
sounded suddenly terribly appealing. "All right," I said.

"Good." She gave me a smile, although it looked like an effort.

She led me through the growing dark to a teahouse with white
fish scale clapboard. Inside I was startled by the mural of a white
dragon that wrapped all the way around the room, both because
it was extremely well-drawn to be a teahouse mural and because

the dragon's eyes seemed fixed on me in a most predatory manner. Dragons were popular in Amaleise folktales, supposed to have
lived among the high peaks of the Mervarnens until they were
killed for the veins of gold and silver that they guarded. It was a
more heroic beginning than the Mervarneise mine companies deserved, with their greed and corruption and callous indifference
to miners' deaths, but I could certainly understand the desire for
a better story.

The Pearl Dragon was obviously the gathering place of the ashe-
noi. The women outnumbered the men by three to one at least, and
several of them called greetings to Chonhadrin as we came in.

She answered them cheerfully but was not diverted from her
path to an empty table in one of the oddly shaped niches along the
back of the room. "Sit down, Celehar," she said. "I'll get the tea."

I sat, finding the spindly wooden chair shockingly comfortable.
I closed my eyes against the lamplight and did not open them until
Chonhadrin said, "And here we go," setting a tray down not quite
with a thump. She dropped into the chair across from me and said,
"I ordered stuffed rolls, as well. They'll be out in a moment."

I hesitated in reaching for the tall, rough pottery mug, trying to
think how much money I had in my pockets, and Chonhadrin rolled
her eyes. "We can divide the bill, or I can pay. I have to eat dinner, too."

"You're very decisive," I said, and she laughed.

"The word is 'bossy.' But at this point, I don't think I'm likely to
change."

I took a cautious sip of tea. Its strong ginger bite seemed to wash
some of the dreadful taste out of my mouth, though it could do
nothing for the headache.

Chonhadrin said, "I'm also nosy. What were you doing in that
hangar that they wouldn't let anybody in?"

I had not been sworn to secrecy. I said, "Othalo Zanarin believes
that the explosion was not an accident, and she is seeking evidence
for her theory from the dead."

Chonhadrin's eyes widened, and her ears flattened a little. "Oh.
And you . . ."

"I am a Witness for the Dead," I said with a shrug and took another sip of tea.

"How awful," she said. "Or does it not bother you anymore?"

"It will always bother me," I said. "I can't follow my calling if it doesn't. If you numb yourself to the horror of it, you can't talk to the dead at all."

Her ears were even flatter. "Are there many old Witnesses in your calling, Celehar?"

"We burn out," I said, "like a candle wick drowning in a pool of wax. I probably have five years or so before I can't hear them any longer."

"Will that be a relief?"

"I don't know."

I was glad that the stuffed rolls arrived then, and not only because I was ravenously hungry. They were very good, soft rolls stuffed with ham and tangy white cheese and then heated just enough to make the rolls crispy on the outside and to melt the cheese on the inside. They were impossible to eat tidily, but the staff brought a stack of napkins to the table with the plate, and the rolls went very well with the aikanaro. My headache began slowly to abate.

We were silent for several minutes, and then I said, "You wanted to speak to me about something."

"Yes," said Chonhadrin. "I did. Although . . ."

"Yes?"

"Perhaps it is an inappropriate time for personal concerns."

"It is not wrong to wish for a distraction," I said. "I would frankly welcome one."

"I suppose," she said, but she hesitated a long moment before saying abruptly, "You know, of course, that it is about the letter."

"I am at least not surprised. What troubles you?"

"Everything!" she said, with an exasperated gesture that nearly knocked over her mug. "I do not wish to be unkind to Osmer Thilmerezh, for he seems very lonely and in truth unhappy, but I am afraid that if I answer his letter, I will break my grandfather's heart. My Deleneise grandfather, I mean."

"The man who raised your mother as his child."

"Yes."

"Have you spoken to him?"

"He lives near Cetho. And I have tried to start a letter to *him* six or seven times." Her ears drooped sadly. "I do not know what to do."

I said cautiously, "Do you feel you need your grandfather's permission?"

"No," she said. "It isn't that. It's just . . ."

"You must be unkind to either Osmer Thilmerezh or your grandfather, and naturally you wish to be unkind to neither."

"Yes," she said, sounding relieved. "I don't . . ." I finished eating while she thought hard for several minutes. A very old prelate in Lohaiso had taught me that people often solved their own problems, if you simply listened to them well enough.

Finally, Chonhadrin said, decisively, "I must write to my grandfather first. I cannot spring it on him later."

I nodded and poured more tea into my mug.

"But I think I must also write to Osmer Thilmerezh," she said, "even if my grandfather disapproves. For in fact, since he was exiled, he is not truly to blame for deserting my grandmother."

"One assumes she could have gone with him," I said. "Many wives did."

"But she didn't even marry him, and from his letter, he sounded as if he very much wished she had."

"She must have been a . . ." I hesitated. "A lady very strong in her purpose."

"What a lovely way of saying she was a stubborn old pickaxe," said Chonhadrin. "But, yes. Once my grandmother had made up her mind, nothing could sway her. And she was afraid of nothing that I ever saw."

I thought of the young Osmer Thilmerezh, banished to Tanvero and discovering his lover did not love him enough either to fight for him or to follow him. No wonder he had chosen to become town historian rather than marrying.

"There," said Chonhadrin, with satisfaction. "Thank you. You are a good listener, Celehar."

I smiled at her, although the expression felt stiff and strange on my face. "I am a Witness," I said. "It is my nature."

)(

That night I slept soddenly and woke feeling still heavy and slow. I had several petitioners (they came sometimes in flurries), two of whom did not need *my* help in particular and could be directed to their district ulimeire, two of whom I could not help at all, and one who allowed me to leave my office, however briefly, to find out from his dead wife whether her death was accident or suicide. All morning, I dreaded the afternoon, knowing that if I did not go back to the Second Production Hangar, Othalo Zanarin would merely send a novice to find me. I could not face lunch again, though I knew I would regret not eating.

It was a beautiful day, sunny, with great billowing white clouds sailing grandly across the sky. Anora would be busy all the afternoon burying the victims of the explosion, and one reason I had to go back was so that the remaining bodies could be buried tomorrow. The families' grief deserved that much from me.

Othalo Zanarin looked grim and exhausted. We did not speak to each other. I knelt beside each of the bodies in turn, saying the prayer of compassion for the dead, and touched the forehead. Each body gave me the same answers of pain and terror. None of them had any guilty knowledge. None of them had intended what had happened. After the last body, my head full of noise and burning, I sat back on my heels and said, without looking at Zanarin, "It was an accident. An honest accident, no matter how dreadful."

Othalo Zanarin said, "Do you know how many people died, Mer Celehar?"

"Too many," I said. "But it makes no difference. A terrible result does not always have a terrible cause." It still wasn't worth insisting

on my proper rank, especially since my guess was that Zanarin
would welcome a fight.

"Then *what happened*?" she snarled.

"That is a question for Witness Parmorin," I said. "The dead have
no answers."

"Thank you, Mer Celehar," she said, her voice colder than ice.
"We have no further need of your services." She walked away, toward where Parmorin was standing surrounded by twisted frag-
ments of airship. Instead of leaving, I followed her.

Parmorin saw Zanarin approaching and stopped what she was
doing to stand, arms folded, and wait, scowling ferociously. "Well?"
she said when Zanarin was in earshot. "Did you find your malice
worker?"

Zanarin ignored the question. "What have you found?"

"Nothing that suggests a mechanical device," said Parmorin.
"And without such a device, no one could have ignited the eisonsar
without being caught in the explosion. And we gather"—she cocked
her head inquiringly at me—"that no one caught in the explosion
bore any responsibility?"

I shook my head.

"There was a leak in one of the eisonsar tanks," said Parmorin,
"and then there was a spark. It takes so little to ignite leaking eisonsar that we hesitate to guess what that spark might have been. The
explosion tore the *Excellence of Umvino* apart, sent bits of metal
flying in every direction, and started three fires."

Zanarin said nothing for a long time, long enough that Parmorin
stopped looking angry.

I said, "No one intended harm."

"No," said Parmorin, "airship work is dangerous."

Finally, Zanarin said, although she sounded as if it hurt her, "So
we shall say in our report to the Amal'othala." She bowed, barely, to
Parmorin, and stalked away.

Parmorin and I stood, looking at the wreckage around us.
"Sometimes that is all you *can* say," said Parmorin.

"Sometimes there is no malice to be unmasked," I said.

"No," said Parmorin, "there is no evil at work here. We are sorry it took Othalo Zanarin so long to accept that."

I shrugged. "What if she had been right?"

Parmorin said, "She wasn't right, and she knew it yesterday. She was just too proud to admit she was wrong."

I sighed and pushed my hair back from my face. "And your investigation, Witness Parmorin? What will you say in your deposition?"

"The truth," said Parmorin. "It was an accident."

)(

Although Zanarin seemed to have forgotten about the matter of depositions, Parmorin and I went together to the Amal'theileian and gave depositions before Judiciar Erimar, Parmorin having formally asked me to make a supporting deposition. All that negative evidence Zanarin had amassed was, on its obverse face, important supporting testimony for Parmorin's findings. Afterwards, she thanked me, saying, "We believe that your part in this investigation was even more unpleasant than our own."

"It is our calling," I said.

She gave me a stern look. "That nonsense had nothing to do with your calling and everything to do with Othalo Zanarin being a fanatic. Don't play word games with her part in this."

"It is no matter," I said uncomfortably.

"Why?" said Parmorin, with a Witness's gift for asking the worst possible question. "Because you were the only one suffering?"

"We weren't—"

"We have eyes," she said sharply. "We were convinced more than once yesterday that you were going to faint. Your proper calling isn't meant to be used like that, and you know it."

"No," I said reluctantly, "it isn't."

"You should make a complaint to the Amal'othala."

"We don't need to," I said. "Zanarin's failure will hurt her prestige enough."

"Maybe *we* should make a complaint," Parmorin said.

The idea was horrifying. "We beseech you, do not."

She gave me a long, measuring stare, and finally said, "All right. We will let it go. But only because the idea seems to distress you so greatly."

"We want the Amal'othala to notice us *less*, not *more*," I said, with more truth than I had intended.

She laughed. "We can understand that. Good day to you, Othala Celehar, and be well."

"And you," I said.

She went left; I turned to go right and walked straight into a knot of newspapermen: Goronezh and Vicenalar and two others whom I did not know.

"Othala Celehar!" Goronezh said, plainly delighted to have a target. "What can you tell us about the *Excellence of Umvino*?"

"The explosion was an accident," I said. Erimar had ruled it as such before we even left his office. "Nothing to do with the Curneisei or the *Wisdom of Choharo*."

"Are you sure?" one of the other newspapermen said. He sounded disappointed.

"Quite sure," I said. "The investigation was most thorough."

"Is it likely to happen again?" asked Vicenalar.

"That is a question for the Amal-Athamareise Ashenavo Trincsiva," I said.

We all knew the answer was yes.

※

The next morning brought—along with the newspapers and the varying degrees of skepticism with which they regarded the verdict of accident—an elven family who wanted to bury their great-grandfather according to the old forms, but it had taken all their money to buy him a burial plot in a cemetery with the proper consecrations. They could not afford the prelate's fee, even for a burial at noon.

I was paid by the Amalo prelacy. I cost my petitioners nothing.

This petition was not strictly within the scope of my mandate, but there was nothing that forbade it, either. And I wanted to do something that was simple and straightforward. I agreed.

With great relief, the new patriarch of the Selimada told me that as the prelate was the only thing lacking and his great-grandfather had now been dead several days, they were prepared to hold the funeral that evening. I said truthfully that I had had no plans, and therefore could not be inconvenienced. He drew me a careful, well-labeled map of how to find the cemetery from the nearest tram stop. I thanked him, we bowed to each other, and I was left with the afternoon free.

It was a chance for which I was grateful, as I had wanted for some time to talk to the president of the collective of Ulchoranee and find out how Min Urmenezhen had ended up in their cemetery. After eating lunch at the Red Dog's Dream, I walked to Ulchoranee, where the placard at the entrance told me the president of the collective was one Mer Ozeva Trathonar. I set out in search of him.

It did not take long. An inquiry at a neighboring shop gained me the information that Mer Trathonar was a butcher two streets over, and his shop was in fact impossible to miss, for the sign emblazoned TRATHONAR AND SONS was nearly the same size as the shop window and painted in cream and scarlet, which I thought perhaps a slightly untactful reminder of the bone and blood that were Mer Trathonar's livelihood.

Inside the shop, I found a tired-looking elven woman, her hair escaping its pins, and her attention clearly divided between the front of the shop and the back room, where a child was crying. "Good afternoon, othala," she said. "How may we help you?"

"My name is Thara Celehar, and I am a Witness for the Dead. I am looking for Mer Trathonar."

"He isn't here," she said. "He's probably in the Bramblepony, if your business is urgent."

I felt my eyebrows go up, and she blushed rose-pink. The Bramblepony was a teahouse notorious for also being an illicit gambling house. The rumor was that the proprietor paid the Vigilant Brotherhood not to investigate too closely.

I said, "Actually, you might be just as able to help me."

"Me?" she said, taken aback.

"I'm interested in a young woman named Inshiran Avelonaran. She was recently exhumed from Ulchoranee."

"Yes," said the elven woman. "Ozeva—that is, Mer Trathonar was very upset. I'm sorry, othala, just a moment, please." The child's crying had suddenly reached a new intensity; she disappeared into the back room. I heard an exchange of voices over the crying, which slowly began to taper off. Then Merrem Trathonaran—for she could be no one else—said, "No, it's not your fault," and reappeared with a white-haired elven toddler on her hip, and an older elven child, maybe five or six, following her, although he stopped at the doorway. The toddler's breath was still hitching, but his blue eyes were wide with interest, and he had clearly forgotten what he had been crying about.

"Your sons?" I said.

She smiled shyly and said, "Ozevis and Panezhet. And I am Mevizho Trathonaran. I can tell you about Inshiran, at least a little bit." She hesitated, then seemed to make up her mind to something. "Would you like some tea?"

⋊⋉

She closed the shop and led me up the tiny corkscrewing staircase at the back to a cramped flat, slightly chaotic in the way that any residence of a small child is chaotic. She put a five-zashanei coin in the gas meter and lit her single burner, then filled the kettle at the tap and put it on to heat.

We sat down at the small table, Merrem Trathonaran with the toddler on her lap and Ozevis standing hesitantly behind her, watching me as if I might prove to be a danger. I said, "I am witnessing for Merrem Avelonaran on behalf of her family, and they are naturally anxious to learn what they can of how she died and how she ended up in Ulchoranee."

"Of course," said Merrem Trathonaran. "I do not know very much, for they did not live here for very long before she died."

"How long?"

"Three months? Maybe four? And she was sick for most of that time. She said it was the early sickness, and it may have been, for women do die of that."

It was a moment before I decided how to answer her, but I was witnessing for Inshiran Urmenezhen, and that meant not telling lies about her. "Actually, she was murdered."

And Merrem Trathonaran said instantly, "Mer Avelonar killed her."

"You are very certain," I said.

"I did not want to think it," she said, "and indeed it is terrible to think that she could be murdered so slowly and no one do anything to stop it, but he was very callous, both about her illness and about her death. He arranged her funeral as quickly and cheaply as he could, and he haggled with Mer Cremorezh, the stoneworker, about the cost of adding the child's name to the stone." She was clearly still shocked by this.

I found it shocking myself. "How did she come to be buried in Ulchoranee?"

"She stipulated it in her will," said Merrem Trathonaran. "Mer Avelonar was angry about it, for of course it meant he had to pay for her burial. He and Ozeva had an argument about it."

"Mer Avelonar seems to be a miserly sort of man," I said.

"Oh yes," she said. "My grandmother would have said he was a man to charge his own shadow for the right to stick to his heels."

The kettle sang, and Merrem Trathonaran was very busy for a couple of minutes with teapot and tea leaves and cups and saucers, and when she returned to the table, she had a plate of the hard Amaleise ginger biscuits, called venevetoi, that never seemed to go stale. She gave one to each of her sons.

I had developed a weakness for venevetoi in my time living in Amalo. I took one while the tea steeped and asked, "Do you know where Mer Avelonar went?"

"No, only that the funeral was at noon and he was gone by sundown."

"Noon?" I didn't know why I was shocked. Mer Avelonar had already proved there was no depth to which he would not sink, and murder was far worse than skimping on the funeral arrangements.

Merrem Trathonaran nodded, her eyes wide. "It was the cheapest funeral either Ozeva or I could ever remember seeing. Poor Merrem Avelonaran. She deserved better."

"Her family gave her proper burial," I said.

"Thank the goddesses," she said, and obviously meant it.

I asked a few other questions, but Merrem Trathonaran had told me all she knew. We drank cups of boronat, and I let her tell me about her family. Ozevis lost his shyness enough to chime in, and Panezhet fell asleep on his mother's lap.

※

When I left, Merrem Trathonaran gave me the next pieces of information I needed: the name of the neighborhood cleric and where to find him.

His name was Radora Husavar, and he lived and worked in the back rooms of his wife's tea shop on Winter Street. He was elven, short-statured; judging by the thickness of his spectacle lenses, he was nearly as myopic as Anora.

I explained myself again. "Her family is naturally anxious to learn whatever they can about how she died."

"Naturally," agreed Husavar. "But I do not think you will want to give them many details of her death. In truth, othala, she suffered horribly, vomiting until there was nothing left in her stomach and then being racked with cramps. I tried every remedy I know."

"She was being murdered with calonvar," I said.

Behind their thick lenses, his eyes went wide. *"Calonvar?"*

"Most likely by her husband."

"He was cold enough for it," Husavar said grimly. "He never turned a hair the entire time—which of course he wouldn't if he was the one causing it. I try neither to like nor dislike my patients and their families—as I'm sure will sound familiar to you, othala—but him I disliked very much. But there was nothing that made me suspicious."

"What did you think it was?"

"She was pregnant. Some women, the early sickness just takes over their bodies and wrenches them and wrenches them until they die of it. Her symptoms matched that all too closely." He sighed. "She was so worried about her baby that I'm not sure she ever really understood that she was in danger of dying herself. But Mer Avelonar cared about none of it."

"What was he like? Can you describe him?"

"He was a young elven man, not much taller than I am. I did not notice his features particularly, although I think I would recognize him if I saw him again."

"That might be very important," I said. "We believe this is not the only time he has murdered a wife."

"How dreadful," said Husavar with obvious sincerity. "He kept to himself—she was much friendlier, even though she was dying. He seemed to resent every zashan he had to pay me. I don't think he ever asked me what was wrong with her, or why I couldn't help her, or any of the questions that a husband usually asks. I heard that he kept his funeral arrangements as cheap as possible, as well."

"That is my understanding," I said. "And it seems likely that he murdered her for her money."

"*Dreadful,*" Husavar said.

"Merrem Trathonaran told me that Merrem Avelonaran stipulated in her will that she be buried in Ulchoranee. Do you know why?"

"I know they fought about it. He wanted to bury her in Ulvanensee, and she had a horror of it, while she wanted to be buried in her family's cemetery, and he would not stand for the expense. She chose Ulchoranee as a compromise, and he was *still* unhappy about it."

"So she stipulated it. If she had a will, she must have gone to a lawyer. Do you know who that might be?"

"I have no idea," Husavar said apologetically. "I knew that she had a will, but nothing more than that."

"I suppose it was too much to hope for," I said. "Thank you, othala, you have been very helpful. If we find this man, would you be willing to come confirm that he is the man you knew as Croïs Avelonar?"

"Of course," said Husavar. "I only regret I cannot do more to help. As I have regretted not being able to help Merrem Avelonaran. But without knowing it was calonvar, truly I do not think there is anything I could have done. Even if I had known . . . no, in that case I would have proceeded in a completely different manner, starting with demanding that the Brotherhood arrest him. I imagine her symptoms would have cleared up remarkably quickly after that."

"Yes," I said. "I think you are right."

𝍌

There was time in the afternoon for one more thing. I had promised Coralezh that I would make a pilgrimage to the Sanctuary of Csaivo for the people of Tanvero, and it had been nagging at me that I had not had time to do it. It had been my intention to make that pilgrimage after I delivered Osmer Thilmerezh's letter, but that had become manifestly impossible.

I could, however, do it now. From Ulchoranee to the Sanctuary was a suitable distance for a minor pilgrimage, and it was a lovely day. I followed Winter Street to Beryl Road, then walked north to Princess Havaro Square and west, through the bustle and clamor of the Greenmarket, and thus over to Bridge Street, where I kept to the Zulnicho tramline past the Marigold Rookeries, then cut east again, walking past the great bulk of the Chelim'opera, the largest opera house south of the Mich'maika, and following the curve of the road around until I came to the gates of the Sanctuary. There, rather than either going to the main building entrance or wandering in the gardens, I climbed the stairs that wound around the outside of the central building, stairs that had been mended and replaced and mended again and replaced again in a nearly constant process for longer than the Sanctuary had had written records—at least three thousand years. It was not a wide staircase, and the bannister was an obvious afterthought, probably no more than four or five hundred years old. I was grateful for it, as I was not fond of heights.

The top of the central building did offer a stunning panorama of the Airmen's Quarter—full of apartment buildings and warehouses and manufactories, the enormous domes of the Amal-Athamareise Airship Works visible to the south—and up to the wall of the Veren'malo. I did not approach the edge to look down at the Sanctuary gardens or the dark water of the Mich'maika. Instead, I followed the spiraling path laid out in white and black marble tiles to the center of the rooftop. There, as Coralezh had asked me to, I said prayers for the people of Tanvero, with particular reference to ghouls. Then I knelt and took a pilgrimage token from the recessed pit, a gilded elesth leaf. I put it carefully in an inside pocket and started back, with no little dread, toward the stairs. My only other option was to stay up here until I starved to death; moreover, I had a funeral to conduct.

On my way home to change, I stopped by Estorezh's and picked up my purchases from the day the *Excellence of Umvino* exploded. Estorezh himself, a tall, elderly elven man, was behind the counter. "I thought you had forgotten, othala," he said mildly as he fetched the neat parcel of my new belongings.

"No," I said. "I've just been . . . busy."

"That yellow coat sold the first day I put it out."

"I'm not surprised," I said. "It was of no use to me, but it was a fine coat."

He looked at me, sharp blue eyes under tufted white eyebrows. "Next time I get a black coat in, I'll put it aside for you to look at."

"That's very kind of you," I said, surprised. "Thank you."

He brushed it aside with a flick of his ears. "You do a great service for our city. I can do a small service for you in return."

"Thank you," I said again and left, so flustered that I almost forgot my parcel.

※

The Selimada lived in a part of the city I had visited only infrequently—north of the Old City toward the mountains—but the young man's map was good. I reached the cemetery at the appropriate time.

The family gathered around the gravesite ranged in age from three months to nearly ninety years. They were all somewhat shabby, but I recognized the air of intense and determined respectability from some of my own neighbors. Everyone was properly dressed in black, even the baby, and Merrem Selimaran, the new patriarch's wife, had some onyx mourning beads wound in her hair. I was probably the most out of place thing in the entire scene.

The family seemed pleased enough, however. After the Devotion of Fours had been performed, and the new patriarch and his brothers had filled in the grave, they invited me back to their house for the traditional vigil dinner. It still wasn't as if I had anywhere else I was expected to be. Besides which, this hospitality wasn't offered as lightly as that of the Orshaneisei; I knew I would offend them all if I refused. I accepted with gratitude.

The vigil dinner wasn't quite the same as a wake, although the two practices had much in common. Whereas a wake involved dancing and sometimes singing and was intended to help the dead person's spirit find rest, the vigil dinner was simpler and quieter and had begun as a vigil to be sure the dead person didn't rise as a ghoul. Unlike the people of Tanvero, the Selimada didn't have to worry about that *literally* coming true—in that sense, the wakes held in other neighborhoods of Amalo and the vigil dinners were exactly the same. I thought some of the younger members of the Selimada might have preferred a wake, but the elderly aunts and uncles were very pleased. I got buttonholed by a pair of them—sisters, I thought, although I might easily have been wrong—who wanted to tell me how many Ulineise prelates these days didn't even know what the Devotion of Fours was. It was in desperation that I turned the conversation to suspicious or surprising deaths.

I couldn't have chosen a better topic. I was still trapped between

them, but now only as an audience, as they collectively went back
through—as best I could tell—every funeral that either one of them
had ever attended. I had learned early in my novitiate how to listen
attentively to parishioners, no matter how much I longed to be doing something else, and that training was rewarded by a litany of
deaths—illness, accident, childbirth, murder—but all of the mur-
ders they related were simple affairs: drunken brawls; a man who
had beaten his wife to death found standing over her body, weeping; a woman who went mad and killed her infant. Nothing like
Avelonar's careful isolating of his victim, his subtle method of murder. I did not know whether I was disappointed or not.

A little later, young Merrem Selimaran came by and rescued me,
and a little after that, someone started to sing.

✕

In the morning, back in my office, I thought owlishly that the
Orshaneisei were right: I did need to do something about getting
more sleep. With no petitioners, I dozed all morning, horrified at
myself and knowing it would serve me right if someone walked in,
but no one did.

That afternoon I decided I could do no better than to track down
the items Min Shelsin had pawned and see if they could tell me
anything. I had taken the whole collection of tickets with me when
Pel-Thenhior and I and all those stolen gowns had left Min Shelsin's
rented room, and I had organized them as best I could into a series
of packets, each for a different pawn shop.

They were all shops in Cemchelarna except for one ticket that
belonged to a shop in the Zheimela. It was interesting proof that
Min Shelsin had been in the Zheimela before the night she died,
and I was sorely tempted to ignore the others and just go haring
after that one. But I had learned to be wary of coincidences and that
one seemed far too good to be true.

I wanted to ask Pel-Thenhior to come with me, since he might
at least recognize some of the pieces and possibly remember who

gave them to her, but I remembered what he'd said about rehearsal beginning after lunch. I debated the matter while I ate and finally decided that I could do no harm by asking. Therefore, after lunch I went to the Vermilion Opera, that being the only place I knew to find him.

Either he truly was there every day, or I was lucky, for I found him in the lobby, arguing with Mer Olora again. Relief lit up his face when he saw me, and he broke away from the disgruntled singer.

"Othala Celehar!" Pel-Thenhior said, striding across the lobby to meet me. In a bare, uncarrying whisper, he added, "Please tell me you need me for something. Anything."

I wanted to laugh. I said, "I was hoping you might be able to visit some pawn shops with me this afternoon, to see if we can find Min Shelsin's jewelry."

"Of course!" said Pel-Thenhior, his voice cordial but not nearly as effusive as his face. "Today is all costume fittings and memory practice, and Thoramis can take that as easily as I can. Just a moment!"

He bounded away into the auditorium, and Mer Olora followed with a sour look at me.

I waited, grateful not to have Mer Olora's company, and Pel-Thenhior returned after a few minutes, shrugging into an overcoat. "Was that true or were you just taking pity on me?"

"No, it was quite true," I said.

"Excellent," said Pel-Thenhior. "Let us go forth, then, and investigate."

X

I soon discovered I had been even wiser than I expected to bring Pel-Thenhior, for he was known and liked in all the pawn shops we visited in Cemchelarna, and no one objected or grumbled about bringing out the pawned items, even knowing we weren't going to redeem them.

Although all of the pawned jewelry was expensive, it varied widely in quality, from painfully ostentatious diamond rings (inscribed on their inner surface *to my Arveneän, from her Milparnis*) to a lovely, delicate choker necklace of faceted emeralds. Pel-Thenhior kept a tally of the prices in the flyleaf of the book he happened to have in his pocket, and when we reached the end of Cemchelarna's Pawn-brokers' Row, he said, "Where was all this money *going*? She had at least a year's salary in pawn—maybe more, since I'm quite sure she did not get the value of some of those items—and we know it wasn't on clothes or lodging."

I had several theories, but the most likely was the simplest. "Did Min Shelsin gamble?"

"I have no idea," Pel-Thenhior said. "She didn't bring it to the Opera if she did, which was wise of her."

"You don't approve of gambling?"

Pel-Thenhior made a complicated face. "Well, I don't see the point of it. But it causes bad feelings, and what exactly do you do if one of your tenors bankrupts the other between acts? So I don't allow it in the Opera, but I can't control what people do when they're not there, and of course if she *was* gambling, she wouldn't have told me."

"Of course," I said. "Who might know? Min Balvedin and Min Nochenin? The clerks?"

"I doubt it." Pel-Thenhior thought for a moment. "She might have told Veralis. They didn't like each other, but I know he *does* gamble."

"She might have told him or he might have seen her."

"Yes," Pel-Thenhior said, and added sourly, "she must have worn those gowns *somewhere*."

I went through my packets of pawn tickets. We'd accounted for all of them except the one that had come from the Zheimela. I said, "Are you willing to go farther afield?"

"Of course! Where?"

I showed him the ticket. "A pawn shop in the Zheimela."

Pel-Thenhior's eyebrows shot up. "How intriguing," he said. "I wonder if they remember her."

※

As it turned out, they did.

The proprietor was a young elven man, ferret-faced as elves often were. He lived in the back of his pawn shop, and stayed open from sundown to sunrise, providing his services to the gamblers who were preyed on by the nearby gambling houses, and he remembered Arveneän Shelsin distinctly.

She had come in with an elven man, he said, both of them the worse for drink. He remembered her because of the eye-catching quality of her pledge and because she was so rude.

"That sounds like Arveneän," Pel-Thenhior said.

She had unclasped a necklace, gleaming silver and sapphires, and pawned it, all the while flirting with the man who accompanied her. The pawnbroker brought out the necklace, which I thought rather gaudy, and said, almost apologetically, "She could have had a better price if she'd been paying attention."

"Do you remember anything about her companion?" I asked.

"No, othala. I'm sorry. But"—he brightened—"I know they came from Tivalinee." He nodded across the street.

Tivalinee was a famous gambling house, patronized by the Ponichada and the Alchinada. "Play must be very steep," said Pel-Thenhior, frowning.

"Yes," said the pawnbroker. "Most of my business comes from over there. They don't accept pledges or stakes in kind."

"Too steep for Arveneän," Pel-Thenhior said to me.

"Maybe she was only there the once," I said, though not very hopefully.

"Maybe," said Pel-Thenhior. "And maybe they let her walk into the trap before they sprang it."

〤

By the time we emerged from the pawn shop, the afternoon was fairly over, the shadows lengthening into dusk.

Pel-Thenhior said, "The Opera does not perform tonight, and I'm starving. Let me buy you dinner."

"What?"

"Dinner. You have to eat, don't you?"

"Well, yes, but—"

"We won't go anywhere fancy. But I hate to eat alone, and I flatter myself I'm not bad company."

His face was so hopeful that I did not refuse as I had intended to. I said, "All right," and Pel-Thenhior's answering smile was almost blinding.

We took the tram back to the Veren'malo, and then I followed Pel-Thenhior through a succession of courts and alleyways until we came to a teahouse called the Torivontaram, after a kind of helpful talking animal in Barizheise folktales.

Inside, it was clear—as I had not been able to see in the dark outside—that the teahouse had been built in the ruin of some much older building, and a row of flying buttresses were the ribs of the roof. Someone had turned the buttresses into a mural of trees along the wall.

Immediately as he came in, Pel-Thenhior was involved in a voluble exchange of Barizhin with a rail-thin and rail-straight Barizheise lady who barely came up to his shoulder. Her hair was iron gray, several shades lighter than her skin, which it had probably matched in her youth, and her round, slightly pop eyes were honey-gold, the same color as his.

I spoke some Barizhin, enough to conduct a service for the dead, but certainly not enough to follow that conversation. It didn't help when they both started laughing.

Pel-Thenhior said, "Othala Celehar, this is Nebeno Pel-Thenhior, my mother. Mother, this is Othala Thara Celehar, who is trying to find out who killed Arveneän."

Merrem Pel-Thenhior's eyebrows rose slightly, but she said, "Be welcome, othala."

"Did you know Min Shelsin?" I asked.

"I knew her when she was a child, and have seen her occasionally since. But it was no more than a passing acquaintance." She smiled at me and said more kindly, "Come sit down. Iäna says you have not eaten yet."

"No, but—"

"I'm still buying," said Pel-Thenhior, "and Mother won't overcharge us."

"You are a dreadful child," Merrem Pel-Thenhior said in Barizhin. She herded us gently to a table for two in one of the back corners, where I would have preferred to sit in any event.

We sat down, and Merrem Pel-Thenhior brought a teapot and two glazed pottery cups. The tea was a Barizheise green, smoky and deep. Pel-Thenhior poured carefully.

Pel-Thenhior said, "Many of the Opera come here, so don't be shocked if you see someone you recognize. They won't bother us."

I choked on the words *Are you* courting *me?* and by the time I had recovered, had thought better of asking. If he said no, I would have embarrassed myself beyond bearing. If he said yes, I would be trapped into having to insist that he had made a terrible mistake and having to leave. But I still needed his help and his goodwill if I was to have any hope of answering the many questions about Min Shelsin's death. And I liked Pel-Thenhior.

I liked Pel-Thenhior, and I was lonely.

His mother returned, bearing a tray with two bowls of soup and a plate of brown rolls. The soup was thick with noodles and vegetables and pieces of chicken, and the smell told me how hungry I was.

Merrem Pel-Thenhior said, "You bless our house, othala," in Barizhin, and I answered in the same language, "Your kindness is a blessing on me."

"You speak Barizhin?" she said in delight.

"Only a little," I said.

"Nevertheless," she said, and added to Pel-Thenhior, "I like this one."

I blushed as if my face were catching fire, and Pel-Thenhior said, "Mother, don't torment Othala Celehar."

She laughed. "I beg your pardon, othala. Please enjoy your dinner."

She added something sharp in Barizhin to her son and went back to the kitchen.

Pel-Thenhior said, "She said not to drive you away."

"Does that happen often to the people who dine with you?" I said, as if I were a courtier and could play the game of elegant conversation.

"I have had some spectacular arguments," Pel-Thenhior said, which was not entirely an answer.

We ate for a while in silence. The soup was as good as it smelled, and the rolls were crisp and chewy, served with soft white Barizheise cheese.

Pel-Thenhior said abruptly, "I'm really not angling for anything more than company. You are far more restful than most of the people I know."

"Restful?" I said doubtfully. And was that denial the truth? Had he recognized my alarm? Or was he denying preemptively so that he didn't have to admit the truth, either?

"Opera singers," he said, and rolled his eyes. "Every splinter is a five-act tragedy. And most of them talk and talk and talk." He mimed jabbering with one hand and laughed. "I'm just as bad, as I'm sure you've noticed."

I said nothing, and he laughed again. "That was your cue to deny it, but I am glad you are an honest man."

I felt that I had to offer something, and said, "I have found your conversation illuminating."

"I choose to take that as a compliment," Pel-Thenhior said, but his smile was brilliant.

)(

When I got home that night, my hands were shaking so much that I was barely able to get my key in the lock.

I went inside, hung up my coat, and sat down on the bed, where the shaking enveloped my entire body like an ague. I fought the tremors long enough to take my shoes off, so that I could huddle against the wall. I swallowed hard, curled up as tight as a dormouse, and then I did my best to sit quietly and wait it out. Eventually, I fell asleep and dreamed that all the ghosts on the Hill of Werewolves had Evru's face.

⅜

I woke up with a pounding headache, and my eyes were as bloodshot as if I'd been awake all night.

I washed my face and braided my hair back severely, and walked to the Hanevo Tree for breakfast, including a two-cup pot of strong orchor. It wasn't enough, but it was the best I could do.

The goddesses were merciful, although I did not deserve it: I had no petitioners that morning. I could not face food at noon; I thought about going to the Opera, but I did not know what to say to Pel-Thenhior, and in truth I did not know what questions to ask anyone else. What I needed to know were Min Shelsin's gambling habits: How often and how much? Was that the explanation of all those pawn tickets? It seemed likely, but still left me short of being able to explain the murder, much less identify the man who had committed it.

But perhaps her patrons knew.

I had been avoiding the task of talking to them, hoping that it might not be necessary, that I could find out who had killed her without intruding on the world of wealth and blood. It had been a vain hope from the outset; at the very least I needed to talk to Borava Coreshar and find out what he knew about what had happened on the last night of Arveneän Shelsin's life.

⅜

I knew from previous witnessing in Amalo that my best chance of talking to Min Shelsin's patrons was to find them away from their homes and guardians like Mer Dravenezh. I also knew that the best places to find them away from their homes were the fashionable teahouses along General Shulihar Street: the Pig of Good

Fortune, the Curling Vine, and of course the empress of teahouses, the oldest teahouse in Amalo, Sholavee. I could not afford Sholavee's prices, but I often wished I could.

Even my silk coat of office looked shabby in Sholavee. I walked from table to table, looking for Min Shelsin's patrons. Eyebrows rose and ears twitched, but no one demanded to know my business or called for the staff to come throw me out, and at a table far in the back of the ground floor, I found Borava Coreshar, playing bokh with an elderly elven man whose rings were gold and emeralds.

I could see that the game was nearly over (Osmer Coreshar was losing); I found a vacant table and sat down to wait.

An elven server approached, smiling as if threadbare prelates were her usual customers. When I said I was waiting for Osmer Coreshar, I saw his ears dip, although he did not turn around.

"Of course, othala," said the server. "Are you in need of anything while you wait?"

"No, I thank you," I said. She smiled and bowed and went to the next table to see if they needed more hot water.

I waited no more than a quarter of an hour before Osmer Coreshar had to concede defeat, tipping over his bokhrat with a rueful laugh. I had been curious to see whether he would admit he knew I was there, but after a few moments' conversation with his opponent, he got up and came over to me, saying, "I am Borava Coreshar."

"My name is Thara Celehar," I said, rising, "and I am a Witness for the Dead, witnessing for Min Arveneän Shelsin."

His ears dipped, but he stood his ground. "How may I help you?"

"You are the last person I know to have seen her alive," I said, and watched to see how he took it.

It clearly staggered him; his eyes widened and his ears went flat. But after a moment, his chin came up, and he said, "I assure you I did not kill her."

"I don't believe you did," I said. "But I need to know anything you can tell me about that night. Please, sit down."

He sat as if he was grateful for the chair. He said, "We . . . we went first— Do you want *all* the details?"

"Yes," I said.

"We went first to her boardinghouse, where I waited in the carriage while she changed her clothes. We always did that; she would never go out in the evenings in the clothes she wore to rehearse."

I thought it was more likely the other way around: she couldn't wear to the Opera the gowns she stole to wear in the evenings. But I said nothing.

Osmer Coreshar continued, "I will grant her that she was extremely efficient in the matter. She said it was the result of doing costume changes in a tearing hurry. When she came back—the dress was green velvet with embroidery of flowers on the cuffs—we went for supper at Haramanee. She was . . . very much in her usual spirits. Afterwards, we went to Bonashee."

That was at least informative. Bonashee was the gambling house closest to the Canalman's Dog—at least, the closest of the sort of gambling house to which Min Shelsin would be interested in going. "How long did you stay there?"

"*I* stayed until midnight. I don't know about Min Shelsin. I lost track of her."

"Was that unusual?"

He shrugged one shoulder. "I play pakh'palar at Bonashee, and all my attention is on the game. It has to be. Usually she was there when the game was over, but sometimes not. It depended on how *her* night had gone."

"So you weren't surprised?"

"No. I looked for her, but when I didn't find her, I went home."

"Was that an early night for you?" I was a little surprised; gambling houses like Bonashee stayed open until dawn.

He colored faintly. "I suffer from sick headaches, and I invariably have one if I stay out too late. I always go home at midnight."

Making him, I thought, the perfect escort down to the Zheimela for a young woman who had, perhaps, a midnight meeting at the Canalman's Dog. He wouldn't notice when she left, and she could rely on him not to invest too much time in searching for her.

"Did you see anyone that you knew? Anyone who might know when she left or where she was going?"

He considered the matter. "I know Danila Ubezhar was there. She would have spoken to him if she saw him. But predicting what Min Shelsin will do is—was always difficult, and I do not know whom else she might have known."

"A fair answer," I said. "What else can you tell me about Min Shelsin?"

"What do you mean?" he said warily.

"The more I know about her, the more likely I am to be able to find her murderer," I said. I had learned over the course of many witnessings to be patient with the reflexive fear most people felt when questioned about a murder victim. "You need not tell me anything private. I merely want to see her from a different angle."

He considered again; either he was weighing his answers to me very carefully or he was a person who habitually thought through his words before speaking. He said, "Min Shelsin was very beautiful and very accomplished. She was ambitious—she wanted to be principal at the Amal'opera. She was very lively."

Which could mean almost anything. "Did she gamble often?"

"We often went to gambling houses, but I was not with her always. I do not know what she did on other nights." He hesitated, then added, "She lost a great amount of money."

"Do you know of anyone who might want to kill her?"

"Iäna Pel-Thenhior," he said promptly. "They hated each other with a passion."

Pel-Thenhior had admitted as much, but it was still discomfiting to hear.

"Thank you, Osmer Coreshar," I said. "You have been very helpful."

"I hope you find the man who did it. Arveneän will be much missed."

I noticed that he did not say *he* would miss her and gambled with a tactless question: "Did you love her?"

He was visibly taken aback. "No. Not *love*. I enjoyed her company, and of course I admired her singing."

"Did you give her many gifts?"

There was another long pause, long enough that I thought he was going to refuse to answer, but then he said, "I knew of her habit of draining her patrons dry, and I did not intend to be another of them. I gave her gifts of a quality and at a time of my choosing. She had not yet grown impatient, but my friends assured me she would soon enough." His ears flattened, and he said, "But now, of course, she won't."

"Do you think any of the men she ruined were angry enough to seek revenge?"

I thought it unlikely; Osmer Coreshar considered the idea politely, but said, "No. Of the three that I know of, two were shipped off to other family branches, and poor Elithar still believes he can come about with enough luck at the gambling table."

"Thank you, Osmer Coreshar. Is there anything else you can think of that might help me find her murderer?"

He considered that question for a long time, and finally said, "If it is not Pel-Thenhior, and I gather from your questions that you do not think it is, then the only reason I can think of that anyone would murder her is that she liked to find out . . . I suppose one would call them secrets. Things she wasn't supposed to know and that one had not confided to her. And she was not . . . if she knew a secret, she gloated. And some secrets *are* enough to drive a man to murder."

"True enough," I said. We bowed to each other, and I retraced my steps to Sholavee's entrance.

Osmer Coreshar's assessment matched with that of Min Shelsin's colleagues; her love of secrets might be enough to have gotten her killed. I thought of Min Leverin. She had acquiesced to blackmail when Min Shelsin discovered her secret, but who was to say others would react the same way? Or might someone have chosen a different method to protect their secret?

The question was: *what* secret? Or, perhaps more trenchantly: *whose* secret?

I remembered that piece of paper in Min Shelsin's pocket, illegible and falling apart with canal water. Had that been someone's secret? Had it gotten her killed? That was nothing but speculation; it did, however, make sense of the midnight meeting in the Zheimela, and why Min Shelsin might have agreed to such a thing.

I wondered if there was any way to figure out how bad her gambling debts had been.

And then there was the other option. Even if Pel-Thenhior hadn't killed Min Shelsin himself—his whereabouts would be easy to prove—there was nothing to say he hadn't hired someone else to do it. You could find men in the Zheimela who would do anything if you could meet their price, and they wouldn't talk about it, either. I didn't think Pel-Thenhior would have any difficulty in finding such a man.

But I also thought the reason he gave for *not* murdering her was persuasive. He had needed her voice, and if I had assessed his character correctly, that was far more important to him than any personal hatred of her.

I could admit to myself that I did not want Pel-Thenhior to be responsible, and I knew better than to trust my own judgment. Evru had sworn to me that his wife's disappearance was not his doing, and I had believed him.

I had believed him and had been proved most grievously wrong. My personal feelings were of no evidentiary value; whether I liked Pel-Thenhior or hated him made no difference to my witnessing. The question was only, how much truth could I dig up?

)(

I found Mer Csenivar in his father's place of business. He was haggard, as if he had not been sleeping, and when I told him my errand, he was almost pathetically pleased to have an excuse to talk about Min Shelsin.

He had adored her; he had asked her to marry him more than once, and she had managed to refuse without offending him. She had obviously never tried to blackmail him. He listed the gifts he had given her; they were all familiar from my foray through Amalo's pawn shops. He could not have known about her gambling debts or he would almost certainly have offered to pay them, and I wondered why she had not taken advantage of him in that way when she clearly had no qualms about accepting—and using—his gifts.

Perhaps, like Osmer Elithar, she had believed she could still fix the situation by her own efforts.

Mer Csenivar did not tell me anything new about Min Shelsin, nor had I expected him to. He did tell me the best places to find her other patrons, since he seemed to have watched them almost as obsessively as he watched her.

This alarmed me, and I said, "Where were you that night?"

"When I should have been saving Min Shelsin's life?" he said bitterly, completely missing the implication that he might be a murderer. "I was right here, helping prepare for the annual audit. The auditors arrived the next morning."

"You were very busy."

"Very. My brother and I didn't reach our beds until dawn—we sent the clerks home at midnight."

Which strongly suggested he had not been in the Zheimela at midnight murdering Min Shelsin.

"Can you think of anyone who would have wanted to kill her?"

"How *could* anyone have wanted to kill her? She was so beautiful and so gifted." Tears welled in his eyes, and he blinked them away. "She had terrible arguments with Osmer Ponichar. Screaming matches, really. I asked her why she continued to accept him, but she just laughed and said they understood each other. She hated Iäna Pel-Thenhior, though. They were always fighting about something, and she'd stay mad at him. She wouldn't at Ponichar."

"Do you think Pel-Thenhior would murder her?"

"I don't know," said Mer Csenivar. "*She* hated *him,* but I don't know how he felt. Min Shelsin could be very . . . dramatic about her feelings for people."

I thought "dramatic" was probably a tactful word, but I had gathered that part of what drew Mer Csenivar to Min Shelsin was the intensity of her emotions and the somewhat overwrought pitch at which she lived her life. For a merchant's dutiful son, she was exciting. I wondered if he would have eventually come to find her exhausting.

That, too, was something that would never be discovered.

Using Mer Csenivar's advice, I was able to find Osmer Ponichar without difficulty. He, however, refused to speak to me about Min Shelsin or anything else. All he would say was, "I know nothing about her death." Since I had no evidence of any kind to suggest that he was lying, I had no grounds to insist that he answer my questions—or at least no grounds that the Amal'othala would find impressive if Osmer Ponichar complained of being harassed. And from his flat stare and the angle of his ears, I thought he *would* complain.

I was not going to jeopardize my witnessing for Osmer Ponichar's information, especially when—unless he suddenly confessed to the murder—it was so unlikely to be useful. I went in search of Osmer Elithar instead.

I found him in a gambling house near the Vermilion Opera. His eyes were bloodshot and his hands restless, and although he spoke to me quite willingly, I never had his full attention. He told me nothing except how beautiful Min Shelsin had been and how charming. He did not seem to see her as the author of his downfall, and I left wondering if she had in fact bled him dry or if his own extravagance was to blame.

That left Dach'osmer Cambeshar, whom I could not find among the teahouses and gambling dens. His town residence was in a block of flats carved out of the old Brenenada compound, and the gate was guarded. No one could go in without permission, and if the page came back and said, "Dach'osmer Cambeshar cannot see you today," there was nothing to be done about it.

But when the page came back, he said, looking more than a little surprised, "Dach'osmer Cambeshar can spare you a few minutes."

The compound was as beautifully maintained as if the Brenenada still lived there, and each door we passed bore a different signet. Members of the Zhivenada, the Tativada, the Rohethada— Dach'osmer Cambeshar was in high company. I felt even smaller and shabbier than I had felt in Sholavee. The liveried servants we passed looked as surprised as the page.

Dach'osmer Cambeshar's flat was on the second floor of the south wing. We crossed a broad rooftop courtyard to get there. It had probably served as a ballroom in the spring and early summer; I had heard that the old Amaleise nobility had had a penchant for such things.

Dach'osmer Cambeshar's flat fronted on this tiny plaza. The first room was airy and light and full of lovely wall hangings and beautiful elesthwood furniture. Dach'osmer Cambeshar rose from a chair by the bank of arched windows and said, "Othala Celehar, we understand that you wish to speak to us."

The weight of his attention made me feel cold. He was tall, intensely elegant, with green eyes which he wore jade in his ears to accentuate. His hair was dressed with amber and gold, but it did nothing to make his presence warmer.

I knew immediately, as one sometimes knows things that cannot be proved, that if he had killed Min Shelsin, her body would never have been found and I would never have come to this jewel-like room.

"Dach'osmer Cambeshar," I said, "thank you for agreeing. We will not take many minutes of your time."

He raised his eyebrows, whether skeptically or encouragingly I could not tell.

"We are witnessing for Arveneän Shelsin," I said, "and we are speaking to all of her patrons. Do you know of anyone who might have wanted to kill her?"

"No," he said. "But we know very little of Min Shelsin save the beauty of her singing. She did not confide in us." The dryness of his voice said he preferred it that way.

I considered him a moment, trying to think past my instinctive aversion. "Do you know anything of her gambling debts?"

"Did she have them?" he said with another unreadable lift of his eyebrows. "We are not surprised to hear it. She was . . . reckless."

It was a condemnation; Dach'osmer Cambeshar was not a man who did reckless things, nor would he sympathize with someone who did.

He sympathized with no one. Despite the warmth of the sun, I felt cold, and despite the light in the room, I felt as though I were groping in the dark. I said nothing for a moment, then decided I had nothing to lose and asked, "Did she ever try to blackmail you?"

He laughed. "Was *that* her game? No, we keep our secrets far more carefully than that."

I believed him. But I thought of one other question. "Did you attend the Vermilion Opera's performance of *General Olethazh* on the ninth?"

"The night she died? As it happens, we did."

"Was Iäna Pel-Thenhior there?" I had to ask someone, and I had no fear that Dach'osmer Cambeshar would lie, as a singer might.

"He was," said Dach'osmer Cambeshar, and did not ask why I was asking.

I said, "Thank you for your time, Dach'osmer Cambeshar. We appreciate your assistance."

"We have hardly given any," he observed. "But you are welcome, othala. We are sorry we could not offer you more information."

"Even a lack of information tells us something," I said, and he rang the bell for a page boy to see me out.

☿

I had at this point, I thought, a relatively well-rounded picture of Arveneän Shelsin. She was an ambitious woman—ambitious professionally, financially, socially. She was, as Dach'osmer Cambeshar said, reckless, unheeding of the consequences of her behavior. Hence the gambling and hence the alienation of her colleagues. Only with Min Nochenin and Min Balvedin had she seemed to care what they thought of her on a personal level. I wondered if she had sought out the two clerks to be her friends *because* she had alienated the singers, or if she was one of those people who could not see colleagues as anything but competition.

She gambled recklessly, she was bad with money, and she had a wild hunger for more—more beautiful clothes, more prestige, more everything. More secrets. Although I had only the one blackmail

victim (so far), I had a general agreement that she would not draw
back from blackmail, and I thought it was the most likely explanation for the circumstances of her death: the midnight meeting in
the Zheimela, the murderer's use of the canal. He might not have
come intending to kill her; that rush in the darkness, that sudden
burst of force, might have been an explosion of overwhelming anger. Certainly she had had no idea that she might be in danger.

But then, she was reckless and bad at considering other people's
reactions. Maybe he had planned it. Maybe her death had been his
goal from the beginning.

That question was unanswerable. More to the point was a more
basic question: who was he?

Not Pel-Thenhior, whose whereabouts I knew, and presumably
not anyone who had performed in the opera that night. There at
least was a question I could find the answer to, and with some reluctance I returned to the Vermilion Opera.

※

It was late afternoon. Pel-Thenhior and the singers were rehearsing *Zhelsu* while Thoramis took frantic notes. I found a seat in
the row behind him and watched.

They were rehearsing the final scene, in which Zhelsu, rather
than submit to the caresses of the lecherous overseer, throws herself
into the machinery of the manufactory. Min Vakrezharad seemed
to be dubious about the jump; I heard Pel-Thenhior saying, "A *stack*
of mattresses, Othoro," from the stage piece which represented the
catwalk over the machinery of Zhelsu's manufactory, while Mer
Olora, playing the overseer, stood center stage and glowered.

Pel-Thenhior and Min Vakrezharad came down from the catwalk
stage piece, and Mer Olora and Min Vakrezharad walked through
the movements of the overseer stalking Zhelsu across the stage and
up the stairs that would put Min Vakrezharad in the right place to
jump at the right time. It seemed to be a complicated maneuver, re-
quiring careful timing, and of course they would be singing as well.

They went through the sequence three times, with Pel-Thenhior shouting words at specific points, which I presumed were the words they would be singing. Then they went through it once singing themselves, although softly. And then Mer Olora started a fight with Pel-Thenhior.

I could hear enough of the words to know it was about something technical, and I could see by their ears and posture that they were both genuinely angry, but why the matter enraged them so I could not tell.

They were soon standing almost nose to nose, shouting at each other, Mer Olora's voice booming through the auditorium, and Pel-Thenhior's, slightly higher, not far behind.

And then, as suddenly as it had started, it was over, Mer Olora stalking into the wings and Pel-Thenhior coming down to the plank bridge, his expression like a thundercloud.

When he saw me, his ears lifted and he smiled as if he was truly glad to see me. "Othala Celehar! What brings you here today?"

"The night Min Shelsin was killed," I said, "who was performing?"

"The top half of the adult chorus. *General Olethazh* is a small cast for principals—not like *The Siege of Tekharee*, with a part for everyone and then some. Just Nanavo and Cebris and Shulethis. We wouldn't perform it if it weren't so tiresomely lovely."

"Thank you," I said. That left more people unaccounted for than I had hoped. "Could I speak to the singers?"

"Of course," said Pel-Thenhior, then shouted, "Everyone on stage, please!"

A surprising number of people came flocking out of the wings; I was lucky in my timing. I crossed the plank onto the stage and asked straight out: "How many of you knew Arveneän Shelsin was a blackmailer?"

After a long hesitation, hands started to go up. About half the company raised their hands, shame-faced, including Mer Telonar, the junior tenor. Almost all the women had known.

I wanted to ask why none of them had told me, but I knew the answer. Either they were keeping a secret for a friend or they were keeping a secret for themselves.

"Thank you," I said. "I have no wish to expose anyone's secrets. How many of you knew that she gambled?"

This time a much smaller array of hands went up. Mer Telonar again and Min Vakrezharad and four or five women from the chorus. "She told us all about Tivalinee one afternoon during fittings," said Min Vakrezharad. "I think she regretted doing so later."

"Does anyone know the extent of her gambling debts?" I was looking at Mer Telonar, and he shook his head.

"We talked about playing pakh'palar," he said. "She wasn't very good, so if she played often, she must have lost a great deal of money."

"Yes," I said. "Yes, she must."

Then someone—one of the chorus members whose name I did not know—called a question back: "Is it true that you spent the night on the Hill of Werewolves?"

"Yes," I said.

"Is it true the Duhalada offered you mortal insult?" asked somebody else.

"What? No, that's not true at all."

"They *did* insult you," Pel-Thenhior said.

"Well, yes, that part is true. But Mer Duhalar apologized."

"That and a zashan will buy you an apple," someone said from the back.

"Are all the stories exaggerations?" said Min Vakrezharad. "You did really find the Curneisei who were plotting against the emperor, didn't you?"

"Yes, that story is true," I said. "But it was much more boring than the newspapers made it sound."

Pel-Thenhior laughed. "We're embarrassing you horribly. But *did* you prove the Duhaladeise will false?"

"I did," I said. "The deceased Mer Duhalar remembered who his heir was."

That unsettled everyone enough that I was able to take a step backward and say, "Does anyone know anything else about Min Shelsin that might help to explain her death?"

They were silent; I bowed and took my leave.

I was on my way out of the auditorium, feeling that I had made no real progress, when Telonar came panting after me. "Othala! May I speak to you for a moment?"

"Of course," I said, and stepped out into the foyer.

Telonar followed me and looked around nervously before he said, "What you said about blackmail . . ."

"Yes?"

"It's true. She was blackmailing me."

"How much did you pay her?"

His elven complexion showed a deep blush. "I couldn't pay her. Gambling debts."

"So what was she blackmailing you *for*?"

"Secrets. Other people's secrets. I hated . . . but if she went to Iäna with what she knew, I would've been out and the door locked after me."

Here was another possible motive. I said, "Where were you the night she died?"

"*Me?*" His voice squeaked with surprise and horror. "I could never—"

"I'm not saying you did. But if you can tell me what you were doing, it makes things easier for both of us."

There was a long pause before he said, reluctantly, "Playing pakh'palar at Indamura's—it's a gambling house about five blocks from here."

"That's good," I said. "That means there are people who can confirm your story. How late were you there?"

"I don't know," he said. "It wasn't dawn yet when I went home, but it was close."

Well after Arveneän Shelsin had died. "Who were you playing with?"

He gave me four names, still reluctantly, and said, "Indamura himself was seeing someone out when I left. He can tell you what time it was."

"That's very helpful," I said. The owner of a gambling house might be more or less likely than fellow card players to lie for Telonar, but if their stories all matched, it would be a good sign that he was telling the truth. "Now, can you—"

But at that moment, a member of the chorus poked his head out between the auditorium doors and said, "Veralis, Iäna says you should—"

"VERALIS! ARE YOU OUT THERE?" Pel-Thenhior's voice rolled out through the open door like thunder and retribution, and Telonar clearly took it as such.

"I'm sorry, othala, I must go. I've told you all I can," he said hastily, and disappeared into the auditorium.

I thought about going after him, but decided against it. I would not get him to tell me anything more either by getting him in trouble with Pel-Thenhior or by calling attention to the fact that he had spoken to me privately. Perhaps next time I came to the Vermilion Opera, he would be willing to speak further.

)(

The post waiting for me at my office in the morning included a letter from Dach'othala Ulzhavar saying that he had news of "Avelonar," and would I come to the Sanctuary at my earliest convenience.

That afternoon, after confirming Telonar's alibi with Mer Indamura, who seemed, if anything, amused to be asked, I returned to the Sanctuary of Csaivo. The first thing I did was to walk around the central building to one of the many tiny shrines hidden in the gardens. There I knelt and said prayers for Coralezh and the other cleric of Tanvero and for the clerics I had met at the Amal-Athamareise Airship Works who had been following their calling with such determination and grace.

The shrine was exquisitely lovely, a filigree of stone around a jade michenotho of Csaivo, and the gardens were full of peace. It was with some reluctance that I got up again and walked back around the central building to the doors.

I felt vulgar and encroaching, but the novice on duty seemed to think nothing of my asking for the Master of the Mortuary. Ulzhavar himself seemed sincerely pleased to see me when I found him in the vaulted autopsy room, watching Denevis finish the autopsy of a drowned child. "Othala Celehar! Come in! I regret immensely that there are no chairs. I don't need one and if the novices sit down, they either fall asleep or they forget I can still see them and, well, they're still young enough to get distracted. But you're here about Min Urmenezhen. Merrem Avelonaran, I suppose I should say, but it feels disrespectful."

"Her family would definitely prefer that you call her Min Urmenezhen," I said. "And, yes, I got your letter this morning."

"Yes, good," he said. "One of my clerics has discovered something." He went to one of the chests of drawers and fetched out a sheaf of palimpsest pages. "His name is Temet Golharad, splendid fellow, he's been the cleric of Aishan's Grove for twenty years at least."

I recognized the name of the district. It was at the far western end of the city, where I rarely had cause to go.

"He had a most remarkable story," Ulzhavar said, "about a man named Segevis Michezar, who came to Aishan's Grove with his newly married bride Drachano. He was polite but unfriendly. She was shy and clearly very much in love. And then she died."

"How?"

"An illness. Short and very violent. Temet said the poor woman was racked with cramps and bouts of vomiting. Her death, when it came, was a mercy."

I made a warding gesture in reflexive horror.

"The odd thing, Temet says, was Mer Michezar's reaction."

He waited, eyebrows raised, until I said, "Which was?"

"Nothing," said Ulzhavar. "No grief, no horror, not even anger—which I'm sure you know is very common."

"Yes," I said. I had been called a ghoul and a vulture and all sorts of terrible things, and I knew it was worse for Csaiveise clerics, who were often blamed for deaths they were helpless to prevent.

"But nothing of the sort from Segevis Michezar. He organized Drachano's funeral as quickly—and cheaply—as he could, and then he vanished."

"Vanished."

"Completely. Temet never saw or heard of him again."

"How long ago was this?"

"Almost five years."

"Do you think it's the same man?"

"I think it very likely," said Ulzhavar.

I hesitated. "Do you think you could learn anything from Merrem Michezaran's corpse?"

"I certainly intend to try. Do you want to come with me?"

"Yes," I said. "Yes, I do."

※

Merrem Michezaran had been buried in the precinct of the municipal ulimeire of Aishan's Grove, in the paupers' quarter, a wide, flat, barren stretch of ground, as desolate as the people who were buried here. Her headstone, a flat square, said only DRACHANO—the bare minimum allowed. The prelate of the ulimeire, a tired-looking middle-aged elven man, who recognized me immediately although I had no memory of ever seeing him before, was somewhat skeptical of the idea that Merrem Michezaran could have been poisoned, but he also recognized Ulzhavar and bowed to his greater authority. He even came with us to dig up the grave himself. "My sexton," he said, "is the biggest gossip in Aishan's Grove. I would certainly prefer to keep this quiet, and I'm sure you feel the same."

I said, "It would defeat our entire purpose if Mer Michezar read about this in the papers."

"The vulture-eyed old people will complain," Othala Bonshenar said. "But the poor girl had no family that we know of, so there's no one who will be truly distressed. She barely lived a week after they moved here. Not long enough to make friends."

"With two Ulineise prelates and a cleric, we can hardly be more respectful," said Ulzhavar. "And I must believe that Merrem Michezaran wants her murderer caught."

"Are you sure it's murder?" Bonshenar said plaintively.

"We won't be until we look," Ulzhavar said.

I took off my coat and helped Bonshenar dig. It wasn't long before our shovels struck wood. Mer Michezar had paid for only the shallowest of graves.

"Such prudent economy," Ulzhavar murmured darkly, then shook himself. "We may not need to do more than open the coffin. If he used calonvar, we'll be able to tell."

"All right," said Bonshenar. "Let's find out."

The grave was shallow enough that Bonshenar had no difficulty in prying the coffin open. He and I said the prayer of compassion for the dead, and we lifted the coffin lid and set it aside. The woman inside was beautifully preserved, looking, as Bonshenar said, as if she'd only died yesterday.

"Calonvar," Ulzhavar said simply.

Only her face and hands were uncovered by her winding sheet, proving that she had been buried according to the rites of the Ploraneisei, one of the two most prominent sects in Amalo. She was sallow and gaunt, but it was something of a toss-up whether that was the result of death or of the sickness that had killed her.

"All right," said Ulzhavar, "let me look at her hands. Then we can be certain."

I stood back from the horse-faced young woman in the coffin, wondering grimly if Mer Michezar made a specialty of the plain ones, for Mer Urmenezh had admitted once, as if it pained him, that his sister had been as plain as a doorknob and that she had despaired of ever finding anyone who wanted to marry her. *Were they grateful, Mer Michezar? Did that make it all the easier for you to woo and win and kill them?*

"Yes," said Ulzhavar. "Those scaly patches along the fingers.

They're small, probably because he killed her so quickly, but they're definitely there."

"Calonvar?" said Bonshenar.

"No doubt about it. It must have been a terrible dose."

"Maybe she was the first," I said, feeling sick. "Maybe he didn't know how much he needed."

Ulzhavar looked up at me, pale gray-green eyes sympathetic. "Is there anything else you need here, Othala Celehar?"

"No," I said. "I think the signs of calonvar poisoning are clear enough, and the other parts of Merrem Michezaran's story sound all too much like what happened to Min Urmenezhen."

"Was there a will?" Ulzhavar said.

"Yes," said Bonshenar, surprised. "They went to Mer Chelavar the first day they were here. He was the only person who attended her funeral, and he was very distressed that she had died so soon after she made her will. Distressed, too, at how cheaply Mer Michezar chose to bury her. In truth, it made him indiscreet. He was fuming, later, that she should have left all her money to her husband and he repay her in such base fashion. She had stipulated no more than that she be buried according to Ploraneisei rites, you see, and he did that."

"So he did," Ulzhavar said in a grim aside.

Bonshenar's ears dipped, but he continued. "And Mer Chelavar never said anything to indicate that he suspected murder."

"Did he say how *much* money was involved?" I asked.

"A lot," said Bonshenar. "Enough to surprise Chelavar, and he was pretty much unflappable after all those years as a lawyer."

"Might we speak to Mer Chelavar?" I said.

"He died two years ago," Bonshenar said apologetically. "But if he had suspected murder, he would most certainly have done something about it." He hesitated, then added, "Enteric fever is very common in the part of Aishan's Grove where they were living. There was nothing surprising about her death, merely sad that she had been married such a short time."

"If Merrem Michezaran had money," said Ulzhavar, "why were they living in such a poor quarter of Aishan's Grove?"

"They were saving," Bonshenar said. "Or, at least, that was what Mer Michezar told me at the funeral, that they had been saving to purchase a house."

"Presumably he told her the same thing," Ulzhavar said, and shook his head as if to dislodge a biting fly.

"I understand about murder," Bonshenar said as we filled in the grave, "but the cruelty of it!"

"Maybe calonvar is the only poison he knows," Ulzhavar said. "It's certainly easy enough to come by."

That was true. Calonvar was used in all kinds of preparations, from hand lotion to hair tonic, and pure calonvar was readily available as rat poison. It would come easily to an intending murderer's hand.

We finished filling in the grave, and Othala Bonshenar— probably glad to see the last of us—pointed us in the direction of the tram stop.

As we walked, I asked Ulzhavar, "Does any of this get us closer to finding him?"

"It depends," said Ulzhavar. "If either Michezar or Avelonar is his real name—and I think Avelonar almost certainly is not—or if he's used one or the other again, we may be able to find him that way. Or someone who knows him. Otherwise, all we can do is keep collecting stories. Knowing the pattern won't hurt our chances."

"At the moment," I said grimly, "it seems to be the only chance we have."

※

I returned to the Sanctuary with Ulzhavar, in order, as he put it, to round up a panel of clerics so that we could give sworn depositions about what we had discovered in examining Merrem Michezaran's body.

The first three senior clerics we found—two in the Sanctuary's library and the third in a workroom with the half-dissected corpse of a pig—grumbled at being dragged away from their work, but none of them seemed genuinely resentful, and they listened attentively as Ulzhavar dictated an account of his findings to the junior cleric he'd collared to serve as scribe. Ulzhavar clearly had had a great deal of practice in giving depositions; he spoke at a steady pace, pausing regularly to let the scratching steel nib catch up, and marshaled his facts in logical order. When he had finished, the panel asked questions, but not many. Then Ulzhavar read over the junior cleric's transcription, while I in turn deposed before the panel. My deposition confirmed Ulzhavar's, and the clerics' questions all concerned the investigation in Min Urmenezhen's case that had led us to Merrem Michezaran.

The junior cleric wrote a tolerable secretary hand, and he was an accurate scribe. "They all have to take a turn at it," said Ulzhavar. "We give depositions nearly as frequently as Witnesses do. It saves any number of nightmares later, when the family decides there was something suspicious about the death."

"Of course," I said.

I signed the deposition, and the clerics signed as witnesses. I walked out of the Sanctuary into the waning gray-gold of an autumn afternoon.

I found a canalside teahouse, the Splinter of Stonanavee, and sat in the back corner with a scone and a pot of green tea, appropriately enough from the same canton as Stonanavee itself. The tea was smoky and denser than I usually liked, but today it suited my mood.

After the first cup of tea and half a scone, I felt able to take stock of the situation.

First, I was officially separate from the Ulistheileian, which gave me some of the same relief as having a headache go away. The Amal'othala had authority over me, but he did not have the authority to dismiss me from my post. Only the Archprelate could do that, and I had confidence that he would support me if someone from Amalo complained of me. And behind *him*, I knew that the emperor would listen if I wrote to him—which I had no intention of doing, but it was good to know that last resort was there.

Second, I had fulfilled my promise to Osmer Thilmerezh.

Whether, in Chonhadrin, he got what he desired was not a problem I could solve.

In the case of Min Urmenezhen, I had another probable victim, but still nothing that seemed likely to be the murderer's *real* name, and nothing I could think of at the moment to do.

That left Min Shelsin and the Vermilion Opera. And Pel-Thenhior, who had frightened me badly through no fault of his own.

Irrelevant, I told myself. The issue was finding Min Shelsin's killer, not my personal feelings, and the Opera was still the most likely place to find someone she had confided in. Gambling was clearly where all of Min Shelsin's money had gone, and it seemed fairly clear that blackmail—an ugly word for an ugly practice—was where at least some of it had come from. Thus, the question was, how much she might have admitted and to whom?

Not to her friends. Min Nochenin and Min Balvedin had admired her too deeply. They would have been the *last* people she would have told about something so sordid. And, of course, maybe she had been one of those rare people who felt no need of a confidante. Maybe the answers were all dead with her.

Maybe I was of a melancholic disposition and prone to despair.

I finished my scone and drank tea slowly, watching the teahouse custom bustle around me. A tableful of adolescent elven girls, flushed with excitement at being grown-ups without nannies or governesses or parents to supervise, were doing their best to suppress their giggles and behave appropriately, but I thought they were fighting a losing battle. At the next table, a middle-aged elven woman sitting alone was looking wistful, as if remembering her own girlhood. Two courting couples were sitting by the window, an elven man and a half-goblin woman leaning over the table to talk together intently, and a goblin pair who were having a lighthearted conversation in Barizhin.

I drank my tea and finished my scone and acknowledged that I did not know how to solve any of my problems.

X

That evening, in desperation, I sought Azhanharad out in his preferred teahouse, the Vedrivcise Gambit. As the name suggested, it was a haunt of bokh players. I did not know if Azhanharad himself played bokh; my suspicion was that he merely liked the intense quiet to be found in most of the rooms.

He did not look pleased to see me, but I did not expect him to. "Othala," he said, getting up. "Let us go to a room where we will not disturb anyone with our conversation."

I followed him into a long, narrow room that had obviously started as a corridor. There were several doorways and a number of patrons and servers walking in and out, so that although the two-person tables were perfect for bokh, there was no one playing.

"Sit," said Azhanharad. "Would you like tea?"

"No, thank you," I said. Common politeness made him ask, but accepting would have implied a social quality to this meeting that we both knew was lacking.

He had brought his cup and teapot with him, and I waited while he poured tea into the cup and took a first cautious sip. Then he said, "What can we do for you, othala?"

"We are witnessing for a woman who was murdered by her husband," I said, "and there is more and more evidence to show that she was not his only victim."

"That is very alarming," said Azhanharad.

"He changes his name," I said.

Azhanharad made a ritual gesture of aversion. "Then how do you expect to catch him? For we assume he is not in your custody."

"No, he is not. We were wondering if the Vigilant Brotherhood might help."

"When you have found him, we will arrest him. What more can we do?"

"Could you not ask your brethren if they know of cases of young women, recently married, dying of what looks like enteric fever?"

He stared at me. "That is not within our remit."

"But you could do it," I said.

"Celehar, do you know how many people die of enteric fever in this city every day? And it is not within the remit of our brotherhood to go poking about in people's private lives. We arrest criminals and hold them until their case can come before a judiciar. And we carry out the sentence."

"You patrol the streets," I argued, although I knew it was hopeless.

"The streets, not people's *homes*." He sounded sincerely scandalized. "No, if you find your murderer, we will arrest him so that you may take your case before a judiciar. More than that, we cannot do."

"Good evening, Subpraeceptor," I said, and left him to drink his cooling tea.

ℵ

The next afternoon I went back to the Sanctuary of Csaivo to tell Ulzhavar that we would get no help from the Vigilant Brotherhood. As I came in the door, Ulzhavar was coming up the stairs from the autopsy room. He said, "Othala Celehar, you come in good time! I am just on my way to meet a cleric who has what sounds like a most interesting story. Do you want to come along?"

"Of course," I said.

The meeting place was only two tram stops away, a teahouse called the Rose Minuet. "Why here?" I said. "Why not come the rest of the way to the Sanctuary?"

"Mmm," said Ulzhavar. "Othalo Darnevin has a somewhat checkered history, and she was reluctant to come to the Sanctuary, which for her is full of bad memories. And it does me no harm to get out."

With that introduction, I was not sure what to expect from Othalo Darnevin, but she proved to be a perfectly unremarkable elven woman, middle-aged, with crow's feet around her pale blue eyes and laugh lines bracketing her mouth. I liked her on sight.

She stood when she saw us and said, "Othala Ulzhavar, thank you so much for coming."

"Nonsense, Aisharan," said Ulzhavar. "This is Othala Celehar, who started us after this hare."

"Othala," she said.

"Othalo," I said in return.

"Sit," said Ulzhavar, sitting down himself. "Aisharan, tell us your story."

"It happened maybe five, maybe seven years ago," she said. "A young couple, just gotten married, and the woman got sick. Vomiting and purging and racked with cramps. She'd have an episode, and then she'd get better for a day or two, and then she'd be horribly sick again. I couldn't figure out what was wrong with her, and I was trying every remedy I knew, and nothing seemed to help. The poor woman—girl, really—was scared as well as most miserably ill, but the strange thing was that her husband didn't seem worried at all. 'It's just his way,' the girl told me, but I thought then and think now that it was a very strange way to behave when your wife was dying."

The server approached us and Ulzhavar ordered a pot of kolveris for the table, and a family plate of steamed buns. "I forgot to eat lunch," he said, "and I hate to eat alone."

I remembered Iäna Pel-Thenhior saying the same thing and pushed the memory away.

"You are very kind," said Othalo Darnevin.

"There is nothing that says I can't be kind if I want to," Ulzhavar said unanswerably. "Go on, Aisharan."

"She was dying," said Othalo Darnevin, "and nothing I tried made the slightest difference. It took almost a month, and I have never felt so incompetent, so *helpless*. She turned seventeen the week before it finally killed her, and she might have died of simple exhaustion. And again, her husband behaved so strangely. He made all the funeral arrangements as efficiently as a secretary, saw his wife buried without shedding a tear, and disappeared like a mirage the next day."

Ulzhavar raised his eyebrows at me, and I nodded. It sounded like the same pattern. "What was his name?" I said.

"Broset," she said. "Broset Sheveldar. I will never forget it."

Ж

The tea and the steamed buns arrived, and we shared our information with Othalo Darnevin. I told her about Min Urmenezhen and Ulzhavar described the exhumation of Merrem Michezaran. Her eyes got wider and wider as she listened. "Then you think Mer Sheveldar *murdered* his wife."

"It seems unpleasantly likely," Ulzhavar said. "Did the thought of poison never cross your mind?"

"I asked Merrem Sheveldaran about what she ate, of course," said Darnevin. "But she and her husband ate from the same dish, drank tea from the same pot, and he was perfectly healthy. I couldn't see how it *could* be poison."

"Mer Sheveldar must be very deft," Ulzhavar said. "Or perhaps he was in the habit of bringing his wife a hot drink at bedtime, and she never thought to mention it to you. *She* must not have been suspicious at all."

"She was very much in love," said Darnevin. "She would never have believed it of him."

"But you do," I said.

"I don't know how he did it," said Darnevin, "but if he is in truth this man you are hunting, I admit it does not surprise me."

"She was seventeen," said Ulzhavar. "Was he much older?"

"He might have been twenty. Not more."

"So this might have been his first," said Ulzhavar.

"Was there any money?" I said. "Did he gain anything by her death?"

"Not that I know of," said Darnevin. "She was a manufactory worker, so there can't have been much money between them."

"This was his first," I said. "He killed her because he wanted to. He figured out it could be profitable later."

"How horrible," said Darnevin.

"But probably accurate," said Ulzhavar. "And thus Broset Sheveldar might be his real name."

I understood at once what he meant. "Do you know a maza who can do that?"

"As it happens," said Ulzhavar, "I do."

X

The maza was an elderly elven man named Lenet, and he and Ulzhavar were clearly friends of long standing. He listened to our convoluted story attentively and said, "Well, it is certainly worth trying."

Among the arcana of the mazei, the specialty of name-magic was particularly arcane. Lenet Athmaza wrote the name "Broset Sheveldar" on a slip of paper the length and width of my little finger, folded it, and put it in a filigree silver ball on a long silver chain.

He spread out a beautiful map of the city of Amalo, each district neatly labeled, then began swinging the silver ball back and forth over the map, murmuring under his breath. Little by little, the arc of the ball changed and narrowed, until finally it was perfectly still over the district of Penchelivor.

"So," said Lenet Athmaza. "From here we must walk."

X

Penchelivor was south of the Zheimela, a quiet, law-abiding district full of artisans and legal clerks and manufactory managers. Lenet Athmaza and Ulzhavar and I made a strange trio amid all that respectability, Lenet Athmaza in his blue robe, swinging that little silver ball on its chain; Ulzhavar with his green robe kilted up as usual to allow him freedom of movement; and me in my black coat of office and my hair escaping from its braid. People stared politely, sidelong—and I reminded myself that Broset Sheveldar could have no idea that we were hunting him.

I said, "Do you believe the Vigilant Brotherhood will listen to us when we have found him?"

Ulzhavar laughed. "They'll listen. Whether they believe or not is a different story, but they will listen to a maza. Once the gentleman is in jail, we can assemble a great many witnesses to identify him, whether as Sheveldar, Michezar, or Avelonar. And we should exhume poor Merrem Sheveldaran, though I have no doubt what we'll find."

"Best to be thorough," Lenet Athmaza agreed.

"Yes," said Ulzhavar. "But I want this vanishing gentleman in a place where I know he's not wooing another wife."

"Or poisoning her," I said.

"Exactly," said Ulzhavar.

The trouble, we found, with the dowsing ball was that it wanted to move in straight lines and the streets of Penchelivor twisted and forked and dead-ended, so that it took us a disproportionately long time, given that Lenet Athmaza knew exactly where we were going, to get there. It turned out to be a boardinghouse, flying the green-and-silver banner and with a boldly lettered ROOMS TO LET sign in one front window.

"We should have brought Othalo Darnevin," I said, realizing. "None of us knows what he looks like, and we don't know what name he's using."

"I will know him," Lenet Athmaza said.

"Yes, but we don't want to confront him," I said, then realized how nervous I sounded, although I was quite certain we had nothing to fear from a man who worked by poison. "And we've no idea where the Penchelivor watchhouse is."

"These are all surmountable problems," Ulzhavar said. "Let's walk on before we make anyone in that boardinghouse nervous, and we can work out a plan."

"Your excursions are always interesting, Ulzhavar," said Lenet Athmaza, "but seldom very well thought out."

⋊

After discussion, we all took the tram to General Parzhadar Square and the one member of the Vigilant Brotherhood who I knew would listen to our outlandish story and might allow himself to be persuaded by it. After all, he had told me he would arrest the murderer if I could find him.

Azhanharad listened carefully to our story. At the end, he said, "If we understand correctly, the only thing you can prove is that this man is Broset Sheveldar, which so far as we know right now he isn't denying."

Put like that, the entire thing sounded like a nightmare Ulzhavar and I had dreamed up between us.

Ulzhavar said, "We have witnesses who can also identify him as Segevis Michezar and Croïs Avelonar. We can prove that Merrem Michezaran and Min Urmenezhen died of calonvar poisoning. And we expect we can prove the same thing for Merrem Sheveldar, if we can find her grave. And the one thing the three of them have in common is Mer Sheveldar. We think he merits a judicial examination."

I did not think Azhanharad entirely believed us, but he knew the remit of his brotherhood, and he had no desire to offend Ulzhavar, who outranked him much as a star outranks a streetlight. "All right, dach'othala. We will come arrest Broset Sheveldar for being Broset Sheveldar."

"It will do," said Ulzhavar. "The rest will come quickly enough."

※

We returned to the boardinghouse: Ulzhavar, Lenet Athmaza, and I, accompanied by Azhanharad and two watchmen, both of them half goblins built like brick walls. Clearly Azhanharad believed enough not to want to take chances.

Azhanharad sent one of his men around to the back of the boardinghouse, in case our quarry tried to escape that way. The rest of us clattered up onto the porch, and Ulzhavar was about to knock when the door was opened by a middle-aged half-goblin woman who was at a guess the landlady.

"Good afternoon," said Ulzhavar. "I am Csenaia Ulzhavar, and I am looking for a man named Broset Sheveldar. I have reason to believe he lives here."

"No, othala," she said in a strong Barizheise accent. "No one by that name among my boarders."

"It's possible," said Ulzhavar, "that he is using another name."

She had taken in the sight of Azhanharad and the watchmen. "Is he a criminal? I don't want anything like that in my house."

Ulzhavar considered her for a moment, either genuinely debating whether she could be trusted with the truth, or pretending to, before saying, "He is a murderer."

She made a warding gesture and said, "Then I hope you catch him. The only one of my boarders who is home is Mer Nilenovar. I will fetch him."

"You're sure he's here," Azhanharad said to Lenet Athmaza.

"If he weren't, we wouldn't be here, either."

The landlady returned with an elven man, young, slightly built, with his hair in a single, sober bun. He was good-looking, though not dramatically so, and did not look like a murderer, as murderers generally did not.

"May I help you gentlemen?" he said politely.

"That's the man," Lenet Athmaza said.

"Is your name Broset Sheveldar?" said Ulzhavar, and we all saw the name hit him like a blow.

But he stood his ground. "No, I'm sorry, you gentlemen must have—"

"No?" said Ulzhavar. "How about Segevis Michezar? Or Croïs Avelonar?"

"How many men do you think I am?" he said, still trying to deflect.

"That depends," said Ulzhavar. "How many men have you been?"

Sheveldar took a step back, turning, and Azhanharad said, "You'll run straight into one of my men at the back door."

For a moment, it looked as though he was going to try it anyway; then his shoulders slumped and he said, "I suppose you're here to arrest me."

"On suspicion of murdering Min Inshiran Urmenezhen," said Azhanharad, "and at least two other women."

He shook his head. "You can't prove it." But he allowed Azhanharad to shackle his wrists.

"Mer Nilenovar," said the landlady, "what should I tell Min Tavalin?"

"You might as well tell her the truth," he said.

But what kept me from sleeping that night was the casual evidence that he'd already started again, that in arresting him we were almost certainly saving Min Tavalin's life.

I lay awake wondering how many brides Broset Sheveldar had had, how many women we hadn't been fast enough to save.

)(

The next day, Chonhadrin came to the Prince Zhaicava Building to find me.

"I don't have a petition," she said. "Are you going to throw me out?"

"No," I said. "Not unless a petitioner shows up, and I doubt they will."

"Your job seems miserable," she said frankly.

"It is not," I said, "although I understand why you say so. I get a few petitioners a week, sometimes several, and in the meantime, I have plenty of reading material."

I nodded at my row of novels, and she laughed.

"But you must have come to find me for a reason."

"I wrote to both my grandfathers," she said, "and I have received letters back. My grandfather Delenar is horrified that I have found out the family scandal, so I must write back to him and assure him again that I am not angry. It would have ruined my mother's life, but it has little meaning for mine." She shrugged her shoulders, like a woman shrugging off a heavy coat. "I am ashenin, and no one cares if my grandparents were married."

"And Osmer Thilmerezh?"

"My grandfather Thilmerezh," said Chonhadrin, "missed his calling as a novelist. He has written me *pages* about Tanvero and the people there. He told me all about the ghoul."

"Um," I said, and she laughed.

"Your ears tell me you don't want to talk about it."

"I don't," I said, "but if you have a question, I will try to answer it."

"How likely do you think it that another ghoul will rise in Tan-vero?"

"It depends," I said. "If they organize themselves to tend their cemeteries, it's unlikely. Did he say if they found Merrem Balama-ran's grave? Her original grave, I mean?"

"They did. He says it wasn't even in a cemetery, just a clearing in the woods."

"Vikhelneise. They don't believe cemeteries are necessary."

"I don't think I understand Vikhelno's teachings at all," said Chonhadrin.

"He was a goblin," I said, "and lived far to the south, where ghouls do not rise. And he was quite legitimately angry at the corruption that had crept into the Barizheise priesthood, particularly among the prelates of Ulis. But he came to see priests, all priests, as a kind of excrescence, both unnecessary and harmful. When the goblins came north in the gold rush, they brought his teachings with them, and there are apparently a lot of people who would like to do with-out priests altogether."

"But how can they think ghouls don't exist?" she said, almost plaintively.

"I can't explain belief," I said. "I can't explain why anyone lis-tened to Vikhelno, except that they, too, were angry at their priests. And once you decide your priests are parasites and their teachings are worthless ... the Vikhelneisei are proud of not believing in anything that they haven't seen themselves."

"They aren't atheists, are they?" she asked, almost whispering.

"No, Vikhelno didn't go that far. He was quite clear that the work of the gods is visible all around us every day. But anything that was a reason you might need a priest, he dismissed as so much perni-cious falsehood. He said that corn mazes should be uprooted and that pilgrimages were ridiculous. And of course he didn't believe in ghouls. Most people don't, south of Veshto."

"And I suppose that once you actually see a ghoul, it's too late to change your beliefs."

"Mostly they're very slow-moving, and it takes them several months to go from eating the dead to eating the living. So, assuming you were alert, you'd have time to rethink your philosophy."

"How many people did the ghoul in Tanvero kill?"

"Two that I know of—unless Osmer Thilmerezh says they found more bodies."

"He didn't mention it."

"Good," I said. "Then probably those two were its only victims."

"*They* didn't have time to rethink."

"I think that ghoul had been risen too long. It had gotten faster and more cunning than they usually do. Certainly far faster than any of the other ghouls I have quieted."

"How many is that?"

"Five," I said, "and a sixth that we caught as it clawed its way out of its grave."

"*Where?*" she said, eyes wide.

"Well west of here," I said. "A town called Aveio, where the population had been shrinking for generations, so that they had more people in their cemeteries than they did in the town. And the stone they had for headstones was too soft. It wouldn't hold a name properly."

"How horrible."

"I do not miss Aveio," I admitted.

She nodded, then briskly changed the subject. "But what I wanted to ask is, do you think it's safe to travel to Tanvero? My grandfather Thilmerezh has invited me to visit him."

I could not help my eyebrows going up. "Even for an ashenin, that is a long journey to make alone."

"That doesn't bother me," she said. "And my grandfather has a housekeeper, Merrem Olharad, so there is nothing improper in my visiting him."

"But you are worried about ghouls."

"I am concerned," she said, a little stiffly.

"I do not think you need to worry," I said. "The new cemetery caretaker seems most conscientious, and I believe the citizens will be taking other measures to ensure the cemeteries are maintained. Tanvero should be as safe as anywhere else."

"That is a relief. Thank you, Celehar."

"I hope you will give Osmer Thilmerezh my greetings," I said.

"Of course. He spoke very highly of you in his letter—he said the othas'ala wanted you to stay."

"He did. But Tanvero is not my calling, and Othas'ala Deprena was . . . mistaken in his assessment."

"Your judgment of yourself is very harsh."

"No, just honest. Othas'ala Deprena needs a prelate with skills I do not have. I am much better suited to this office and the people of Amalo."

"If you think you are suited to this office," she said, with a wave of her hand indicating our surroundings, "then your judgment of yourself is harsh indeed."

She surprised me into laughing. "No, no one is suited to this office. But the work that I do in Amalo is rewarding to me and makes full and proper use of the skills I have." I almost said, *I would rather talk to the dead than to the living,* but bit it back in time.

Chonhadrin looked as though she had heard my thought. She said hesitantly, "May I come tell you about my visit when I return? No one else will understand or care."

"Of course," I said. "I would be very pleased." And it was even the truth.

⋊

I received a note from Dach'othala Vernezar, asking me to meet him at the shrine in the catacombs. Although I had denied that he had any authority over me, it seemed both imprudent and spiteful to refuse. This time I went alone.

Vernezar was also alone, although I was sure there was at least a novice waiting for him somewhere just out of earshot. "Othala Celehar," he said. "Thank you for coming."

"Dach'othala," I said.

"We, ah, we trust that you were not . . . that is, we hope you will not . . . We bear you no ill will, Celehar, and we hope that you bear us none."

"Of course not," I said.

"Good, good," Vernezar said, not meeting my eyes. "It's only natural that there should be some confusion. After all, there's never been a post quite like yours—appointed directly by the Archprelate—before."

"No," I agreed.

"And we would hate to think that any such *confusion* should be misinterpreted as . . . as anger. Or hostility."

"We did not make that interpretation," I said warily. There had been no interpretation necessary.

"Othalo Zanarin is . . ." He hesitated for long enough that I began to think he would be unable to continue. Finally, he said, "Intemperate. We have suggested to her that perhaps she needs to spend a season in isolate devotion in the Chapel of Floods."

Hypocrisy, from a man like Vernezar, but Zanarin's reach had exceeded her grasp, and retaliation was inevitable. Power was a dangerous game. And I had to admit I felt a surge of relief, that at least for a season, I would not need to worry about encountering Zanarin, either in the Amalomeire or simply on the streets.

I said, "It is very cold in the Mervarnens in winter."

"Isolate devotion is not a *punishment*. We have told her to wait until spring."

Isolate devotion was exactly a punishment—except for those few who were called to it—but I had no desire to argue with the Ulisothala of Amalo about that or anything else. I said nothing.

"In any event," said Vernezar, "we hope for nothing but peaceful relations with your, ah, office."

As if I were a foreign country. I said, "There is no reason for anything else."

"Very good," said Vernezar. "And you won't . . ." He eyed me sidelong.

Here was the matter he actually wanted to discuss with me. A pity that I had no idea what it was.

I waited, and he said, "We would hate for the Archprelate to gain an . . . *inaccurate* picture of matters here in Amalo."

"We are not in communication with the Archprelate," I said blankly. "We have no reason to be."

"Oh come, Celehar," said Vernezar, sounding almost annoyed. "There's no need to pretend you don't report to him."

"We don't," I said. "We do not expect the Archprelate to take an interest in our very mundane dealings."

He stared at me as if I'd told him I could hear fishes singing.

I still had no way to prove a negative. I sighed and said, "We will not tell the Archprelate anything injurious."

"Thank you, Celehar," said Vernezar, who now of course believed all the more firmly that I wrote reports for the Archprelate about the religious goings-on of Amalo.

"Dach'othala," I said, and was grateful to make my escape.

※

Lord Judiciar Erimar was given the case of Broset Sheveldar. It took him a week to read all the depositions, plus the statement from the lawyer Mer Sheveldar had hired (doubtless with the money he had inherited from his victims), and quite a crowd gathered in the Amal'theileian when he announced he was ready to pass judgment. I was there, and Ulzhavar, for once in his formal robes, Othalo Darnevin, Othala Bonshenar, and a number of other people whom I did not know and whose connection to the case, if any, I could not guess. Some of them might be family of the murdered women, for I saw the glint of Mer Urmenezh's pince-nez near the back.

Lord Erimar was an elven man in his sixties, very erect of carriage and needle-sharp of mind. He looked at all of us, his eyes lingering for a moment on Mer Sheveldar, who was attending shackled between two massive goblin Brothers, then said, "This case is quite unlike any other we have ever judged. We have read depositions from Witnesses for three women, each of them murdered with calonvar in the weeks or months following her marriage to this man, who has called himself Broset Sheveldar and Segevis Michezar and Croïs Avelonar and we doubt not other names besides. The statement presented by Mer Sheveldar's lawyer notes that in each case there is no proof that Mer Sheveldar is the murderer, but either he is guilty or someone else is following him from name to name and marriage to marriage and poisoning his wives just when it is most advantageous to Mer Sheveldar that they die. We find this unlikely to the point of absurdity, and the Witness for Mer Sheveldar has been able to find no proof, not even a hint, that this story might be true. We find that Broset Sheveldar is guilty of murdering Livano Sheveldaran, Drachano Michezaran, and Inshiran Avelonaran and her unborn child Ulanu. Sentence will be pronounced tomorrow by Prince Orchenis."

But we all knew already what the sentence would be.

Mer Urmenezh said to me afterwards, "He is truly an evil person."

"Yes," I said. "We are sorry he was not what your sister thought him."

"She wanted it so badly to be true," he said. "We are sure it was the same for the others."

"Except perhaps for the first Merrem Sheveldaran," I said. "She might have known him—or thought she did."

"We only hope Inshiran did not *know* before she died," said Mer Urmenezh. "That is the thought that wakes us at night."

It was unanswerable. Only Sheveldar knew, and he refused to admit his guilt. Never mind the three wives under three different names, all of whom had died in the same way; never mind the vial found when the Brotherhood searched Sheveldar's room, a quarter full and the yellowed label reading CALONVAR. Never mind the deposition of the Witness for Min Chinevo Tavalin, his bride-to-be, which showed clearly the pattern testified to by the Witnesses for his victims. He put forward no explanation, not even of why, if his wives continued to die horribly, he had not *quit marrying*; he would not discuss any of the dead women. He merely insisted on his innocence and declared himself a martyr, although to what was never exactly clear.

"But we wanted to thank you," said Mer Urmenezh. "For you persevered when a dozen other men would have given up. And without your perseverance, Min Tavalin might already be married."

Depending on how fast he worked, Min Tavalin might already be dead. But I did not say so.

I said, "It is our calling, Mer Urmenezh. You need not thank us."

"Nonsense," said Mer Urmenezh. "In Inshiran's memory, we *must* thank you."

That, too, was unanswerable. I bowed to him and said, "Then we accept your thanks."

He smiled and said, "Truly it is an accomplishment to have bested one so stubborn. Thank you, Othala Celehar." He bowed to me, lower than I deserved, and left.

This time, when a newspaperman caught me—Goronezh on his own—I had no hesitation in answering his questions. Mostly what he wanted to know were things such as, how had I found Min Urmenezhen, and had the bodies of the victims told me anything. Which, of course, they had not. He was also very interested in the name-magic that had found Broset Sheveldar, and even more interested in, and horrified by, the list of Sheveldar's names. "How could he do such a thing?" he muttered.

I was not sure if that was meant as a question. I said, "He does not acknowledge that he has done so, except to point out that it is not a crime."

"No," Goronezh said, "because no one thought it necessary to make a law against it. What an insane thing to do!"

"No more insane than murdering three wives," I said.

"No, we suppose not." His ears twitched, their tiny peridot studs glinting in the sun from the tall windows. "Perhaps we should be grateful we do not understand."

"Perhaps," I said, and Goronezh darted away to catch Ulzhavar, stiff in his formal robes. I could speak to Ulzhavar later, back in the autopsy room where we were both more comfortable.

I went instead to talk to Anora.

I found him in the catacombs beneath Ulvanensee, engaged in the endless task of arranging bones in revethmerai and making sure each had its correct name, as the prelates of the municipal cemeteries had been doing for thousands of years. I had followed his bright yarn clew through the windings of the catacombs, the owl-light illuminating the incised names of the long dead. The clew was somewhere between a sensible precaution and a dire necessity, for the catacombs were vast and the maps of them partial, difficult, and sometimes wrong. If one were to become lost, there was no guarantee that one would *ever* be found.

"Is that thou, Thara?" Anora called when I could only just see the light of his lantern. "For I know of no one else who would come so far into the catacombs to find me."

I called back, "Yes, it is Thara."

Anora said, "The judiciar must have reached a decision, then."

"Yes. Sheveldar will be condemned to death tomorrow, for I cannot imagine Prince Orchenis making any other judgment."

"Art thou pleased?"

It was an odd question. "I'm certainly pleased that the monied and unmarried women of Amalo will be safe from him."

"Ah," said Anora, as I rounded the final corner and found him kneeling beside a row of empty revethmerai, carefully taking long bones out of a linen bag and putting them one at a time in the fifth one along. He'd completed four before I found him. "But art thou pleased with thine own part in the matter?"

"I followed my calling," I began, but Anora cut me off.

"Thara," he said sharply. "That isn't what I asked."

It wasn't.

I said, "It's ridiculous to feel guilty. The man is a murderer three times over."

"At least," Anora agreed. "But thou feel'st guilt?"

"Mer Urmenezh pointed out to me today that my stubbornness has gotten a man killed."

Anora sat back on his heels to look at me. "I would wager that is a very free interpretation of what he said."

"And Mer Sheveldar does not admit his guilt," I said.

"And thus thou'rt concerned," Anora said.

"I should not be. I know he's guilty."

"It is thy nature. Thou'rt conscientious to a fault."

"Thy praise is unstinting," I said dryly.

"Thou wilt worry thyself to flinders," said Anora. "And thou needst not. No innocent man would change his name four times. Even the barbarians of the steppes only change their names once."

"He could not offer an explanation," I said.

"Of course not. What will they put on his headstone to keep him from rising before he comes to bone and dust?"

"I suppose it will have to be all four names," I said, though the idea seemed both ludicrous and utterly monstrous.

"Only a monster would value his name so little," Anora said in an eerie echo of my thoughts. "Wilt thou be comforted, Thara?"

"Perhaps," I said.

"Well, what didst think of him? Dost think him innocent? Really?"

"No," I said without any need of pondering the question. "I think him guilty beyond a doubt. But—"

"But?"

"I will not grieve for him," I said. "But there are other murderers I have grieved for and were they not also monsters?"

Anora considered the question. "Art thou positing that all murderers are monsters?"

"Are they not?"

"The *act* is monstrous. But one may commit a monstrous act and not be a monster. Unless, like Mer Sheveldar, one allows oneself to be consumed."

I said nothing, and Anora continued, "If thou grievest not for Sheveldar, it does not make thee a monster, either. But in grieving for a murderer, thou art not grieving for the monstrous. Thou grievest for the man who failed to reject the monstrous act."

I had never asked Anora if he knew about Evru, so that I did not know if he knew how much meaning was in his words. But I felt a burden lifted that I hadn't fully realized I was carrying. "That is a better way of thinking about it," I said, and was glad the shadows kept him from reading my expression.

He probably saw more than I wanted him to, anyway. "Come," he said. "Enough talk of murderers. Come do thy duty as a prelate of Ulis and help me sort out these decent and virtuous bones."

"Gladly," I said, and set my owl-light so that it would illuminate our task.

)(

The next morning, my first petitioner was a familiar one. I rose, more than a little startled to see Min Alasho Duhalin again. She was accompanied by an older woman, both of them grim-faced. Min Duhalin said formally, "We bring a petition to the Witness for the Dead."

"What is your petition?" I said, that being the only allowable response.

Min Duhalin's ears were flat, and she would not meet my eyes. "Because of the forgery, our lawyers insist on following all the old forms for the reading of the will."

"Of course," I said. The old forms, which had fallen out of fashion during the reign of Varevesena, stipulated that the testator have a Witness present to speak for him or her should the need arise.

"You have already witnessed for our grandfather," Min Duhalin continued doggedly, and I realized she was embarrassed as well as angry, "and Mer Ondormezh says that means legally you must witness for him again."

That was true, if intensely unfortunate in the circumstances.

"Of course," I said again, because I could say nothing else. "When is the reading to take place?"

X

That evening, I returned to the Duhaladeise compound. I was accustomed to being an unpopular guest—a Witness for the Dead rarely visited for congenial reasons—but the Duhalada actually drew back from me slightly, as if I were poisonous. I bowed politely and did not approach.

The will was to be read in the receiving room, and as the old forms demanded, the entire family was present, including Nepevis Duhalar, standing between two elven men from the Vigilant Brotherhood. Prince Orchenis had not yet pronounced his sentence; therefore he remained in the Bereth, the jail in the Veren'malo where prisoners of good family were kept.

The lawyer, Mer Ondormezh, was hunched with age, but his eyes were bright and sharp. He did not recoil from my presence, but said, "Oh good. We are glad you agreed to attend, othala."

"Our calling obliges us," I said.

"Ye-esss," said Mer Ondormezh, "but not all prelates would see it that way. The House Duhalada offered you a considerable insult."

"Yes," I said. "But that does not change our duty. And we admit to a natural curiosity."

That amused him. He said, "We are astonished to hear a prelate of Ulis admit to anything so ordinary as curiosity."

"We have as much as any man," I said, "and we have come to have some stake in Mer Duhalar's proper will."

"Nothing like a personal interest," murmured Mer Ondormezh.

His clerk distracted him then with a question, and I stepped back, not wanting anyone to think I was encroaching on Mer Ondormezh's time. The Duhalada continued to skirt wide around me.

It was only a few minutes later that Mer Ondormezh said, "Very well, merrai and merroi. Let us begin."

It took a long time to read a properly drawn-up will, and Mer Duhalar had had a number of very finicky arrangements about his real estate and his share of the company before we reached the question of the money. And then he became even more finicky. I was thinking that this will provided an unflattering but probably accurate portrait of Nepena Duhalar when Mer Ondormezh said, "And to our grandson, Tura Olora, child of our favorite child Daleno, we leave five thousand muranai."

The little susurrus of indrawn breath told me that I had not misheard. Tura Olora, the senior principal bass at the Vermilion Opera, was Mer Duhalar's grandson. Also that my immediate conclusion was correct, and was the reason Mer Olora was not here. Daleno had almost certainly been illegitimate, and thus this bequest, phrased as it was, was a deliberate insult to Mer Duhalar's legitimate Duhaladeise children.

It was also a significant sum of money, more than an opera singer would make in a year, and I could not help wondering if Mer Olora had known of his grandfather's bequest, and if he had known, who else had known? For this would make him a very tempting target to a money-hungry blackmailer like Min Shelsin.

I wondered even more bleakly what secrets Mer Olora might have been keeping that Min Shelsin could have found.

I barely heard the rest of the will—a series of increasingly small bequests to people whose names I did not recognize but who were probably servants—my mind racing as I reassembled the story with this new information.

I had read of Mer Duhalar's death in the newspapers two weeks before Min Shelsin was murdered; that was certainly enough time for her to approach Mer Olora in whatever manner she did so, to make an appointment in the Zheimela, to keep it, and to be killed. I thought of Mer Olora's temper, of him shouting at Pel-Thenhior. I did not know if he could plan murder, but I did know he could be goaded to fury. And if the paper I had found in Min Shelsin's pocket was Mer Olora's secret, whatever it was, it was safe now.

When the will-reading was finally over, I left the Duhalada to the several thorny problems Mer Duhalar's death—and Mer Duhalar's will—had caused them, and then, having taken the tram to the Amal'ostro, walked to the Vermilion Opera, running over this new

truth, wondering if I was mistaken. This story required Min Shelsin
to know something I was sure Mer Olora would not have told her—
two things, actually: the fact that Mer Olora would inherit a substan-
tial amount of money on his grandfather's death and then the secret.

Tonight was the premiere of *Zhelsu*. At least I knew exactly
where to find Mer Olora, even if it would be several hours yet before
I could talk to him.

At the Opera, the ushers recognized me and let me into the dim,
narrow hallway that ran behind all the boxes. Pel-Thenhior's box,
being the last before the hallway ended, was easy to find.

I decided I would cause him greater disruption by knocking than
not. I opened the door just wide enough to slip inside.

Pel-Thenhior twisted around; when he saw me, he beckoned for
me to come sit beside him.

When I did, he leaned over and said very softly, "I'm glad you're
here, although you may not be."

"Why not?"

"They haven't decided what they think yet," he said, then went
back to his notes, leaving me to puzzle out his meaning.

It didn't take long. Unlike my first time here, the audience was
stonily silent; everyone was focused on the stage in a way that was
either flattering to Pel-Thenhior or alarming. I was afraid it was the
latter.

A few minutes later, while Zhelsu and Tebora were singing about
their dream of escaping the manufactory, Pel-Thenhior leaned over
again and said, "I owe Othoro my firstborn child. She's holding the
whole thing together."

Of course, I thought. The singers would be able to read the audience as well as Pel-Thenhior and I could. They would have discerned
this ominous silence, so much worse than the half attention most
of the audience had paid to *The Siege of Tekharee*. And Pel-Thenhior
was right. Min Vakrezharad was singing superbly, almost daring
her fellows to fail her. Thus far, apparently, no one had.

It was nerve-racking to sit and watch the opera with that silent,
judging audience. During the shocking duet between Zhelsu and

her mother, in which her mother tells her she should sleep with the overseer and use his favor to her advantage, I realized my palms were clammy. Pel-Thenhior seemed not to notice at all, except that every so often he would look out over the audience, and his ears would lower another fraction of an inch.

When the end of *Zhelsu* came, it came quickly. The overseer gets her alone and starts pressing his case again. It becomes clear that he will rape her if she doesn't yield willingly. She backs away and away—and I remembered watching them rehearse this, how matter-of-fact and straightforward it had all seemed, nothing like the panic on Zhelsu's face now, the increasing terror in her words—until he has her pinned against the catwalk, and then instead of submitting, she turns and jumps. There is a scream from off stage as the overseer stares in blank astonishment at the place where Zhelsu had been. And the curtain comes down.

The silence held for a long moment while I found my hands clenching. Then someone in the auditorium started clapping, and as other people joined in—I heard one shout of "Genius!"—I thought maybe we had skirted the storm. Then a voice yelled, *"This is an outrage!"* and the entire theater erupted in pandemonium.

Pel-Thenhior said something obscene and heartfelt in Barizhin, then grabbed my wrist and shouted over the rising din, "Come with me! Right now!"

I perforce followed his iron grip on my wrist as he dragged me through the backstage door, turning to bolt it behind us as he yelled at the stagehands, "Don't open the curtain!"

The singers were clustered on stage. The still-increasing chaos in the auditorium was audible, though muffled by the curtain. Min Vakrezharad, a little disheveled from her leap onto the stack of mattresses, called to Pel-Thenhior, "What should we do?"

"Go change," said Pel-Thenhior. "But I think you're safer backstage than trying to leave. I could be wrong."

"How comforting," Mer Olora said dryly.

Pel-Thenhior shrugged, although his ears were still too flat for it to come off as casual. "It's a riot, Tura. I can't predict what it's going to do." At that, several of the chorus made protesting cries, and Min Rasabin said, "Are they really rioting?"

"Oh yes," said Pel-Thenhior. "I am going to have a very unpleasant discussion with the Marquess about the cost of repairs. Assuming, of course, that I live 'til morning."

"Iäna!" protested Min Vakrezharad.

"At least half of the people out there are howling for my head, Othoro. I don't intend to present it to them, but if they find me . . ." His voice trailed off and his shoulders hunched for a moment.

"Well, I'm going to get out of this awful costume," Min Rasabin said practically.

"I have to go warn Wardrobe," Pel-Thenhior said. "Othala Celehar, do you want to come with me, or do you want to take your chances with leaving the theater?"

I needed to talk to Tura Olora, who had already vanished into the backstage darkness. But I wanted to talk to Pel-Thenhior first. "All right," I said.

He went swiftly through the maze. I followed, trying to make some sort of mental map, but I was soon hopelessly turned around again.

In the Wardrobe Department, we found that they were already alarmed. The stagehands were spreading the word, too.

"I think you're safe here, Ulsheän," he said to the wardrobe master, who was close to panicking. "But don't try to leave until someone comes and tells you it's safe." He smiled at her and said, "I'm sure you have ways to occupy your time."

That made her laugh, although it was a choked, hiccupping sound. "I'm sure we do," she said.

Outside the Wardrobe Department's double doors, I stopped Pel-Thenhior and said, "I need to talk to you."

"Of course," he said, puzzled but willing. "About what?"

"Did you know Mer Olora is Duhaladeise on his mother's side?"

"Yes, of course," he said, still puzzled. "Tura makes no secret of it."

"Did you know his grandfather was going to leave him five thousand muranai?"

". . . No," he said, frowning, "but what of it?"

"Mer Olora's grandfather died two weeks before Min Shelsin was murdered."

Pel-Thenhior was no fool. He made the connection quickly. "You don't think *Tura* . . ."

I said, "I think I have to find out."

)(

We found Mer Olora alone in the cramped dressing room shared by the male principals. He had removed the mask-like maquillage that the singers wore in performance and was in the middle of taking off his costume.

"Iäna," he said.

"Tura," said Pel-Thenhior. "Othala Celehar needs to talk to you."

"Othala," Mer Olora said, politely enough although he was beginning to frown. "How can I help you?"

I said, "I was at the reading of Mer Nepena Duhalar's will this evening," and watched with no pleasure as his face changed and his ears flattened. "Did you know of his bequest to you?"

"Yes, but I don't see—"

"Did anyone else know?"

"No!" But he was lying.

"Did Min Shelsin know?"

"I certainly didn't tell her," he said.

"That's not the same thing. Did she *know*?"

He exhaled a hard, slow breath and said, "You can't prove anything. No judiciar in the city will listen to you."

"Perhaps," I said, "but the Amal'othala will." I was bluffing; the Amal'othala was no more likely to listen to my story, with all its holes, than any of the city judiciary. But Mer Olora had just told me I was right. *You can't prove anything* was very different from *I didn't kill her.*

Mer Olora had continued changing while we spoke and was now, in trousers and shirtsleeves, buttoning his waistcoat. He was still in stocking feet; Pel-Thenhior and I were both caught completely off guard when he said, "You'll have to excuse me a moment," and bolted out of the room's back door. After a stunned second, we ran after him.

Pel-Thenhior said, "I don't know *where* he's going. There's no way out back here, even if he wanted to take his chances with the rioters."

Mer Olora clearly had a destination in mind, though, for we could not catch him. He neither slowed nor hesitated nor ran into any dead ends. When we found a narrow open door and could hear feet on the treads of a twisting spiral of stairs, Pel-Thenhior gasped, "The roof!"

If we could have climbed those stairs faster, we would have. But Mer Olora stayed ahead of us all the way to the top and out onto the roof. By the time we caught up to him, he was already standing on the parapet.

"Tura, no," Pel-Thenhior said imploringly.

"I don't know how she knew," Mer Olora said. "I only ever told Veralis and Shulethis, one night when we'd all drunk too much. I swore them to secrecy. But she found out. I know she stole the letter because she told me so, the brass-faced bitch. I made the mistake of sleeping with her once, and she used the opportunity all too well."

"Mer Olora," I said, "please step down."

He continued as if he hadn't heard me. "Meeting at the Canalman's Dog was her idea. An intrigue," he said bitterly. "As if we were characters in a novel. She showed me the letter and said I could have it back for a thousand muranai."

"Oh no," said Pel-Thenhior, though he might not have been aware he said it out loud.

"It wasn't the money," Mer Olora said earnestly. "It was knowing that even after she gave the letter back—if she really did—she would still have me under her thumb. The letter contained my . . . my lover's name." His voice broke. "I would never be free of her smirks and knowing looks, and she would always have the means to make me pay again. She would always be a threat to . . . to my lover."

"So you killed her," I said.

"It was the only way out. The only way to keep my lover safe. And that's why I have to do this."

He stepped sideways off the roof.

"Blessed goddess," Pel-Thenhior half sobbed as we both ran to the parapet. Looking down, I saw Tura Olora's broken body and around it a widening circle of stillness as the rioting opera-goers realized what had happened. The members of the Brotherhood trying to restore peace were suddenly successful.

"I have to get down there," I said to Pel-Thenhior. He looked at me blankly, as if my words made no sense to him. I said, "My duty lies with the dead."

"Of course," said Pel-Thenhior. Then he blinked and seemed to come back to himself. "Yes, of course. This way, othala. We can take a different way down." He winced at the double meaning. "That is, there's an easier set of stairs."

I followed him, as I had been doing all evening, and we descended by a staircase around a square lightwell. At the bottom, Pel-Thenhior had no difficulty in leading me to the front of the Opera and Mer Olora's corpse.

The watchman standing guard was glad to see me. "Othala! We don't know if he fell or jumped, but his neck's broken, either way—along with most of the rest of him."

I went down on one knee beside the body and began saying the prayer of compassion for the dead. This part, ironically, was easy. It was everything else that was hard.

※

The newspapermen—Goronezh, Thurizar, and Vicenalar—found me at some hour between midnight and dawn as I emerged from Ulvanensee, where I had gone with Tura Olora's corpse. The municipal cemetery of the Veren'malo was much smaller than Ulvanensee and had no room—hadn't had room for new burials for fifty

years, so hopelessly behind were they in transferring their charges
to the catacombs. Anora was rightfully asleep, but Vidrezhen, the
prelate assigned night duty, was calm and competent, and I was
feeling as if at least I had gotten one thing done correctly when I
heard Goronezh calling, "Othala Celehar!"

I wanted, very badly, to turn on my heel and go back into
Ulvanensee—and lock the gate behind me as well—but I knew they
would just wait until I emerged again.

"Good morning, Mer Goronezh," I said, and tried not to say it
tiredly. "What may we do for you?"

"Is it true that Mer Olora committed suicide?" Goronezh asked.

Vicenalar, right behind him, said, "Is it true he jumped off the
Vermilion Opera?"

Thurizar, coming around to my other side, said, "Do you know
why he did it?"

I *did* know, of course, and as the Witness for Arveneän Shelsin, I
would tell Azhanharad the whole ugly tangle of the truth later that
morning, but while my calling forbade lying, it did not require me
to cause unnecessary pain. Telling the newspapermen would shout
Tura Olora's shame to the entire city, and neither the Duhalada, the
Olorada, nor the Vermilion Opera would be made better thereby. I
could not deny the suicide—even if I'd wanted to try, no one was going to believe he'd accidentally gone all the way up to the roof—but
I could say, truthfully, "His reason died with him," for Pel-Thenhior
and I had agreed it should. Azhanharad would record the matter
in the Brotherhood's record book, but that book was kept strictly
secret. I wasn't even supposed to know it existed.

"Come now, othala," Thurizar said reproachfully. "You must
have *some* idea."

"His reason died with him," I said again. "We regret, but we cannot tell you anything more."

"You are a sore trial to a newspaperman, othala," said Goronezh.

"We do not know about you gentlemen," I said, "but we would
like to be in bed before dawn. Good night."

They would probably have preferred to shake the truth out of me, but they let me go.

)(

Tura Olora was buried in the great municipal cemetery in the Airmen's Quarter, just as his victim had been. None of his Duhaladeise cousins attended the funeral, nor any Olorada. The mourners consisted of me and Iäna Pel-Thenhior, who looked as if he was not sure he was doing the right thing.

Once Olora was safely buried and his headstone blessed—for suicides are the most likely to turn ghoul—I said to Pel-Thenhior, "May I buy you a cup of tea?"

"No," he said, and dragged a smile out from somewhere. "But I will gladly go have tea with you."

We went to the Chrysanthemum, which was the teahouse Anora favored, and settled with a pot of eladriät. Pel-Thenhior scrubbed both hands up his face and said, "Thank the goddesses that's over."

"You did the right thing in coming," I said.

"Did I? He was a murderer. He murdered one of my singers. Two of them, if we call suicide self-murder."

"He was a man under intolerable stress," I said. "He did what he thought he had to do to keep his secret—and his lover—safe."

"Well, he succeeded in that. I've sorted through all his papers and I don't have the least idea."

"Someone highly placed and vulnerable to scandal, at a guess."

"Yes. And I admit, I don't *want* to know. Tura died to keep this secret. It feels wrong to try to uncover it—but that reminds me. I was going to tell you I know how Arveneän found out about the money."

"Oh?"

"She was blackmailing Veralis."

"Yes, for secrets," I said. "He told me that."

"He told her about Tura's money. He said he was desperate to keep her quiet, and he didn't think she could do any harm with it.

I didn't ask him what *his* secret is, and I'm trying not to learn any more. It makes me angry, and being angry is pointless because Arveneän is dead. And there's no way to fix the damage she did."

"No," I said, "but at least it is at an end."

"I suppose," he said, although he sounded doubtful. "And meanwhile I've got to find a new principal bass *and* a new principal midsoprano. Toïno is doing her best, but she really doesn't have enough voice. Hathet is doing *his* best, but he really was the *junior* bass. This is only his second year with us."

We sat in silence for a few moments, drinking eladriät. Then Pel-Thenhior said, "You are welcome to share my box any time you want to."

"That is very kind of you."

"You needn't sound so surprised. I enjoy your company, and I hate the thought that your last memory of the Opera should be Tura's death."

"All right," I said, and decided there was no point in mentioning the nightmares I'd been having. "I would like that."

"Good," said Pel-Thenhior, and finally managed a real smile. "Now let me bore you to tears by telling you about my new opera."

Acknowledgments

My profoundest thanks go to my Patreon patrons: Laura Bailey, H. E. Wolf, P. Keelan, Garret Reece, D Franklin, Lorna Toolis, Liz Novaski, Jennifer G. Tifft, Lindsay Kleinman, Sarah Ervine, Kate Diamond, Bill Ruppert, Sharis Ingram, Elizabeth Woodley, Gretchen Schultz, Jennifer Lundy, Gordon Tisher, Danielle Beliveau, Hilary Kraus, Clifton Royston, Andrew Lin, Mary and Mikey Reppy, Kris Ashley, Jeff Frane, Paige Morgan, Kitty Marschall, Eleanor Skinner, Sylvia Sotomayor, ScottKF, Sasha Lydon, Erin Lytle, Margaret Johnston, Hannah Albert, Katec V, pCiaran, Laura E. Price, E.S.H., Ruthanna and Sarah Emrys, Katie Jones, Simone Brick, Megan Prime, Danielle B, Brianna Smart, Asia Wolf, Amy Miller, Caryn Cameron, and Liza Furr.

Thanks also go to my editor, Beth Meacham, my copy editor, Christina MacDonald, and the production team at Tor, who do amazing work.

About the Author

Katherine Addison's short fiction has been selected by *The Year's Best Fantasy and Horror* and *The Year's Best Science Fiction*. Her novel *The Goblin Emperor* won a Locus Award. As Sarah Monette, she is the author of the Doctrine of Labyrinths series and coauthor, with Elizabeth Bear, of the Iskryne series. She lives near Madison, Wisconsin.